TO LOVE

IS TO WALK WITH GOD DAILY

Toni Joy

WESTBOW
PRESS®
A DIVISION OF THOMAS NELSON
& ZONDERVAN

WestBow Press books may be ordered through booksellers or by contacting:

WestBow Press
A Division of Thomas Nelson & Zondervan
1663 Liberty Drive
Bloomington, IN 47403
www.westbowpress.com
1 (866) 928-1240

ISBN: 978-1-5127-2174-4 (sc)
ISBN: 978-1-5127-2175-1 (hc)
ISBN: 978-1-5127-2173-7 (e)

Library of Congress Control Number: 2015919950

Print information available on the last page.

WestBow Press rev. date: 12/8/2015

Acknowledgement

There are a few people in my life that I can say that inspired me to put together these devotions; my sister Terri Pearl, Pastor Sonya Longstreet, and my daughter, Darlita.

I looked back all through my life and I can hear my sister's support and encouragement to be led of God without fear. I had been thinking about this book for a while. One day she said to me, "what are you going to do with these devotions? You should put them together in a book." So I did. I thank God for my daughter Darlita for saving every one of my devotions for over 5 years. And truly because of her, here it is...

To Love Life..... Is to walk with God Daily.

I also acknowledge with much appreciation my Pastors Curtis & Sonya Longstreet for being there for me in the hard times – far beyond the pulpit. God's calling on their lives have been the divine ingredients of what God called for in His shepherds for his people. Pastor Sonya has given me more of her time than any one person can ask. As you will see, The "Agape Walk Weekly" and this book has become a wonderful collage of ministry with her personal touch of "My 2Cents". Her wisdom and mentorship are sure to be admired by all – as it is much admired and valued by me. Their voices have become a necessity for me.

I thank God for these three ladies in my life.

But... **I dedicate this book to my mom who loves perfectly!**

All scripture is from the KJV, NKJV, and NIV or otherwise it will be noted.
Editing by Amanda Bryant,
Atlanta, GA

January 1

Toni Joy

Happy New Year

Confession for the Month of January

Print or write out your confession. Place it where
you can see and confess it all month.

This IS going to be a great year; I will be
successful in everything I do because the
Lord is speaking to me through His Word
and by the Holy Spirit. I meditate on His
Voice, His Word (Jesus), His Spirit (Holy
Spirit), His ways, and the steps that are
planned for me. – I surrender to the will of
my Heavenly Father in every area of my life.
This is the year of God's Glory in my life.

*Arise, shine, for the glory of the LORD
is risen upon you. Isa. 60:1*

Happy New Year to you, Happy New to you, Happy New to you dear friends, may it be a good one for you! (Sung to the tune of Happy Birthday).

Can you tell I'm happy about this New Year? That's because I just plain ole like new stuff... but also because I'm working on self-improvements this year. I'd like to share some of the things I'm meditating, focusing on, and working towards this year. These are NOT resolutions. I personally don't make New Year resolutions. But here are my focuses. Maybe one or two of these might be of interest to you.

- Take 100% responsibility for my life.
- Stop making so many excuses.
- I'll not talk about the reasons why I can't and why I haven't.
- Stop blaming outside circumstances.
- Remember the past is the past.
- Seek to solve the problem instead of focusing and dwelling on the problem.
- Remember the outcome of an experience is based on how I respond to it.

Well there you have it. As you can see I have my work cut out for me. I believe I've done my share of complaining and excuse making last year. I need to clean it up. How about you? What have you decided to do to make a better you?

Only Believe!

Luke 8:22 *Now it happened, on a certain day, that He got into a boat with His disciples. And He said to them, "Let us cross over to the other side of the lake." And they launched out.*

The Battle Is Won

Did you know that at the exact moment you make a decision - the battle is won or lost? Believe it. Usually when we make a serious decision, the rest of our thinking will follow that decision. A decision of faith will be surrounded by the Word of God. A decision of fear (or no decision) will be surrounded by everything you see, feel, and hear. *For sure, we will go into battle:* Jesus told His disciples "Let's go over to the other side", that meant "**they were going to the other side, they still had to get in the boat, in the water, and through the storm**".

Go into battle a winner by the right decision.

*So Jesus answered and said to them, "Have faith in God. For assuredly, I say to you, whoever says to this mountain, 'Be removed and be cast into the sea,' and does not doubt in his heart, but believes that those things he says will be done, he will have whatever he says. Therefore I say to you, whatever things you ask when you pray, **believe that you receive them**, and you will have them. Mark 11:22-24 - when faith speaks...thoughts follow. What are we saying?*

One of my favorite quotes in the bible is "**More than Conquerors**" (Rom. 8:37). Because....

A Conqueror is someone who wins a battle - Those of us who are more than a Conqueror have won when we enter the battle.

Be More than a Conqueror today

Meditate today on ...

Trust in the Lord with all your heart
and lean not on your own understanding;
in all your ways submit to him,
and he will make your paths straight.

Do not be wise in your own eyes;
fear the Lord and shun evil.
This will bring health to your body
and nourishment to your bones.

Proverbs 3:5-8 (NIV)

Let your walk today be led by
the Word of God – In everything;
ask yourself, WWJW

Matt. 14:24-30 *Shortly before dawn Jesus went out to them, walking on the lake. When the disciples saw him walking on the lake, they were terrified. "It's a ghost," they said, and cried out in fear. But Jesus immediately said to them, "Take courage! It is I. Don't be afraid." "Lord, if it's you," Peter replied, "tell me to come to you on the water." "Come," he said. Then Peter got down out of the boat, walked on the water and came toward Jesus. But when he saw the wind, he was afraid and, beginning to sink, cried out, "Lord, save me!"*

Don't Lose Sight

We have many avenues that we look to in order to make our way in this life; and we think that's quite something (looking at all the possibilities that this world has to offer....). **God** wants us to look to Him - at the impossibilities that the world *can't* offer.

The Lord knows that some things are going to be hard, but we have to stay focused and not lose sight as to Who is our source, our life, our Lord. When we run into hard things, remember these three things:

1. *Don't do what you're not supposed to do;* ***just stop.***
2. *Do what you are supposed to do:* ***just do it.***
3. *Have faith in God:* ***walk by faith and not by sight.***

If you are having a problem with any of these - Joshua 1:8 says to keep the Word before your eyes day and night and then your way shall be prosperous. The harder your problem, the more time you should spend studying the Word of God. Become a student of God. Study the Word.

*Don't lose sight - be a water walker:
a step-out-in-faith kind of guy!*

My Agape Walk Today

Mention something
about Jesus
to someone You don't know
today

✓ <u>I walked in love today</u>

Meditate today on ...

The Lord is my shepherd, I lack nothing.
He makes me lie down in green pastures,
He leads me beside quiet waters,
He refreshes my soul.
He guides me along the right paths for His name's sake.
Even though I walk through the darkest valley
I will fear no evil, for You are with me;
Your rod and Your staff, they comfort me.

You prepare a table before me
in the presence of my enemies.
You anoint my head with oil;
my cup overflows.
Surely Your goodness and love will follow me
all the days of my life,
and I will dwell in the house of the Lord forever.
Psalms 23 NIV

Walk protected & secure, because you are

2 Cor 9:8-9 *And God is able to make all grace abound to you, so that in all things at all times, having all that you need, you will abound in every good work.*

Seek God, all the time

Whether we are in troubles and trials or walking in our God given calling, we must put ourselves in a position to hear from God, trust God, and believe God – DAILY.

Sometimes we can get caught up in worry or fear and listen to our troubles instead of hearing from God. And on the other end, we can be working the plan of God and get so busy we end up ahead of God doing our own thing. Whichever way we get caught up, we can hurt ourselves, someone else, or lose something valuable.

The disciples asked Jesus to teach them to pray. In the prayer Jesus gave them He said to ask the Lord to give us our daily bread.

P.S. God's waiting on us. ....for your Father knows the things you have need of before you ask Him (Matt. 6:8)... Then He tells us to pray...give us this day our daily bread (Matt. 6:11). He knows, acknowledge HIM

Regardless of where we are this week, let's seek God "daily".

Our Father in heaven, Hallowed be Your name. Your kingdom come. Your will be done, On earth as it is in heaven. Give us day by day our daily bread. Luke 11:2-3

Ps. 122:1 I was glad when they said unto me, Let us go into the house of the Lord.

Ouch

When church started, I was still in a short meeting that was running late, and I heard praise and worship begin.... I had this urge to join in. In my mind I'm thinking, *"I'm missing it - they're worshiping the Lord without me"*.

The meeting ended and I ran in service, to be a little disappointed. I had this expectancy to walk in service and see everyone enjoying what I was missing - but I found a few texting, busy in there purse, talking to someone, etc. I just shook it off and joined in worship. I realized that what I was missing because of a meeting, they were missing too; but not for the same reason.

Have you heard the saying "What you don't know won't hurt"? That is a lie from the pit of hell. What they were missing is definitely going to hurt them. Missing the move of God. I can think of a lot of things we can lose by that; *the move of God can save you money, time, friendship, deliverance, salvation, direction, etc.*

So, if you are one of them that go to church and you're too busy for God - *stop... If this is for you, just say OUCH and...*

Get in the Groove

My people are destroyed for lack of knowledge. Hosea 4:6

Moving Forward

As we move into a new year, I'm expecting great things, I hope you are too. I honestly cannot remember a time in my life when I felt so much expectancy and excitement about the future. Around about August, The Holy Spirit began to deal with me on the subject of **transformation**. He very specifically began to challenge the way I think. I wanted to dig a little further on this subject so I began a study about transformation and thoughts. Through this subject I began to realize in order to fulfill my purpose in life, to be all God has ordained me to be, I was going to have to do some **very real growing** and **changing.** Do you believe The Holy Spirit prepares us for moves of God in our lives? At the time He began dealing with me on this subject, I was desirous of growing, of moving forward. I knew it was time to make some changes. I was meditating on The How... What things did I need to adjust. What things did I need to begin to do.

His dealing with me came, of course, at a point when I was very receptive. Since August I have totally surrendered to The Holy Spirit's nudging to change my thought patterns. I want to change. I'm open more than ever. In September our praise and worship leader introduced me to a song by *Israel Houghton* **(I'm Moving Forward)** that confirmed how I felt about this season in my life. I call it my new theme song.

As we enter into a new year, I dedicate **Israel Houghton's song - Moving Forward,** to all of you. From the CD **Power of One.** I've chosen to move forward, I'm not going back! Only Believe!

It's a NEW YEAR!!!!

Lyrics from Israel Houghton - Moving Forward

What a moment, You have brought me to - such a freedom I have found in You
You're the Healer, Who makes all things New - I'm not going back, I'm moving ahead
Here to declare to You - My past is over - In You all things are made new
Surrendered my life to Christ
"I'm moving, moving Forward"

Meditate today on ...

Let not your heart be troubled: ye believe in God, believe also in Me. In My Father's house are many mansions; if it were not so, I would have told you. I go to prepare a place for you. And if I go and prepare a place for you, I will come again and receive you to Myself; that where I am, there you may be also. And where I go you know, and the way you know."

Thomas said to Him, "Lord, we do not know where You are going, and how can we know the way?"

Jesus said to him, "I am the way, the truth, and the life. No one comes to the Father except through Me."

John 14:1-6

Don't worry or fret; we know someone on the inside...

James 1:26 If anyone among you thinks he is religious, and does not bridle his tongue but deceives his own heart, this one's religion is useless.

Religious? Not, maybe

I always said that "I am not religious" because I viewed religion as having so many hang-ups. There are so many denominations and beliefs that have so many different laws, rules, by-laws. All of them can believe that Jesus is the Son of God. Some of them have gotten so far from God through religion *(this can happen also through following tradition)* that they have the appearance of being spiritual or holy and they are not.

As I was reading James 1:26-27, something caught my eye - **_Pure and undefiled religion before God and the Father_ is this: to visit orphans and widows in their trouble, and to _keep oneself unspotted from the world_**.

I see that religion could be a good thing, but I believe we (people) have given religion a bad name. We have taken religion out of the hands of God. The physical church is supposed to be filled with the "Body of Christ" and/or with those coming to know God and joining the Body of Christ, not with our philosophical spin on religion and what it should be. God doesn't need our help in figuring it out; He handled in "IN Christ".

We may have made it just what the Webster's dictionary defines it as; just a code of ethics and mere philosophy "with reverence toward a god". Webster can be correct, but it can also be misleading if one purposed it to be. Why would one purpose it to be...that's a whole different devotion. **_Now the question is_**:

Religious... are we?

My Agape Walk Today

Be attentive;
do everything
that the Lord
leads you to do today
– expect His guidance

✓ I walked in love today

Acts 3:2-6 And a certain man lame from his mother's womb was carried, whom they laid daily at the gate of the temple which is called Beautiful, to ask alms from those who entered the temple; who, seeing Peter and John about to go into the temple, asked for alms. And fixing his eyes on him, with John, Peter said, "Look at us." So he gave them his attention, expecting to receive something from them. Then Peter said, "Silver and gold I do not have, but what I do have I give you: In the name of Jesus Christ of Nazareth, rise up and walk."

Look on US

Just a thought
As I was reading further down from the passage above, I thought, why are we not seeing this power more today? We need to stir up the compassion of Jesus in us towards others.

We don't need more – we need to move in the power of God that has been given to us.

Matthew 9:36 *But when He saw the multitudes, He was moved with compassion for them, because they were weary and scattered, like sheep having no shepherd.*

*14:14 He was **moved with compassion** for them, and healed their sick.*

*18:27 Then the master of that servant was **moved with compassion**, released him, and forgave him the debt.*

I would love for us to be somewhere walking and see someone in need and say...· Look on US

Most assuredly, I say to you, he who believes in Me, the works that I do he will do also; and greater works than these he will do, because I go to My Father. John 12:14

Martin Luther King Jr.

Excerpt of his speech

"I Have A Dream".... that day when all of **God's children**, black men and white men, Jews and Gentiles, Protestants and Catholics, will be able to join hands and sing in the words of the old spiritual, **"Free at last, free at last. Thank God Almighty, we are free at last."**

I wonder sometimes do the world forget that this man was first, a man of God, second - a Civil Rights Leader.

My thoughts are that it was the call of God on his life that made him such a dynamic leader. It was his obedience to this calling, his faith-filled, non-violent, and integrity of heart that changed the world we live in today... He knew that our fight was not physical, but spiritual (2Cor. 10:3-6)

For though we walk in the flesh, we do not war according to the flesh. For the weapons of our warfare are not carnal but mighty in God for pulling down strongholds, casting down arguments and every high thing that exalts itself against the knowledge of God, bringing every thought into captivity to the obedience of Christ, and being ready to punish all disobedience when your obedience is fulfilled

For our struggle is not against flesh and blood, but against the rulers, against the authorities, against the powers of this dark world and against the spiritual forces of evil in the heavenly realms. **Eph. 6:12-13**

"Armed We Are" Part 1 of 9

When we were born again, we were translated from the power of darkness to the kingdom of light. This puts us in authority, a higher spiritual plane than the enemy. We are still in this world, but not of this world, but we do have to decide, whose plane to ride on. In God's kingdom (seeing that we are at war), we have "Immunity" against evil, disease, poverty, depression, etc. When it comes our way – **we are fully armed, standing as Ambassadors of Christ.**

Ambassador's with Immunity

I love when King David went into battle as a kid with a sling shot; he took off the King's armor and went in with the power of God. That rock struck Goliath in the head and killed him - a spiritual force was with that rock.

Funny, Mother's words were, "Don't throw rocks; you can put someone's eye out."

The work of victory is done, but it's the devils job to lie to us and say it ain't so. The work was done before the rock left the sling. Our sling and stone are faith/acting/speaking the Word of God. This is what David said to the enemy:

"You come against me with sword and spear and javelin, but I come against you in the name of the LORD Almighty, the God of the armies of Israel, whom you have defied."

Let's stop fighting the enemy on his terms, playing his games. For though we live in the world, we do not wage war as the world does; the weapons we fight with are not the weapons of the world.
Learn how to fight through Christ in the next 8 devotions.

Therefore put on the full armor of God, so that when the day of evil comes, you may be able to stand your ground, and after you have done everything, to stand. *Stand therefore....* **Eph. 6:13**

"Armed We Are" Part 2 of 9

<u>Key Note</u>: Put on the full armor of God. When God created us He gave us everything we needed to walk in this life. But after the fall He made coats of skin for Adam and Eve to be clothed (Gen. 3:21). *They knew their nakedness, so for their own protection, they had to be covered.*

God has given us clothes (armor) for the spirit man (for our protection). Because of the fall, the devil is out to kill us. Even though the fight is won (and the devil is defeated), it is only won through Jesus Christ. So "In Christ" is our shield against the enemy. We are no match for the enemy without it.

*But **put** on the Lord Jesus **Christ**, and make no provision for the flesh, to fulfill its lusts. Rom. 13:14*

For example, look at the dress code today; we walk around half naked not knowing that we are fighting a losing battle. This is a sex craved world! Yet, we wonder why relationships don't last anymore? We are hell bound in this area. We can understand not being clothed or should I say "unclothed" physically is one of the enemy's weapons to feed into lustfulness. By being clothed in Christ, we expose and defeat his plan to destroy families.

The whipping we are getting for not being clothed is truly grieving the Holy Spirit. Ponder on this scripture.

There is therefore now no condemnation to those who are in Christ Jesus, who do not walk according to the flesh, but according to the Spirit. Rom. 8:1

Don't Get Caught Half-Dressed – Put on the Armor

Toni Joy

Stand firm then, with the belt of truth buckled around your waist...
Eph. 6:14

"Armed We Are" Part 3 of 9
Jesus answered, "I am the way and the truth and the life. No one comes to the Father except through me." John 14:6

When you have truth, you are released from the world and grounded in **GOD** - you're unshakable, free from the coulda, shoulda, what ifs – Jesus is not just the right answer, He's the only answer; Jesus said ...*for this cause I came into the world, that I should bear witness unto the truth, everyone that is of truth hears my voice" John 18:37.*

Knowledge can establish a fact. A fact can establish perspective (not always the right perspective).
Truth establishes power, freedom, and life. *The world goes by facts; facts can change, lose, be low, be high, etc. Facts are not stable.*
Facts hold you to circumstances - Truth frees you from it

The bible is more than just a story or history that is true; it's truth, life, liberty. Without it, hope and faith are ineffective; they have nothing to stand on. Truth is absolute; Jesus said that He is the way, the truth, and the life.

Now that we the established the truth... **wrap yourself in it**. It's a gift given to you. This piece of armor holds you together.

John 8:31-32 *to the Jews who had believed him Jesus said "If you hold to my teaching, you are really my disciples. Then you will know the truth and the truth will set you free."*
Just think – we have something absolute on our side

Truth takes you out of the world and brings you *to the Father*. It is wisdom, knowledge, and power in your hands. Truth makes a way out of no way. You go from bending to standing, from death to life, from nothing to something, from not knowing to knowing, from empty to full, from alone to loved, from being bound to free, from lack to abundance. *It's your firm foundation, your solid rock.* **What do you want to be free from? Where do you want to go? Get Truth**

However, when He, the Spirit of truth, has come, He will guide you into all truth; for He will not speak on His own authority, but whatever He hears He will speak; and He will tell you things to come. He will glorify Me, for He will take of what is Mine and declare it to you. All things that the Father has are Mine. Therefore I said that He will take of Mine and declare it to you. John 16:13-15

....with the breastplate of righteousness in place. **Eph. 6:14**

"Armed We Are" Part 4 of 9

Superman & Spiderman wore an "S" on their chest to signify/ proclaim their virtue or state of being. We are to wear an "R" for the Righteousness of God.

When the superheroes appeared, we knew something spectacular was about to happen; we are the superheroes (or supposed to be) of the present time. Not with our unrighteousness but with the righteousness of God – His virtue and state of being.

When you wake up every morning to begin to deal with the hustle and bustle of life; clothe yourself with the righteousness of God. We have the right to invade the territory with power and authority. We are sitting in heavenly places with in His righteousness (Ephesians 2:6). Put your hand on your hips and let your back-bone slip.... oh, sorry, went to a song we used to sing as kids; but think about it, put the kid in you in charge. He or she would put the "S" on their chest and take charge; no longer thinking of who he or she was but the right given to them. Did you play cops and robbers as kids, or mom and dad? Well, they were in charge.

We are to do the same. We are to take our place everywhere we go in the righteousness of our God displaying the right standing given through salvation and His grace. How else are we to live the supernatural life?

We are in charge. We have families to raise, jobs to do. They look to us to get them through. Everyone should expect the supernatural to happen when we walk in room. Let them see Christ Jesus in us. They should desire the God in us. They see the world - it shows itself every day on TV/News, etc. What should they see when they see us?

Let us be sober, putting on faith and love as a breastplate, and the hope of salvation as a helmet. For God did not appoint us to suffer wrath but to receive salvation through our Lord Jesus Christ. 1 Thes. 5:8-9

My Agape Walk Today

Find time to

pray for a few

minutes in the

middle of the day

✓ I walked in love today

....and your feet shod with the preparation of the gospel of peace. **Eph. 6:15**

"Armed We Are" Part 5 of 9

Rom. 10:15 *And how can anyone preach unless they are sent? As it is written: "How beautiful are the feet of those who bring good news!"*

Eph. 6:15 helped me understand Rom. 10:15. I just didn't get what feet had to do with the gospel? I guess I was seeing only five toes and a heel. What connected it for me was that all of them referenced peace, the gospel, and salvation. How beautiful are the feet of those that carry the gospel i.e., the Spreader of the gospel. Peace is a word that is sound and comforting - it brings, holds, and carries safety. Your paths have been cleared (worries evaporate). It holds the power of tranquility, understanding, and wholeness.

What does shod mean? Participle of shoe, an anchor of the feet. So if our feet are shod (clothed) with the preparation of the gospel of peace - our direction is set. Our hope and future is solid with an agreement with God.

Jeremiah 29:11 *For I know the thoughts that I think toward you, says the LORD, thoughts of peace and not of evil, to give you a future and a hope.*

I guess you say "how is this a weapon of our warfare? The devil would love for our peace to be disturbed, our confidence to be shaken in God fighting our battles. What is it then, should we walk trembling, with fear - wondering whether our enemies or foes will have the upper hand? Should we concern ourselves with what tomorrow will bring? If we knew our tomorrow was in perfect hands - or our next moments; how would that change your thoughts of life, your future, your present – your walk?

The battle is won - but you must go through certain areas to get to the Promised Land... to get to your desires. Walk like a giant, or sleep on the boat like Jesus did. *Make a treaty with yourself To take a free ride, plant your feet in understanding and the wisdom of God - you have already been given passage to win If God is for us, who can be against us? Rom. 8:31*

....above all, taking the shield of faith, wherewith ye shall be able to quench all the fiery darts of the wicked. **Eph. 6:16**

"Armed We Are" Part 6 of 9

The next few weapons are all in conjunction with the phrase *"above all"*. They are not separated from the ones already mentioned but this is a work that WE must put forth. ***This is important*** because I don't want us to "hit and miss" in the goodness of God.

(Lazarus' sister Martha talking to Jesus) Lord, if thou had been here my brother would not have died (John 11:21).

Jesus told her that He was the resurrection and the life and if you believe this you will not die, then He asked her, ***"Believe Thou This?"*** This question stuck with me for years. Every time Jesus asked someone a question on their faith or I'm in a situation where I have to choose this or that, this phrase "Believe Thou This" always rings in my ear. It's a challenge question for me - like *"I dare you to trust God"*, like Jesus is in front of me saying, *"Do you believe this Toni Joy?"*

We have to walk in faith *On Purpose* every day with Jesus in our ear. "Believeth Thou This?" We have to apply this in the small, big, and hard matters of life.

Right before Jesus raised Lazarus from the dead, He reminded her again "said I not unto thee that, if thou wouldest believe, thou shouldest see the glory of God? He prayed and said "Lazarus come forth" and he that was dead came forth.

In Eph. 6:16 it says "above all, taking the shield of faith" Imagine Jesus standing there with you 24-7 giving you His Word and saying "Believeth Thou This?". ***It's a "yes or no" question***.

I really want you to get this; He asked her twice. We find ourselves saying, "If only you Lord? *Can* you Lord? Will you Lord?"

When you get in a spot and fiery darts are flying, let your faith be a shield: ***Yes Lord, I believe You***; *and act on what you believe.*

1John 5:4 for everyone born of God overcomes the world. This is the victory that has overcome the world, even ***our*** faith.

....and take the helmet of salvation, **Eph. 6:16**

"Armed We Are" Part 7 of 9

Romans 1:16-17 *For I am not ashamed of the gospel of Christ; for it is the power of God unto salvation to everyone that believeth; to the Jew first, and also to the Greek. **For therein** is the righteousness of God revealed from faith to faith; as it is written, The Just Shall Live By Faith.*

Hard Hats

Everyone knows, for our protection, when we enter a construction area we must wear hard hats because of the work that's being done. *We are in this world but not of this world* (John 17:14) which puts us in an atmosphere where we need protection; we need hard hats - The Helmet of Salvation. Look at the scripture above *"for therein" that is, **in** our salvation is the righteousness of God revealed from faith to faith. In Christ is our salvation, deliverance.*

The helmet signifies protection in the work arena

The bible says to "**work out our salvation**" by faith. If we go further down in Romans (2:13); "for not the hearers of the law are just before God, but the doers of the law shall be justified".

We are going to work regardless of what we think, need, desire, or whether we want to work *or not*. Either it's works toward righteousness or un-righteousness. There is no in-between. You can't serve two masters (Luke 16:13).

Walk the Walk and Talk the Talk

James 1:22-25 *Do not merely listen to the word, and so deceive yourselves. Do what it says. Anyone who listens to the word but does not do what it says is like someone who looks at his face in a mirror and, after looking at himself, goes away and immediately forgets what he looks like. But whoever looks intently into the perfect law that gives freedom, and continues in it—not forgetting what they have heard, but doing it—they will be blessed in what they do.*

Don't forget your work is insured by the blood of Jesus

....and the sword of the Spirit, which is the word of God. **Eph. 6:16**

"Armed We Are" Part 8 of 9

2Cor. 4:13...and since we have the same spirit of faith, according to what is written, "I believed and therefore I spoke," we also believe and therefore speak.

This is so important to our life "Now". In **Heb. 11:1** is says that *"Now faith is the substance of things hoped for and the evidence of things not seen".*

NOW - when all visual evidence is contrary to what we speak
Now: at the present time, at this moment, at once.
Faith brings what is hoped for into existence; that's why it's "NOW" – that's why we speak - I am healed – all my needs are met, I am more than a conqueror... *It's brings it*

Without speaking the Word of God it makes void so many promises and the hope that we have in Jesus as our Lord and Savior.

We have twenty one *(21) "by faith"* statements in Heb. 11. All those battles and situations were won *by faith* and speaking the Word of God. It's our word against; ***against what***? *If God be for us, who can be against us?* (Rom. 8:31) But we are against ourselves when we don't **Speak the Word of God, Walk in the Word of God, and Act on the Word of God**.

Shield of Faith + Helmet of Salvation + Word of God
Rom. 4:18-25 Therefore, the promise comes by faith. Against all hope, Abraham in hope believed and so became the father of many nations." Without weakening in his faith, he faced the fact that his body was as good as dead—since he was about a hundred years old—and that Sarah's womb was also dead. Yet he did not waiver through unbelief regarding the promise of God, but was strengthened in his faith and gave glory to God, being fully persuaded that God had power to do what he had promised.

Read Hebrews 4:12 and Hebrews chap. 11

...praying always with all prayer and supplication in the Spirit, and watching thereunto with all perseverance and supplication for all saints... **Eph. 6:18**

"Armed We Are" Part 9 of 9

Now we are all armored up, ready for battle, and all dressed up; so, where do we go? To God in prayer; it's were the battle is won.

If you are like me, you're asking, if the battle is won in prayer and it is all in the power of God, why can't we just skip the armor and get on our knees and get God involved? We can all just pray a lot.

It would be like giving a loaded gun to a 3 year old. Would you trust your life to a man that didn't know truth, righteousness, peace, faith, salvation, how to go to God in prayer, intercede for you, or hear from God or know what to do with the blessings or inheritance of God? We have to know what's on the inside of us, the power we have and how to use it to be led and hear from God every moment. For example; without the love of God working on the inside of me, I would only see with my eyes, hear with my ears, and speak what little I do know – not a good picture.

We are the vessel God uses – we're nothing without Him
Our Relationship & Communication With God Are Key!

We are God's children and He wants to give us the desires of our hearts. We have to grow up in Him and learn what the inheritance is about. The devil took it once from Adam and Eve. God is showing us how **not** to allow the devil to steal it back again.

*For those who are **led** by the Spirit of God are the children of God. The Spirit you received does not make you slaves, so that you live in fear again; rather, the Spirit you received brought about your adoption to sonship. And by him we cry, "Abba, Father." The Spirit himself testifies with our spirit that we are God's children. Now if we are children, then we are heirs—heirs of God and co-heirs with Christ, if indeed we share in his sufferings in order that we may also share in his glory. Rom, 8:14-17*

Now we are all dressed up and there's only one place to go... to God in Prayer – Read 1 Thes. 5:16-18 & 1 John 5:14-15

Meditate today on ...

He who dwells in the secret place of the

Most High

Shall abide under the shadow of the

Almighty.

I will say of the Lord, "He is my refuge

and my fortress;

My God, in Him I will trust."

Ps. 91:1-2

Stop, take a moment and get in your

rightful place - meditate;

OK, now proceed with your day.

My Agape Walk Today

Say a specific
Prayer for
Yourself
Today

✓ I walked in love today

Acts 8:3, 4 As for Saul, he made havoc of the church, entering every house, and dragging off men and women, committing them to prison. Therefore those who were scattered went everywhere preaching the word...

The First Missionaries

How do you think some of the missionaries became missionaries? They were pushed out. Some of them didn't go out into the world until they were beat and sought out to be put into prisons... *"Therefore they were scattered abroad"* They were put on the mission field. *How about that...pushed by the enemy to spread the Word.* Have you ever heard the saying "for what the devil did to hurt us, God used for the good"? *My brethren, count it all joy when you fall into various trials...* James 1:2

Every time tests and trails come our way, let it move us to mission

(When Jesus' cousin, John the Baptist, head got cut off, Jesus went about healing the sick and delivering people from sin).

*First Jesus, then the disciples, **now us**...*
That we might be a kind of first fruits of His creatures....James 1:18
Just remember as we go into the mission field (the world)
God had not given us the spirit of fear; but of love, power, and a sound mind. 2Tim. 1:7

Don't let the tests and trials of life push us down but to push us up to 24 hour missionaries

And He said to them, "Go into the entire world and preach the gospel to every creature." Mark 16:15

Meditate today on ...

Jesus said to him, "If you can believe, all things are possible to him who believes."

Immediately the father of the child cried out and said with tears, "Lord, I believe; help my unbelief!"

Mark 9:23-24

Choose to believe and give your doubts to God; don't let your doubts stop you from receiving

Mark 7:28 "Lord," she replied, "even the dogs under the table eat the children's crumbs."

What does it take?

Jesus left that place and went to the vicinity of Tyre. He entered a house and did not want anyone to know it; yet he could not keep his presence secret. In fact, as soon as she heard about him, a woman whose little daughter was possessed by an impure spirit came and fell at his feet. The woman was a Greek, born in Syrian Phoenicia. She begged Jesus to drive the demon out of her daughter. "First let the children eat all they want," he told her, "for it is not right to take the children's bread and toss it to the dogs." "Lord," she replied, "even the dogs under the table eat the children's crumbs." Then he told her, "For such a reply, you may go; the demon has left your daughter." She went home and found her child lying on the bed, and the demon gone. Mark 7:24-30

We have a woman wanting Jesus to perform a miracle before it was time for the Gentiles to receive *(He had to fulfill the law first)*. It's almost like He provoked her (on purpose) to pull out of her, her intense desire for deliverance/the power: He knew the zeal that was in her; I believe everything Jesus did and said was for a reason.

My daughter said something when we were studying this that was so profound.... She said: <u>So the woman was a lawyer?</u> The woman found a loop hole to receive before it was time!

My daughter noticed that the woman fought for justice for her daughter. She saw a savior, an answer, the solution to her problem and pressed Jesus until she got it.

What that woman fought for then is rightfully ours now. Why don't we get it when we need it? We love our family just like this woman did. She had the same devil, the same pressure.

Is it pride, is it fear, is it keeping up with the Joneses? What is the cost? Are we willing to take what Jesus died to give us?
She had to <u>*find a way*</u> to get <u>*what we already have.*</u>
What does it take for us to save ourselves and/or our families?
Fight the good fight of the faith. Take hold of the eternal life to which you were called when you made your good confession in the presence of many witnesses. 1Tim. 6:12

"What does it take" to see the manifestation of my dreams, and certain answers to my prayers? I usually have this conversation with myself when the answer or manifestation has been a long time coming, seemingly delayed. There are several prayers I've been waiting literally years to see answered. It's a new year, and so a few days ago, I was reminded that those particular prayers had not come to pass in my life yet. Ouch! That reminder didn't feel good.

As I was talking with a buddy and was reminded of the story of the Persistent Widow in Luke 18. There was a godless judge with great contempt for everyone. A widow of that city came to him repeatedly appealing for justice. The judge ignored her for a while, but eventually she wore him out, she drove him crazy. He finally gave her justice, because of her constant requests." Then the Lord said, "Learn a lesson from this evil judge. Even he rendered a just decision in the end, so don't you think God will surely give justice to his chosen people who plead with him day and night? Will he keep putting them off? I tell you, he will grant justice to them quickly! But when I, the Son of Man, return, how many will I find who have faith? Luke 18:1-8 NLT

What does it take? **Persistence and faith**. We've got to keep believing. I said, 'Self, ya gotta keep believing **anyway**.' Regardless of what I see, I must keep fighting the good fight of faith. Sometimes it looks like we're fighting against unbeatable odds, but I know for a fact -- there is nothing too hard for God. And even though I'm still waiting for some particular answers, I will continue to dream big, and fight. I'm completely sold on the power of God and His goodness. One day those prayers will come to past and I'll be somewhere shouting about His goodness and dancing like there is no tomorrow. **Wait, I already dance like that.** Anyway, I'll be testifying how important it is to wait on the Lord. **Wait, I also already testify to that**. Well, anyway, I'll be doing what comes natural for me when I see the hand of The Lord move on my behalf.

I know His Hand is moving for me right now. I might not be able to see it, but it's happening. I'm waiting for big stuff and when it comes, I'm gonna bust a move out of this world. Oh wait, I do that practically every day.

Only Believe!

Toni Joy

Confession for
the Month
of February

Thank you Lord for saving me and my family.
For loving us, and taking care of us.

I receive prosperity in our finances, our
body, our mind, and our spirit.

I thank you that everything we put
our hands to will prosper.

I thank you for favor with our peers, teachers,
and supervisors. I thank you for promotion
on our jobs and good grades in school.
I receive favor going in and favor going out.

Beloved, I pray that you may prosper in all things and be in health,
just as your soul prospers 3 John 1:2

Rev.3:8 I know your deeds. See, I have placed before you an open door that no one can shut. I know that you have little strength, yet you have kept my word and have not denied my name.

He knows

God said "He know thy works" so why do we try to make God's works match our works when in truth, we should make our works match God works. Because He made us and we did not make ourselves.

God's way is not letting our good be evil spoken of, for God said that the kingdom of God is not food and drinks, but righteousness, peace, and joy in the Holy Ghost.

We try to make God agree with our lifestyle instead of us agreeing with His lifestyle. We make excuses for what we believe and how we think things should go because it's easier, the way the majority does it, or because it feels good for the moment. It may **_seem_** to be a blessing, but it stops the power of God from moving in our lives.

Example: how many of us will allow a mistake on the retailer's part in giving us too much money back or charging the wrong amount and say, "that's a blessing from God". Sometimes we use a mistake for a blessing instead of correcting a mistake and letting God bless us.

We make up in our own minds what we want it to be like and put a stamp of God's approval on it when in actuality it is forgery or robbery of righteousness. It is powerless, temporary, and isolated incidents that don't lead to anything or build upon true life.

Let us live our life everyday purposely walking in righteousness that build towards the next day's blessing; Going from faith to faith, glory to glory, blessing to blessing. Let the word of God speak.

Luke 22:44 And being in anguish, he prayed more earnestly, and his sweat was like drops of blood falling to the ground.

Certain Pain

How do I describe this? Most of us don't recognize this pain. It's the pain that we don't want to endure but must in order to grab hold of the prize. It's the pain that we cover up with the world (medicines that don't heal) – medicine we think will make us feel better, like; relationships, work, drugs, alcohol, etc.

It's the pain we know when we make the choice to let go of the world and take hold of the cross. Most of us think that it's the pain that comes from sickness, sin, etc. That is not the pain God speaks of when he say *"pain may endureth for a night, but joy cometh in the morning" (Ps. 30:6)*. We don't get joy from sickness/sin. It's the pain that comes from shedding sin and sickness, and not allowing these things to keep you. It's the chiseling off of self.

That certain pain is the space between starting and finishing growth spurs.

The picture I have of that certain pain is the poem of "footprints in the sand". I was going through a tough time in my life and I saw a picture of Jesus carrying someone through the sand. I remember saying "that's me - I'm in your arms right now because I can't make it alone; but I know you will get me through". You have to be willing to trust God with your life. If you have to cry all night, keep going forward knowing in your heart (not your head) that **_everything is going to be alright_**.

Don't hide from certain pain, but embrace it; fixing our eyes on Jesus Fixing our eyes on Jesus, the Pioneer and Perfecter of faith. For the joy set before Him He endured the cross, scorning its shame, and sat down at the right hand of the throne of God. **Hebrews 12:2**

My Agape Walk Today

Compliment

Someone

Today that

You don't know

✓ I walked in love today

Meditate today on …

Do not be afraid nor dismayed because of this great multitude, for the battle is not yours, but God's.

2Chronicles 20:15

What you are facing today is not too hard for God; fear not

Phil. 4:6-7 Do not be anxious about anything, but in every situation, by prayer and petition, with thanksgiving, present your requests to God. And the peace of God, which transcends all understanding, will guard your hearts and your minds in Christ Jesus.

Don't Worry, Be Happy

Sometimes we question ourselves as to whether we are in the Lord's will. I say don't worry, be happy. We don't have to figure that out; let the word do the work. Our job is to walk by faith, not worry; worry starts with what we think, but the

Just shall live by faith.
Faith in what? In God, His promises, His Word
In God being there for us
Listen to every Word that proceeds out of the mouth of God
How do we live by every Word?

....and be not conformed (follow after, imitate) this world, but be ye transformed (moved, changed) by the renewing (re-learn, re-educate) your mind, that ye may prove (know, not doubt) what is the good, acceptable, and perfect will of God. Rom. 12:1-2 (AMP)

Trust in the Word and be holy, everything else will fall into place.

It takes a made up mind (choose) and determination (dedication). Even when we make mistakes (don't worry) because it takes time to change and renew our mind. Just don't stop the process of trusting God; He is always there. Jump on the right track and smile. In the book of James, it states,

"Consider it pure joy, my brothers and sisters whenever you face trials of many kinds, because you know that the testing of your faith produces perseverance. Let perseverance finish its work so that you may be mature and complete, not lacking anything." James 1:2-9 (AMP)
Trust the Word to work out the kinks in our mind.
If we could do it, we wouldn't need Jesus.
Casting all your cares upon Him, for
He cares for you. 1Peter 5:7
Don't worry, just walk by faith...

Heb. 10:24,25 And let us consider one another in order to stir up love and good works, not forsaking the assembling of ourselves together, as is the manner of some, but exhorting one another, and so much the more as you see the Day approaching.

Dressed Up and Out

I was thinking about the 12 disciples and the saints *(after Jesus rose up to be with the Father)* - when they came together, did they consider how they dressed? I can't help to think that how they were dressed was not the most important part of their gatherings.

I am not against looking good — but what's the most important reason we come together. I started thinking about "what were the things that was most important to them when they got together;

Worship and Praise - Blessing God and Being Blessed by God
The Salvation and deliverance of others - Blessing each other
Learning more about the Father, Jesus, and The Holy Spirit
Learning more about the Kingdom of God on earth
how to work, where to go, and what to do
Learning more about who they were in Christ; How to live
there are so many good reasons

I wondered what we think is important when we come together;

How we are dressed
how someone else is dressed
who is here, who is not
I wonder what happened to them - who they with - where they going
who should I talk to, who shouldn't I talk to
why are they doing that, I should be doing that
there are so many not-so-good reasons
Do people notice the Holy Spirit in us or just our holy apparel?
Let's look good, but most important...· Attract people to God
By the way; there is no perfect church (not even in the early church). **Acts 5:1-5**

My 2 Cents

What is our focus to be when we come into the House of the Lord? Now, I'll admit I have spent time in church admiring some of the absolutely gorgeous attire in which some of the women are dressed because I enjoy fashion. I enjoy seeing women with the ability to pull an outfit together. And some women in church do it better than some supermodels. I'll also admit, some of them have made me look twice or more in the mirror at my own outfit and second guessed what I wore to church.

But, being attired in the anointing is far more important. You can look pulled together on the outside and be as empty and dead on the inside as an old dried up tree branch and not have enough power to pray yourself out of a paper bag.

"It's more important for you to be clothed in the anointing; new clothes will not set anybody free."

Did that change my perspective? You better believe it did. I can't tell y'all how many times since I have rolled out of bed on a Sunday morning and eyeballed a pair of jeans, wanting so badly to wear them to church. I haven't done it yet. I have to work up the nerve. Yes, I'll dress them up at least. I understand, it's not about what's on the outside, it is what's on the inside that makes all the difference. Jesus said this to the Pharisees—Then the Lord said to him, *You Pharisees are so careful to clean the outside of the cup and the dish, but inside you are still filthy--full of greed and wickedness! Luke 11:39 NLT* I like in that same passage Jesus also said, in verse 36, *If you are filled with light, with no dark corners, then your whole life will be radiant, as though a floodlight is shining on you.*

That's what I want. I want Luke 11:36 to be my look; and quite honestly - to look fashionable while being full of His light.

I'm sold on the idea we can have both. *Only Believe!*

By the way, I wore jeans to church on Sunday. Yep, I dressed them up. Wore one of my favorite starched white shirts, a pearl necklace with diamonds, matching bracelet and 3 1/2 inch heel boots. Oh and a tweed jacket made in Italy. (Long story about the jacket). Anyway, I was kinda, sorta comfortable. Not something I would make a habit of. I don't see anything wrong with wearing jeans to Sunday Worship Service. It is not about what you wear. Wearing jeans did not affect my worship at all. Hallelujah! Really, in my opinion, you can wear whatever you want to worship service <u>unless</u> it's your pajamas or daisy duke shorts.

Only Believe!

My Agape Walk Today

Call someone

you haven't

talked to in

a long time

<u>a family member</u>

<u>or close friend</u>

✓ <u>I walked in love today</u>

Meditate today on ...

Blessed is the man
Who walks not in the counsel of the ungodly,
Nor stands in the path of sinners,
Nor sits in the seat of the scornful;
But his delight is in the law of the Lord,
And in His law he meditates day and night.
He shall be like a tree
Planted by the rivers of water,
That brings forth its fruit in its season,
Whose leaf also shall not wither;
And whatever he does shall prosper.
Ps. 1:1-3
Talk to someone who knows God today, not someone
who will tell you just what you want to hear

Mark 11:24 "Therefore I say to you, whatever things you ask when you pray, believe that you receive them, and you will have them".

"Wake up Everybody"

No more sleeping in bed. No more backwards thinking – time for thinking ahead. The world has changed so very much from what it used to be. There is so much hatred, war and poverty.

A song from way back in the day – but it still stands true today, even more so now!

My work schedule has changed so much over the years, which has affected every part of my life, especially getting up in the morning to pray. I had to adapt changes to my time with family, cleaning the house, cooking, eating, sleeping, etc. But the most important thing I had to learn, and still make myself follow, is to be consistent in prayer.

I was meditating on what I was believing God for one Sunday morning while I was making breakfast – *you know that when-God-when kind of thing*; and it came up in my spirit that everything I wanted and needed was in prayer. Because of my schedule I was getting away from my daily routine of praying. I was reminded that prayer needed to be consistent.

I had to wake up to the reality that the salvation of my children is in prayer; the souls of the sinners are in prayer, the wisdom of President Obama is in prayer; prosperity is in prayer, etc." *(That should make us get up in the morning, tired legs, eyes and all, and pray).*

Regardless of what is "*inconsistent*" in our lives, prayer needs to be <u>consistent</u> <u>& first</u> and this will affect every area of our lives and others for the good.

Wake up and Pray – first and foremost...Daily

"If My people who are called by My name will humble themselves, and pray and seek My face, and turn from their wicked ways, then I will hear from heaven, and will forgive their sin and heal their land. Now My eyes will be open and My ears attentive to prayer made in this place". 2 Chron 7:14-15

Revelation 20:3 and he cast him into the bottomless pit, and shut him up, and set a seal on him, so that he should deceive the nations no more till the thousand years were finished. But after these things he must be released for a little while.

Practice Makes Perfect

I was on a cruise a while back and thought about the time during the millennium, that it will be a time of perfect leadership with no influence of evil. The Devil will be locked up for 1000 years and Jesus will reign on earth. As I was gazing at the water and clouds I thought about what it was going to be like:

> ***To go about life without pressure or the appearance of evil***
> ***To have twenty-four hour godly guidance, wow...***

Why not live like that now? The influence of evil is here but *"greater is He that is in us than he that is in the world" (1John 4:4).*

Why not practice reigning with Jesus now? He lives on the inside of us. We **DO** have twenty-four hour godly guidance. We have the righteousness of God,

I think about the bold "sweet and swag" that the world thinks they have in living everyday life. Where is our boldness? Jesus has given us all things that pertain to life and godliness. Let the Word of God and Holy Spirit reign in us so the world can see the Glory of God and choose life.

<u>**We have the real "sweet and swagness" of life.**</u>
Let's make our environment "Jesus Ready"
Usher in the millennium now! Practice makes perfect

But if Christ is in you, then even though your body is subject to death because of sin, the Spirit gives life because of righteousness. For I do not do the good I want to do, but the evil I do not want to do—this I keep on doing. What a wretched man I am! Who will rescue me from this body that is subject to death? Because through Christ Jesus the law of the Spirit who gives life has set you free from the law of sin and death. And if the Spirit of him who raised Jesus from the dead is living in you, he who raised Christ from the dead will also give life to your mortal bodies because of his Spirit who lives in you. Romans 7:15-8:11

Happy Valentine's Day

Be my valentine

Give out candy today

Or a healthy sweet

✓ *I walked in love today*

Rom. 12:18 *If it is possible, as far as it depends on you, live at peace with everyone.*

Don't Receive It

I had the opportunity to be part of a group of people in a class for eight weeks and I watched the negative and positive attitudes on display. I noticed how the attitudes transferred from one person to the next.

I told my oldest daughter (years ago) when she got in high school to just sit back in class for a while and pay attention to people, don't just jump up and start hanging with people - learn a little about them. This helped her to make very good decisions regarding who she chose as friends (my youngest daughter recently graduated high school, now she couldn't slow down enough to pay attention to herself less alone others - much prayer went forth there...)

You can learn a lot by sitting back and paying attention.
I also know that we believers, even the ones that are very kind, which seems like nothing ever bothers them are not special. We too will have to be in the company of people that have attitude issues. We will soon have our day being the victims of these negative attitudes. It doesn't matter how sweet you are. **It's at this moment, you will find out if you're made of sugar and spice and everything nice?**

Will you receive it? Will you follow that train of behavior and get caught up in what can cost you dearly? Study on the example of Christian love. We are supposed to be un-movable and have self-control, letting the Holy Spirit lead us. The Word says we can do all things in Christ. W**e** **_can turn_** the other cheek and walk in love towards those that are un-fair, discriminatory, or abusive in their behavior towards us. I'm not saying that sometimes we won't have to take steps and actions for certain matters - this is where wisdom must play a big part.

In a perfect world, we are witnesses of God who are making the world know Him by our behavior, not being moved by negative and contrary attitudes.

Our motivation and hope are to reach for the perfect world while living in an in-perfect world
Therefore let us pursue the things which make for peace and the things by which one may edify another. Rom. 14:19

Half-Steppin

Matt. 6:33 *But seek first the kingdom of God and His righteousness, and all these things shall be added to you.* We need to examine this scripture very closely... I think sometimes we say it, only looking at the "**And all these things shall be added to you**". It's not in small print, but we look over the "**Seek first the kingdom of God and His righteousness**".

Do we really do that? When we're up against the wall, do we really seek His righteousness? We skimp on little things that God expect from His Children and want Him to just look over them and understand. But we still want to hold Him to His Word on the *"adding things"*. He is such a loving Father that I'm quite certain if He could, He would look over some things; but, because He loves us, He can't. Yes, He does forgive us and give us chance after chance to seek His righteousness.

When we skimp, we half-step... we compromise our faith. We don't like to think we do, but we do. We think we are in faith because we're looking in the right direction and may be on the right path - but are we walking in the true integrity of "doing it God's way".

Sometimes we don't look at "His Righteousness" as "His Way"... His whole way, all the way

We say "God is Perfect" speaking of His Righteousness like it's just a description of a Good God. We get against the wall and only see what we think or the way the world does things... so we choose the best we can, not understanding that He can't honor our lack of integrity or faith, even if it's super hard for us or don't make sense, or We thought it was no other way. *(A year of tithing got away from me with this one. I repented and settled firmly in the righteousness of God concerning the finances He has blessed me with.)*

Anytime we deviate from His Righteousness (God's Way of doing things), we are walking in our own or the worlds way of doing it.... and we will always fall short and miss out on the THINGS that should come to us. ***Continued with today's devotion on next page.***

What we need to do when we hit a wall is to trust God to reveal the way even if it means breaking routines. That may be what we need even if we think we are losing we are losing to self and winning in Christ. God don't have to show up; He's there! He won't let you fall. I think sometimes we get impatient, thereby, making the situation bigger than what it is. Sometimes it just hurts or we think it will hurt someone else. We can't save everyone from their hurts no matter how much we want to. We over-think it and put God in our pocket We pretend like we still have Him, but tuck Him under our sleeves for a minute to do what we think is best.

Here's a little example: We're believing God to heal us so we speak the scriptures, we pray, we believe God's our healer, and when someone ask us how we feel... we tell them the whole story.... giving a testimony of our situation and not God being our healer; thus giving more attention to the pain/sorrow/pity than acknowledging and standing in faith in the Word of God. When we do this, God has to wait until we get so sick and tired of being sick that we get on our face to God and not think about telling anyone about how we feel. Then **bam...you're healed! Why?** Because you stopped looking at the world and tapped into the kingdom.

I had to realize this to break through some financial matters that I had. I was on the right path. I prayed, cried, believed that I was debt free...did, everything **I** knew to work things out. Things were getting better; but, it was like going forward 3 steps and then 2 steps back, then 3 more steps then 1 step back. It was this vicious cycle that was wearing me down. Revelation here and there.... but this revelation on His Righteousness broke that cycle. I had to check my faithfulness to His Righteousness. I can see why prosperity worked in other areas of my life... *faith in His way, walking in His Righteousness - but I wasn't using it in areas I hadn't matured or completely submitted to yet.*

What's working in your life? What's not? Test the integrity of your faith. Do like I did....

I had to put my whole foot into His righteousness, no half-steppin!

The Lord opened my eyes to this scripture... seek first the kingdom of God and **His Righteousness**, desiring to do things His way, all the way
The Kingdom and His Righteousness is where "the things are"

Matt 18:21-22 Then Peter came to Him and said, "Lord, how often shall my brother sin against me, and I forgive him? Up to seven times?" Jesus said to him, "I do not say to you, up to seven times, but up to seventy times seven.

How Many Times?

Up to 490 times-plus: God is a forgiving God from the simplest matters to the hardest. He forgives our mistakes and broken promises. He forgives the person that hurt or sinned against us; and when we hurt or sin against others, He forgives us.

God is merciful to the just and the unjust: In order to be just, we had to have been unjust. Mercy was applied in an unjust situation to make it just. God says to bless and love our enemies, do good and pray for those that hate us and spitefully use us. In doing this we are the sons of the Father (because that's how He is). *Matt 5:44-45*

God asks us to forgive, as a matter of fact – He demands it. God is straight forward on this subject. There is no need to ask for wisdom for the scripture that says "if we don't forgive men of their trespasses – our heavenly Father will not forgive us". Matt 6:15

Why is That?
When we walk in kindness we are the Children of God; but when we walk in un-forgiveness, we act like the adversary the devil.

I will be kind to those that love me as well as to those that don't. I will walk in loving-kindness because my Heavenly Father is kind to me.

Or do you despise the riches of His goodness, forbearance, and longsuffering, not knowing that the goodness of God leads you to repentance? Rom. 2:4

Presidents Day

Washington's Birthday is a United States federal holiday celebrated on the third Monday of February in honor of George Washington, the first President of the United States.

It is also a state holiday in most states where it is known by a variety of names including **Presidents Day** and **Washington's and Lincoln's Birthday** and officially celebrates, depending upon the state, Washington alone, Washington and Lincoln, or some other combination of U.S. presidents. Some states celebrate Washington and the third president Thomas Jefferson but not Lincoln.

Colloquially, the holiday is widely known as "Presidents Day" and is often an occasion to celebrate, or at least remember, all presidents and not just George Washington and Abraham Lincoln. Both Lincoln's and Washington's birthdays are in February. In historical rankings of Presidents of the United States both Lincoln and Washington are frequently, but not always, the top two presidents. In Washington's adopted hometown of Alexandria, Virginia, celebrations are held throughout the month of February

Excerpt taken from Wikipedia http://en.wikipedia.org/wiki/Washington%27s_Birthday

Therefore I exhort first of all that supplications, prayers, intercessions, and giving of thanks be made for all men, for kings and all who are in authority, that we may lead a quiet and peaceable life in all godliness and reverence. For this is good and acceptable in the sight of God our Savior, who desires all men to be saved and to come to the knowledge of the truth. For there is one God and one Mediator between God and men, the Man Christ Jesus, who gave Himself a ransom for all, to be testified in due time, 1Tim. 2:1-5

Pray for the President, whether you voted for him/her or not.

My Agape Walk
Today

Take a few minutes

and pray that

God give you favor

in everything you

do and say

today

✓ <u>I walked in love today</u>

Matthew 25:1-4 *At that time the kingdom of heaven will be like ten virgins who took their lamps and went out to meet the bridegroom. Five of them were foolish and five were wise. The foolish ones took their lamps but did not take any oil with them. The wise ones, however, took oil in jars along with their lamps.*

Foolish Virgin
I was reading the parable of the 10 Virgins, but I particularly took notice to the
5 foolish ones:
1. It did say they were "Virgins", (this is good).
2. They lacked wisdom (wow, you can be good yet lack wisdom).

This makes me put a lot of **2's** together, example:
....a Christian person with money that don't tithe ....a church goer that parties...an educated person that don't have common sense...a mouth that praises God and curses like a sailor, without remorse....someone that desires to get married and sleeps with every Tom, Dick, and Harry (or Sue, Lois, and Jane). You get the picture/

Some makes sense and some don't. But it's so easy for us to fall into these 2's. But there are so many good people in the world, so many smart people in the world - and these are the same people that will reject godly wisdom. Have you had someone tell you *"there is nothing wrong with taking a drink every now and then - even Jesus drunk wine"*? It boils down to "our owe thinking" - we measure knowledge and wisdom by what **WE THINK**.

The wisdom of the world says:
Do you really think that you can have a relationship without having sex in these days...? God knows my heart... (This is a good one) God gave us our own mind to decide...
you can walk away and say.... "Foolish Virgin"

Set your life apart for "God's use" and be ready when He comes

When your character is challenged, stop and allow the Word of God to correct you.
Let's not be wise in our own eyes and be foolish Virgins.
And the foolish said to the wise, 'Give us some of your oil, for our lamps are going out.' But the wise answered, saying, 'No, lest there should not be enough for us and you; but go rather to those who sell, and buy for yourselves.' And while they went to buy, the bridegroom came, and those who were ready went in with him to the wedding; and the door was shut. **Matt. 25:8**

Meditate today on ...

For His anger *is but for* a moment,
His favor *is for* life;
Weeping may endure for a night,
But joy *comes* in the morning.

Ps. 30:5

And that's a promise
Wake up to His Favor and Joy
Right now, yes "you"

Prov 3:5-6 *Trust in the LORD with all your heart, And lean not on your own understanding; In all your ways acknowledge Him, And He shall direct your paths.*

It's A Supernatural Thing!

Trusting God is not a natural thing to do. It goes against what we see, feel, and think (it went against our nature before we were born again). It's a spiritual thing. So when we make a decision to trust God – expect the natural to put limits on it – but let the super lead the natural and **Let God Be God**.

Abraham trusted God and Sarah had a baby. **Moses** trusted God and parted the Red Sea. **Peter** trusted God and walked on water. **Jesus** trusted God to raise Him from the dead and we became children of God.

Think about it: walking by faith is walking by what God says, which means it's coming from above and not what is physical in this world. Faith is not coming from what we think, feel, or see. We're not dependent on the ways or things that are perishable.

This makes us not subject or bound by poverty, lack, sickness, depression, jealousy, sin, etc.

Let's stop making this choice (which life is best) so hard. God **is a God of miracles -** He is the same today, yesterday, and forever.

Let God be God in our life, receive the super on your natural today.

"For the eyes of the LORD run to and fro throughout the whole earth, to show Himself strong on behalf of those whose heart is loyal to Him."
2 Chron 16:9

Romans 8:28 *And we know that in all things work for the good of those who love him, who have been called according to his purpose.*

Do You Know?

As I read this verse, I wondered how many of us really know that God can handle it; handle our ups and downs, our good and bad, successes and failures, etc. God knows every hair on our head. When we accepted Jesus as Lord of our life we gave Him an inside connection to each of us. *With that, He can work.* He knows us better than we know ourselves. That makes Him a qualified authority to tell us who we are, what we need, and how to get it.

What else do we know?

Now He (Jesus) who searches the hearts knows what the mind of the spirit is, because He makes intercession for the saints according to the will of God. ***He (Jesus) sees us; knows us; stands in the gap applying the answer to our particular life (knowing our particular desire), and set the course for our particular needs, wants, and desires.*** What then shall we say to these things? If God *is* for us, who *can be* against us? <u>*That's why we say:*</u>

Yet in all these things we are more than conquerors through Him who loved us. For I am persuaded that neither death nor life, nor angels nor principalities nor powers, nor things present nor things to come, nor height nor depth, nor any other created thing, shall be able to separate us from the love of God which is in Christ Jesus our Lord Romans 8:39-39

God said that He would give us the desires of our heart (Ps. 37:4). **God is not a liar, Saints**. So if we take Him at His Word, we have to believe that He knows something about our desire... (Just to side track for a minute...if He know our hearts and desires, He knows all the other little secrets too – *HE STILL* sent Jesus. Why? To help us not hurt us!)

Do YOU really think God knows YOU?

Know for sure that Jesus knows the mind of your heart and intercedes for us and takes that particular petition to God.
He told Moses to stand still and see... and Moses did... and God did....
Know that God can handle it – For what are we waiting?
Let's Win, NOW

Gratefulness **One thing I was reminded of while watching the events of Super-storm Sandy-***GRATEFULNESS***. Watching the special news reports on the storm unfolding I found myself continuously thinking, "thank you Jesus that's not happening where I live". Watching that event unfold put in perspective for me and probably a whole lot of other folk what's important and what's not. I immediately became grateful that my power didn't go out during the small wind/rains we experienced here.**

I think (and this is just my opinion) we get so busy living life we forget about the small blessings like having electricity. I have a nephew who lives in New Jersey. I called him Sunday evening to tell him and his family that my family would be praying for them. He said, they had already boarded up his home, purchased lots of bottled water, food, and he had just gotten back from hunting down batteries for his transistor radio. However, his community was not asked to evacuate but some of his adult children that lived nearby had to evacuate and they were coming to his home. You know what he was grateful for? He said, he was happy he had enough room for his adult children and their families to come stay with him as he has a seven bedroom home. That's what gave him joy during the storm; being able to provide for his family and offer some protection. He was **GRATEFULL**.

Talking to him and watching others in those cities endure this hardship put things in perspective for me. Materials things matter not; it's people that matter. Family, friends, loved ones matter. Human life matters. Relationships matter. Material things we can buy again. Every day, we should be grateful for what God has given us. Like the people that experienced Hurricane Sandy; you never know when your life is going to take a quick turn. Be grateful today for even small things like running water in your home, electricity, coming home to family, and the big things like having a roof over our heads. Some of those people lost everything. One young man from New Jersey who had lost everything said: "I still have my health, my wife and my kids." Selah! I spoke with my nephew again on Wednesday, he said, he and his family were good. There were three houses on his block with electricity; his was one of them.

He was praising God. He was GRATEFULL. *Only Believe!*

Meditate today on ...

as His divine power has given to us all things that pertain to life and godliness, through the knowledge of Him who called us by glory and virtue, by which have been given to us exceedingly great and precious promises, that through these you may be partakers of the divine nature, having escaped the corruption that is in the world through lust.

2Peter 3-4

We can partner with Life or Death
Choose today to partner with
Exceedingly great and precious promises

My Agape Walk Today

How Bold Are You

Text someone and

Say that

Jesus loves them

And to have

A blessed day

✓ I walked in love today

John 16:33 *In the world you will have tribulation; but be of good cheer, I have overcome the world."*

The Overlay

Overlay: to lay or spread over or on. To cover the surface of a thing

What is the Life that Jesus wants us to live and how are we to live it in a world of tribulation?

Think about being in a classroom with a projector and looking at the screen as the teacher lay a transparency to view, then adds transparency one over the other to change or add to the view; Jesus said He overcame the world;

So we have tests and trails.... But we also have the Overcomer.

<u>That's the life we are to live</u>

Heaven Over Earth

As you go about your day today, in everything you deal with look at it from the view of the overlay. Literally, change the picture view by laying the Word of God on it to see what God wants you to see. Let the Holy Spirit give you the road map.

Walk in the Overlay today. Add the Word. Add the promise. Add faith. Add love.

···But also for this very reason, giving all diligence, add to your faith virtue, to virtue knowledge, to knowledge self-control, to self-control perseverance, to perseverance godliness, to godliness brotherly kindness, and to brotherly kindness love. For if these things are yours and abound, you will be neither barren nor unfruitful in the knowledge of our Lord Jesus Christ. For he who lacks these things is shortsighted, even to blindness, and has forgotten that he was cleansed from his old sins. Therefore, brethren, be even more diligent to make your call and election sure, for if you do these things you will never stumble; **2Peter 1:3-10**

1Peter 5:7 Casting all your cares upon Him; for He careth for you.

Does He Care?
*I think God gets mad when we walk pass
the color purple and don't notice it*

Right before the above scripture it says "*humble yourselves therefore under the mighty hand of God, that he may exalt you in due time*". To receive His care we must receive Him.

Wherever you cast your cares is where you are looking to take care of them. Where and to whom are _you_ taking your cares?

There are so many scriptures that tell us what to do so that He can bless us: ***praise, pray, faith, trust – basically Know Him.***

The more we know God, the more we know the reasons and secrets of life. For example, God gave us back the dominion that Adam lost, but how can we have dominion over what we don't know or have?

It just messes us up when our children don't listen to us or trust us in matters of life. On the same hand, I can see it should mess God up when we do the same thing to Him; but God is God! And it's a good thing that we can't mess Him up. Like when the Israelites asked for a King like the other nations and God was like.... "Give them what they want" – it wasn't His will – but their choice (*1Samuel:8*).

We do the same thing every day when we acknowledge the things of the world or what the majority do, or our neighbors, co-workers, what other kid's moms/dads let them do verses the things that pleases God.

Let's set our hearts and minds to wake up every morning and notice God's goodness, kindness, and tender mercy... He cares

Because he has set his love upon Me, therefore will I deliver him; I will set him on high, because he knows and understands My name [has a personal knowledge of My mercy, love, and kindness – trusts and relies on Me, knowing I will never forsake him, no, never].
He shall call upon Me, and I will answer him; I will be with him in trouble, I will deliver him and honor him. With long life will I satisfy him and show him My salvation. Ps.91 (Amp.) **Let's stop walking pass the blessing**

Leap Year

Fun Facts

- A leap year occurs every four years. This is because the earth takes about 365 and a quarter days to orbit the sun. After four years, this quarter day adds up to a whole day, which is added to the month of February.

- Ancient Egyptians are smart and figured out that solar calendar and the man-made calendar didn't match up. It takes the Earth 365 days to travel around the sun, but the Egyptians realized that it's roughly "365 days, 5 hours, 48 minutes, and 46 seconds, to be exact." So the extra time amounts to an extra day on our calendar — Leap Year!! Julius Caesar officially added the year into Roman calendars 2,000 years ago.

- Women are traditionally allowed and even encourage to propose to men on Leap Year. This tradition dates all the way back to 5th Century Ireland.

- Since Leap Year and Leap Day only happens once every four years, let's celebrate!! One obvious way is to celebrate your birthday, if you are a Leap Day baby. Also, you can go to Disney!! Disney is open 24 hours on Leap Day!! Go CELEBRATE!!

CONFESSION FOR THE MONTH OF MARCH

Print or write out confession; put where you can see and confess it all month

There is a calling on my life, and only God can direct me in it· I focus on the path that God has put me on, regardless of how contrary this may seem to others – and even to myself at times·

Jesus is the Lord of my life and I live it every day, acknowledging Him in everything I do·

John 8:28 So Jesus said, "When you have lifted up the Son of Man, then you will know that I am he and that I do nothing on my own but speak just what the Father has taught me.

Who Said That?

Whose words are we repeating? Are we repeating the world or the Word (God's Word)? It is through the words of our month that will tell

Who we really serve.

They both will make themselves known to us, but we tend to follow what we see, hear, and feel. The devil is calling out to us 24/7. But guess what; God is calling out to us continually also.

Let's stop taking calls from the devil and answer the call of God.

Do you like what you say? Sometimes do you find yourself wishing you didn't say that? We speak what's on our heart, so fill your heart with the Word of God, then when we open our mouth – the Word of God is what's coming out.

It is so easy to listen to our thoughts, feelings, and the messages that the world sends us. We have to guard our hearts and minds because this is where the issues of our life flow (Prov. 4:23). There will be a certain moment, when it won't matter what anyone else has to say, **only God will have the word that will be the right answer at the right time – and it is that Word that we will need to speak....**

Just a funny example of who are we mirroring: (true story of my daughter and granddaughter.) My daughter told her daughter to do something and she stood there with her hands on her hips like she didn't want to do it. So my daughter said, "Or, you can just go to bed!" She stood there, still, with her hands on her hips and did the longest eye-roll. So my daughter went off! And as she was going off, she noticed her daughter was mimicking her neck-rolling right there on the spot! (Could you picture that? She's three years old.) My daughter had an instant epiphany. It was like a human mirror experience. She noticed that she was picking up "the entire attitude" from her.

Every time we speak, I wonder, "Who Said That?"
A good man out of the good treasure of his heart brings forth good; and an evil man out of the evil treasure of his heart brings forth evil. For out of the abundance of the heart his mouth speaks. Luke 6:45

Right Sister Toni Joy. It comes down to this.....
...Lord are those my words, your words, or his (the devil)?

As much as we work at getting it right, sometimes the wrong thing is out of our mouths before we can stop it. And then it's out there for us to deal. Once it's out there the first order of busy is to correct it by repenting, then rendering those words ineffective, and, if necessary, apologizing.

Apologizing doesn't make us appear weak. As a matter of fact, it takes courage to admit you were wrong. So, if you're able to admit you were wrong; you are courageous. If you've used your words to tear someone down instead of building them up; be courageous today and go apologize. Ask for their forgiveness. Did you know the words of our mouth can be a snare to our soul (the mind, the emotions, the will, and our intellect)? Meaning the words of our mouth can entrap or entangle our soul. If we can entrap or entangle our own souls with the words we speak; how much damage can be done to another by our words?

Charles Capps wrote a very good book on the subject of confession. It's called *"Faith & Confession, How to Activate the Power of God in our Life."*

I've read this book at least three times. It has helped me to discipline my tongue and to confess the Word of God consistently. ***I highly recommend it***. Only Believe!

My Agape Walk Today

Say

"Thank You"

All day Today

To everyone

✓ <u>I walked in love today</u>

Meditate today on ...

Love suffers long and is kind; love
does not envy; love does not parade
itself, is not puffed up; does not
behave rudely, does not seek its
own, is not provoked, thinks no
evil; does not rejoice in iniquity,
but rejoices in the truth; bears all
things, believes all things, hopes
all things, endures all things.

Love never fails. 1Cor. 13:4-7

This is Agape Love that
comes only from God.

Show the world God thru you today

Toni Joy

Gen. 25:31 But Jacob said, "Sell me your birthright as of this day"

Consequently...

Do you sometimes sell yourself short? I wonder sometimes do we even know when we sell ourselves short. You may lose something more than just a missed opportunity or something temporary. Sometimes the consequences can be life changing.

The small decisions we make daily can consequently be bigger than the ones that we think are major; like getting married, having a baby, what college to go too, what job to take.

What about the matters of the heart, walking in love, forgiveness, kindness? What about following the leading of the Holy Spirit. The consequences can be huge and may not even be seen for years. It can cut off our blessings, our health, lose someone valuable, and even our life.

Esau seemingly did something simple that he didn't think through. He was hungry and sold his birthright for some soup that he didn't think meant anything or had spiritual ramifications behind it.

"Look, I am about to die," Esau said. "What good is the birthright to me?" Gen. 25:32

Let's grasp the importance of a thing now, so that we don't have to pay for it later. It can be something as small as "putting something off for tomorrow that you can do today".

Don't take for granted what can bring huge consequences later.

....he burst out with a loud and bitter cry and said to his father, "Bless me—me too, my father!" But he said, "Your brother came deceitfully and took your blessing." Esau said, "Isn't he rightly named Jacob? This is the second time he has taken advantage of me: He took my birthright, and now he's taken my blessing!" Then he asked, "Haven't you reserved any blessing for me?" Isaac answered Esau, "I have made him lord over you and have made all his relatives his servants, and I have sustained him with grain and new wine. So what can I possibly do for you, my son?" Gen. 27:34-36

Gen. 1:3:4 and the serpent said onto the woman "Ye shall not surely die"

He lie, he lie, he lie.......

Mind over Matter

Renew Your Mind.... With the Word of God

The question is....From what are we renewing our mind? The deception the devil wants us to think "reality is", what "life is", or what "works" is. From the very beginning he wanted us to die! He steals our dreams, he kills our desires, and destroys our hopes.

And he is still lying today.....

The Devil tells you, *"You are dying, you can't be forgiven for that, nobody loves you, that sickness is onto death, you will never have nothing, you can't do that, they deserve that, you're better off dead, you can't win, you're a loser, don't get up, it's done, it's lost, it's over, you might as well give up, you messed up too many times – you passed your limit, etc."* **What lies are the devil telling you?**

There is no difference in mind over matter if your mind is **_not_** renewed to the Word of God and the cares/matters of this world are what rule, build, strengthen, create, and mold your mind. Hold up your bible...Say **"this is my reality!"** *Still holding your bible*? **God has given each of us a measure of faith** (you are holding your Bible.... **THIS IS YOUR MEASURE**. How much you let this get in you is what your measure will be.

Renew your mind from old habits, sins, weights, lies and more lies. As you get into the Word of God you will find so many lies that you didn't even know were lies. It sounds good, feels good, looks good - but it's not good. You will be shown in your inner man what is true. The power that raised Jesus from the dead is the same power that resides in you to deliver you from dead works, sick thinking and the power of lies.

*Therefore lay aside all filthiness and overflow of wickedness, and receive with meekness the implanted word, which is **able** to **save your soul**s.*
James 1:21
The Truth of the matter

My Agape Walk Today

Send

Someone

a card in the mail

"U·S· Post Office"

✓ <u>I walked in love today</u>

Matthew 4:4 But He answered and said, "It is written, 'Man shall not live by bread alone, but by every word that proceeds from the mouth of God.'"

Who Knew

So many of us search the world for answers to our problems, for our successes, for our desires, and the truth is:

No one knows the plan of God for our life but God.

I had such a revelation of this in 1Cor. 2:9 *But as it is written: "Eye has not seen, nor ear heard, nor have entered into the heart of man the things which God has prepared for those who love Him."* No one in this world knows what God has for you.... So stop searching

IN THIS WORLD.

Pay close attention to this- It say's *"nor have entered into the heart of man..."* God gave that secret to no one, but wants to reveal it to you (the real you, the spirit you; not the flesh). *Again....* Pay close attention to this – It say's *"the things which God has prepared for those who love Him. "* To live *His way and to love God is to take what He has prepared.* Then later in scripture is says, **But we have the mind of Christ – 2Cor. 2.16.** Sometimes we don't know we have everything we need; or we forget that we do.

God knows what you need, he told us to seek Him first and all these things will be added to you Matt. 6:33. This is important to know because there are things we need to know In Christ and things we need to know in the world; but God says to **seek Him first**, **first**, **first**, and the rest will be added to you. He knows we need it, and He wants to give it to us. Read all of Matthew 6.

Who Knew, the answer was right on the table
In your BIBLE and in our heart.
If you want to know, Only God can tell you

My 2 Cents

As I read what Toni Joy wrote this week, I am reminded of the many ways God speaks to us. He speaks through His Word (Logos) and Rhema (Truth Revealed, An Utterance or Thing Said). Not only can we ascertain His will for us through studying the Word, but God talks! He talks to each of us. Some listen and some turn a deaf ear.

The gatekeeper opens the gate for him, and the sheep hear his voice and come to him. He calls his own sheep by name and leads them out. After he has gathered his own flock, he walks ahead of them, and they follow him because they recognize his voice. *St. John 10:3-4 New Living Translation*

He has various ways He speaks to us to reveal His plan. Has this ever happen to you? You're sitting in service and the Pastor having no clue what you're going through speaks the answer to your problem right in the middle of his sermon? THAT'S GOD TALKING! It's so powerfully spoken and it's so clearly a rhema word just for you; it makes you feel like jumping up and shouting a great big ole hallelujah right then. Oh yeah, when God speaks honey, it will move you. Everything He says has the ANOINTING attached to it. That's one of the ways we can tell if it's Him talking.

Is it peaceable? Is the anointing present?

I had an experience this past week during bible study at church. During bible study last week; while we were praising God, I heard *"ride the wave of My Spirit"*. I said, "Yes Lord". I began to worship God more fervently. Let me just tell you, by the time service was over I looked a hot mess (hair style gone, clothes disheveled). As I rode the *"wave of His Spirit"* others rejoiced with me, but no one experienced the intensity of the presence of God as I did. Why? It was my RHEMA WORD! I went home totally refreshed in my spirit and I'm still enjoying that refreshing. It was exactly what I needed. A spiritual refreshing. I needed a word from the Lord and got it. Have you received a rhema word from the Lord lately?

Only Believe!

James 1:7-8 *For let not that man suppose that he will receive anything from the Lord; he is a double-minded man, unstable in all his ways.*

Compromising positions

Compromising positions.... We face them every day. We are presented with the opportunity or pressure to lie, cheap, or compromise our word, reputation, prosperity, or our trust with others.

Our integrity is on the line

I don't know of anyone who doesn't care if someone trust them or not, or at least would like to look in the mirror and say "I'm a man/woman of my word".

Sometimes the pressures of holding our ground or pursuing our goals squeezes us into compromising positions because we believe it will help our situation when in reality, it will hurt. If not now, somewhere down the line we will lose something; and most likely, something more important than we realize. Some compromising positions are really "light mattered" like; *"my dog ate my homework"*. But some are heavier like telling a spouse, *"I was at my mom's last night"* when you were... nowhere near there. Neither is good. If we start pressuring ourselves to be people of integrity, our goodness will pay off in every area of life and strengthen us for the more difficult matters. It teaches us to deal with life. Anything else would be cheating ourselves and stopping our growth, causing us to stay children and creating immature and untrustworthy adults).

God has given us a position where we can face everything with the truth, even if it hurts. His grace and mercy will take us through compromising positions with honor, grace and favor. And we will always be able to look in the mirror and be well-pleased with ourselves. Maturity equips us to handle the situation with grace regardless of the level of trouble, who is to blame and the setbacks it may cause.

This is why we can tell the truth· This is why we can trust God· This is why we can face our fears, troubles, and trials with boldness·
If you're in a compromising situation... let truth walk you out, God's got your back!
Don't let situations compromise honor

Toni Joy

Rom. 7:16-19...For I have the desire to do what is good, but I cannot carry it out. For I do not do the good I want to do, but the evil I do not want to do—this I keep on doing.

It's not my desire to be disobedient!

If you were to ask my mom, she would say that I'm was not a good student as a child, that, she would tell me what to do, and I would say, "OK Mom," still do my own thing, and would have to pay the consequences later. But again, unbeknownst to my mom, it was not my desire to be disobedient. I had every intention to do exactly what I was told; it just didn't work out that way.

The influence of the world is stronger than man... but there is a greater power in us that can help us to do exactly as we intended.

You, dear children, are from God and have overcome them, because the one who is in you is greater than the one who is in the world. 1 John 4:4

But the lack of knowledge can be devastating. We have to know what we are fighting against or we will be beating the air.

I didn't know for a long time that I wasn't strong enough on my own to fight the forces against me or that I wasn't acting on my own or that it was a sin nature (influence of the enemy) working. ***I just thought I was bad***. What was I to do, the devil had me where he wanted me.

But thanks be to God, who delivered me from my sin nature. Now I am spirit led and not led by the influences of the world.

What do our heart desire? We can be good students and go on to be good teachers.

So I find this law at work: Although I want to do good, evil is right there with me. For in my inner being I delight in God's law; but I see another law at work in me, waging war against the law of my mind and making me a prisoner of the law of sin at work within me. What a wretched man I am! Who will rescue me from this body that is subject to death? Thanks be to God, who delivers me through Jesus Christ our Lord!
So then, I myself in my mind am a slave to God's law, but in my sinful nature a slave to the law of sin. Rom. 7:21-25

Matt. 28:5-6 *But the angel said to the women, "Do not be alarmed and frightened, for I know that you are looking for Jesus, Who was crucified. He is not here; He has risen, <u>as He said [He would do]"</u>.*

Step out the boat
I want to talk about "Be not faithless, but believe".

Then the eleven disciples went away into Galilee, to the mountain which Jesus had appointed for them. When they saw Him, they worshiped Him; but some doubted. Matt. 28:16

<u>And there are 3 things to which we need to pay close attention:</u>
When they saw Him, They worshipped Him, but some doubted.

Haven't we all been in a service before while the anointing was strong and present, but *we weren't connected*? So can you see the doubters in the presence of Jesus? In Jesus' core group, there were some doubters. ***"Be not faithless, but believe."***

At this point in my life, this is how I feel about it: I don't know how much longer we have here and I am getting older. I didn't say I was old, but getting older. As I see the things in the world and how things are going, I have two frames of mind here: 1) Time is moving fast and 2) I see the wickedness of the day. ***I'm steppin out the boat every day, because what do I have to lose? I'm taking challenges more now than I ever have before. Let's all get out the boat and see what is in us and have an adventure with Jesus. What do we have to lose? "Be not faithless, but believe."***

Then He said to Thomas, "Reach your finger here, and look at My hands; and reach your hand here, and put it into My side.

Do not be unbelieving, but believing."
And Thomas answered and said to Him, "My Lord and my God!"

Only Believe

Toni Joy
1 Corinthians 13 From the
Toni Joy's Version (TJV)

Live Life Loving
*I woke up the other night about 3 am and couldn't
go right back to sleep so I wanted to share with
you this scripture, in my own words:*

*Though I speak with the tongues of wise men and of angels, or sing
like a bird but not have love, I am a drum with no beat or a bell
without a ring. And though I know all the secrets and answer all
questions (tell you all you want to hear), and though I believe and
therefore receive, but have not love, I am still empty, lost, alone.
And though I am a great giver and known for my charity,
and will chain myself to the cause (bring home the bacon and
fry it in the pan) but have not love, my giving is my reward – it
brings back nothing.
And though I have skilled hands of a surgeon or a master builder,
but have not love, it will break - I may need a lawyer. Vs. 1-3
What are your words on LOVE, applying it in everyday life
(walking in it as if it had everything to do... with living).*

LOVE by the worlds standards fall short because it is ruled by
imperfectness including our feelings and thoughts.
LOVE by God's standards holds the test of time. It delivers because
it is ruled by truth, power, and perfectness.

*Love is patient, love is kind. It does not envy, it does not boast,
it is not proud. It does not dishonor others, it is not self-seeking,
it is not easily angered, it keeps no record of wrongs. Love does
not delight in evil but rejoices with the truth. It always protects,
always trusts, always hopes, always perseveres.*

Love Like God – Live Life Loving
**Love never fails [never fades out or becomes obsolete or
comes to an end]. 1 Cor. 13:8 Amp.**

My 2 Cents

Some years ago, I learned a very pivotal lesson about unconditional love and loving by choice. One of my co-workers at the time was a *"real piece of work"*. This young lady persecuted me **every single day** that I showed up for work. She persecuted me ON PURPOSE. As if her goal for the day was to see if she could get me to NOT QUOTE SCRIPTURE, but to CURSE AT HER. It was hard to avoid her because her office was near mine. Avoiding conflict with her was something I desired to do. Sometimes when I would look at her I thought I saw horns coming out of her head. That's how much her evil works had convinced me she was the devil in the flesh.

Every morning when I would come in as I passed her desk I would plead the blood of Jesus; and every day in my prayer time I would pray for her. Still nothing changed. For months this girl did or said something to me that challenged my love walk. Regardless of what she said or did, I never said anything out of line back to her **(because you know the bible says, "don't render evil for evil or railings for railings).** I would treat her nice anyway; besides, because of her I learned to quote **Matthew 5:44-46** from memory. One day, she had a phone call; a family crisis that meant she had to leave work early. She came to my desk distraught and asked if **I WOULD COVER** her work assignments that day. I gladly agreed. And told her I would be praying for her, which I did.

She was gone from work for a few days. When she came back she thanked me profusely. And mentioned that I was the only one she felt she could ask to cover for her. **ME????** The one she gave the blues every day. Well, our relationship dynamics changed from that point. I wouldn't call her a friend, but our work relationship became friendly. As I got to know her a little better, she told me she had been molested repeatedly by her father as a young girl and hated him with a passion. He was dead. And one day she said to me, *"every year on the anniversary of my father's funeral, I go to the cemetery to spit on his grave."* So, you see she wasn't just being mean to me; she was a wounded, bitter, and unforgiving, young woman carrying her past around with her and afflicting others with her pain.

Even today, I am glad that I never responded contrary to the Word of God towards her. There was a reason she acted the way she did; I was the only co-worker that didn't treat her the way she treated us. Martin Luther King Jr. said, *"Let no man pull you so low as to hate him. Hate cannot drive out hate; only love can do that."* **T.D. Jakes has a new book called "Let it go".** It's so new I am not sure it's on the market yet. But, I was able to read an excerpt from it and it's basically about forgiveness and what happens in our future if we carry our past hurts and disappointments with us.

Only Believe!

My Agape Walk Today

Go through the day

believing that you

can do all things

through Christ who

strengthens you

✓ _I walked in love today_

St. Patrick's Day

Much of what is known about St Patrick comes from the *Declaration*, which was allegedly written by Patrick himself. It is believed that he was born in Roman Britain in the fourth century, into a wealthy Romano-British family. His father was a deacon and his grandfather was a priest in the Christian church. According to the *Declaration*, at the age of sixteen, he was kidnapped by Irish raiders and taken as a slave to Gaelic Ireland. It says that he spent six years there working as a shepherd and that during this time he "found God". The *Declaration* says that God told Patrick to flee to the coast, where a ship would be waiting to take him home. After making his way home, Patrick went on to become a priest.

According to legend, Saint Patrick used the three-leaved shamrock to explain the Holy Trinity to Irish pagans.

According to tradition, Patrick returned to Ireland to convert the pagan Irish to Christianity. The *Declaration* says that he spent many years evangelizing in the northern half of Ireland and converted "thousands". Tradition holds that he died on 17 March and was buried at Downpatrick. Over the following centuries, many legends grew up around Patrick and he became Ireland's foremost saint.

Saint Patrick's Day, or the **Feast of Saint Patrick** (Irish: *Lá Fhéile Pádraig*, "the Day of the Festival of Patrick"), is a cultural and religious holiday celebrated annually on March 17th, the death date of the most commonly-recognized patron saint of Ireland, Saint Patrick (c. AD 385–461).

Saint Patrick's Day was made an official Christian feast day in the early seventeenth century and is observed by the Catholic Church, the Anglican Communion (especially the Church of Ireland), the Eastern Orthodox Church and Lutheran Church. The day commemorates Saint Patrick and the arrival of Christianity in Ireland, as well as celebrating the heritage and culture of the Irish in general. Celebrations generally involve public parades and festivals, and the wearing of green attire or shamrocks. *Christians also attend church services, and the Lenten restrictions on eating and drinking alcohol are lifted for the day, which has encouraged and propagated the holiday's tradition of alcohol consumption.*

Saint Patrick's Day is a public holiday in the Republic of Ireland, Northern Ireland, Newfoundland and Labrador and Montserrat. It is also widely celebrated by the Irish diaspora around the world; especially in Britain, Canada, the United States, Argentina, Australia and New Zealand

From Wikipedia, the free encyclopedia

Toni Joy

And David said unto God, I have sinned greatly, because I have done this thing: but now, I beseech thee, do away the iniquity of thy servant; for I have done very foolishly. ....And David said unto Gad *(David's seer)*, I am in a great strait: let me fall now into the hand of the LORD; for very great are his mercies: but let me not fall into the hand of man. 1 Chron. 21:8-13

It's A Trick

I had the hardest time dealing with spiritual beliefs (that turn into religious bondage), like:

Reaping what you sow - You deserve it - What goes around comes around

There are so many more that we can add. Not that these sayings are false, but they can be taken out of context and can be used at the **will of man**, allowing even our own self to condemn us.

Sometimes we let others judge us and will also judge ourselves (we are harder on ourselves to the point of not forgiving ourselves - even when God has). *We are not perfect beings.* Even a mature Christian can be plagued with "spiritual beliefs". Issues such as divorce, wayward children, death of loved-ones are hardships on the family and weigh heavily on our hearts. It is only through the Love of God and the guidance of Holy Spirit that we escape the bondage of religion (which can be disguised as righteousness).

I have two things to say to that and two things we can do for that:
(1) The Grace of God by the Love of God
(2) Let go and let God with repentance and rejoice

Whether the burden is easy or hard, light or heavy, your fault or not (or even carrying someone else's burden), I have learned you don't want to leave it to yourself or others to judge it. You must deal with it with God. Whether you're getting a light spanking or a sho-nuff whopping, **get it and move on as David did**. There is a work that God has chosen us to do. He knows every hair on our head and still chose us.

Let's not figure it out – Let God do His job.

It's a trick of the enemy to use our own spirituality to hang us up.

Brethren, if a man is overtaken in any trespass, you who are spiritual restore such a one in a spirit of gentleness, considering yourself lest you also be tempted. Gal. 6:1

My 2 Cents

Another **trick** of the enemy that disturbs me greatly is this one of **judging others**. When the devil is able to get us to judge each other the end result is usually destruction. Beautiful relationships have ended because of passing judgments. I am of the opinion (and this is my opinion) that women can be some of the greatest offenders of passing judgment **against each other.** Instead of encouraging each other we can tear each other down in a New York minute.

And we can be petty with it too. We say things like, *"that's not her hair, that's a weave"*; *"why is she trying to wear those stilettoes when she know her feet hurt?"* Small petty things like that can seriously get someone's feelings hurt and a relationship destroyed. I'm being nice about it; there are worst things being said. At the end of the day, after we've said all the ugly little things we've said about others and we look in the mirror we find we're actually no better than the one on which we passed judgment. *The truth is, it is her hair; she bought it.*

Remember what the bible say's *"judge not lest you be judged of the same."* Encouraging others should be priority number one. It goes a lot further than judging. Even, if you don't understand why the sister is wearing her hair the way she does, consider this...she might not understand your choice of hairstyle either. But, there is probably something on which you can compliment her. Look for that and encourage her. One of my mother's favorite sayings was, **"if you don't have anything good to say, don't say anything".** I agree with Sister Toni Joy. Let us extend the Grace and Love of God. Next time, you get ready to fix your mouth to slam a sister, do consider the woman in the mirror first. Because if we don't see Halle Berry, Heidi Klum, or Jesus staring back at us in that mirror, maybe we need to shush it.

Only Believe!

My Agape Walk Today

Take a few minutes

and pray for someone

that God will give them

favor in everything they

do and say today

✓ *I walked in love today*

Meditate today on ...

For My thoughts are not your thoughts,
Nor are your ways My ways," says the LORD.
"For as the heavens are higher than the
earth,
So are My ways higher than your ways,
And My thoughts than your thoughts.

Is. 55:8-9

Get over yourself today – Live better
I love you

1 Corinthians 10:13 No temptation has overtaken you except such as is **common to man**; but God is faithful, who will not allow you to be tempted beyond what you are able, but with the temptation will also make the way of escape, that you may be able to bear it.

"Really···" it's an attitude

Attitude: (Webster) manner of acting, feeling, or thinking that shows ones disposition, opinion, etc. (a friendly, sad, or mean attitude)

Topic: An Overcoming Attitude

*You are of God, little children, and have **overcome them**, because He who is in you is greater than he who is in **the world**. For whatever is born of God **overcome**s **the world**. And this is the victory that has **overcome the world**—our faith. Who is he who **overcome**s **the world**, but he who believes that Jesus is the Son of God? 1 John 4:3-5*

Our attitude influences (plays a great part) in our position in life.

Faith produces an overcoming attitude. You see it done. You see yourself out of the circumstances. Faith will take you where you want to go and the circumstances **must** follow. **You have to see it that way; that's what faith does, it puts you on the other side.**

Let's look at those things that are hard, heavy, burdensome, and strong that hold us back, down, or trap us from moving forward in Christ (those things that are *"Common to Man"*) and let's see that God has an escape!

We, being common to God – are not subject to what is common to man

And the Lord shall make you the head, and not the tail; and you shall be above only, and you shall not be beneath, if you heed the commandments of the Lord your God which I command you this day and are watchful to do them. Deut. 28:13 (Amp. Version)

Your attitude should change knowing you're above, not beneath?
I have this picture in my head of a man (6' tall) with his arm stretched out, holding back a 3' tall with the palm of his hand - while this smaller man is swinging at the air trying to hit him. And the tall man just looking at him saying "Really?"...
Couldn't you see yourself saying "Really?"
Be that tall man and let your troubles/problems be short.

My 2Cents

John C. Maxwell said in his book *"Attitude 101"*, "There is very little difference in people, but that little difference makes a big difference. The little difference is attitude. The big difference is whether it is positive or negative."

In my <u>very</u> early years of working in the ministry I had GREAT BIG ATTITUDE. I was used to working in Corporate America and how things were done...usually very efficiently. When I started working in the ministry and saw how slow church projects can get off the ground or NOT, I think I was shell shocked at how some church people regarded the house of God.

I started working in the church full-time thinking the House of God was a priority for all saved folks. Did I get a rude awakening? I had grandiose plans. I was going to give God my best. I was going to be the dictionary definition of EXCELLENCE. The problem was, I didn't get much cooperation. My attitude changed. I started slacking too. I even vowed to quit working in the ministry and go back to Corporate America. I told that to anyone that would listen, mostly to God though. Thankfully, I mostly gripped about it to Him. <u>He got me straight</u>. He got me straight with this...

***"For as he thinketh in his heart, so is he."* Proverbs 23:7**

Attitude is what's on the inside showing up on the outside. ***Basically*** my attitude was affected by my environment. I was internalizing stuff. I'm saying ***basically*** because I had control over my attitude.

Our attitude **can** be affected by our environment. We choose whether we will be negative or positive. I like this story about the two shoe salesmen who were sent to an island to sell shoes.

The first salesman, upon arrival, was shocked to realize that no one wore shoes. Immediately he sent a telegram to his home office in Chicago saying, "Will return home tomorrow. No one here wears shoes." The second salesman was thrilled by the same realization, immediately he wired the home office in Chicago saying "Please send me 10,000 pairs of shoes. Everyone here needs them."

How's your attitude lately? Are people starting to refer to you as *Tyler Perry's Ma Dear character*? (If they are, you do know that's not good right?) Is it a hot mess? Are you allowing your environment to affect you in a negative way? Or are you and your attitude in the Zone?

Only Believe!

Toni Joy

1 Sam. 17:28 ...When Eliab, David's oldest brother, heard him speaking with the men, he burned with anger at him and asked, "Why have you come down here? And with whom did you leave those few sheep in the wilderness? I know how conceited you are and how wicked your heart is; you came down only to watch the battle."

So They Think They Know Me

I was thinking about the words that David's brother spoke to him. Now we can believe what his brother said about the heart of David or we can believe what God said about the heart of David.

*'I have found David son of Jesse, a **man after** my **own heart**; he will do everything I want him to do. Acts 13:22*

Sometimes even your own family members, co-workers, maybe even someone closer to you, can judge you wrong. We sometimes allow what others think of us rule and even stop us from pursuing our dreams and goals. They tell us what they think and because of who they are, what they have, what they do, and who they know (it may even be someone you admire – even a Christian), we take their word as truth.

But what's really in your heart? What does God say about you?

*Blessed is the one
who does not walk in step with the wicked
or stand in the way that sinners take
or sit in the company of mockers,
but whose delight is in the law of the LORD,
and who meditates on his law day and night.
That person is like a tree planted by streams of water,
which yields its fruit in season
and whose leaf does not wither—*
whatever they do prosper. *Ps. 1:1-3*

P.S. on the other hand, please, let's not be guilty of being judges ourselves; pray for others that God reveal to them their path in life as well as our own.

Meditate today on ...

Therefore I remind you to stir up
the gift of God which is in you
through the laying on of my hands.
For God has not given us a spirit
of fear, but of power and of love
and of a sound mind. *2 Tim. 1:7*
That's right; you are invincible,
powerful, fearless, forgiving, kind,
and most of all
You have the mind of Christ (1 Cor. 2:16)

My Agape Walk Today

How Bold Are You

Treat yourself to Something

Special Today – especially

if this seems to

not be your day

"It don't have

to cost a thing"

✓ I walked in love today

Toni Joy

1 John 5:14-15 *And this is the confidence (the assurance, the privilege of boldness) which we have in Him: that if we ask anything according to His will, He listens to and hears us. And if we know that He listens to us in whatever we ask, we also know that we have the requests made of Him.*

Answered Prayers
When we pray and things don't happen, what do we think?
What about the scripture above?
Was it not God's will? Did we pray right? Do we have to wait? Do we have faith? Did they or we not deserve to get those prayers answered?

So we know He hears us – Do we hear Him?
We, and those we pray for, need very much so to **wake up** to our **answered prayers**.

I believe that we can sometimes block the answer to our prayers when we are not attentive. Have you ever been engaged in a conversation with someone; while looking at them, and not hearing a word they were saying, lost somewhere in your own thoughts and when you regain your focus, it's, "what did you say?"! Sometimes we even pretend like we heard it.

Are we listening when the Lord is talking?
I believe sometimes we see or hear the answer and it passes us by. We glance and keep going, half asleep, missing it like a whisper, and we blow it off.

Answered prayers is a promise! Let's stop sleep walking
Then He said, "Go out, and stand on the mountain before the Lord." And behold, the Lord passed by, and a great and strong wind tore into the mountains and broke the rocks in pieces before the Lord, but the Lord was not in the wind; and after the wind an earthquake, but the Lord was not in the earthquake; and after the earthquake a fire, but the Lord was not in the fire; and after the fire a still small voice. **1 Kings 19:11-12**

Can we hear Him now, Can we hear Him now, Can we hear Him now

Answered Prayers

I specifically want to address steps/process to getting our prayers answered. There are steps to everything: steps to shoe tying, to buttoning our clothes, to learn in order to use Google, to send and receive emails; the **how to** list goes on and on.

Steps - any of a series of distinct successive stages in a <u>process</u> or the attaining of an end.
  (1) **Decide** what you want from God. James 1:6-8 -**Decisiveness is key. It's very important.**
  (2) **Read** scriptures that promise the answer you need. Joshua 1:8
  (3) **Ask** God for the things you want. Matthew 7:7-8
  (4) **Believe** that you receive. Mark 11:23-24
  (5) **Refuse** to doubt. 2ⁿᵈ Corinthians 10:5 - **Never permit a mental picture of failure to remain in your mind.**
  (6) **Meditate** on the promise. Proverbs 4:20-22 See **yourself in possession of what you have asked from God and make plans as if it already were a reality.**
  (7) Give God the praise. Philippians 4:6 - **This final step is to lift your heart to God constantly in gratitude and praise.**

My husband and I used the steps above to buy our first house. Many things happened during the buying process that looked like we were going to be denied. In spite of the obstacles and forecast, we implemented Step #5 and refused to doubt. We are homeowners today because we applied the seven steps. A very close friend of mine used these steps when she needed a new car. As she used these steps, with step # 1 she was very specific about what she wanted. Step # 3 she asked that she not have a car note with the car. Her family talked about her bad. They asked her how on earth did she think she was going to have a car without a car note. Steps 4 & 5 kept her grounded. Not long after my dear friend was driving to work again in her car **without** a car note.

Nothing is too hard for God! Whatever you're praying about (such as healing in your body, financial restoration, a new home, a job, and your children) is doable when God is steering your life's ship. Fight the good fight of faith. Don't give up. See the answers to your prayers manifested. **He loves us**, Only Believe!

PALM SUNDAY

On Palm Sunday Christians celebrate the <u>triumphal entry of Jesus Christ</u> into Jerusalem, the week before his <u>death and resurrection</u>. For many Christian churches, Palm Sunday, often referred to as "Passion Sunday," and marks the beginning of <u>Holy Week</u>, which concludes on Easter Sunday.

The next day a great multitude that had come to the feast, when they heard that Jesus was coming to Jerusalem, took branches of palm trees and went out to meet Him, and cried out:

"Hosanna! 'Blessed is He who comes in the name of the Lord!' The King of Israel!"

Then Jesus, when He had found a young donkey, sat on it; as it is written:

**"Fear not, daughter of Zion;
Behold, your King is coming,
Sitting on a donkey's colt."**

His disciples did not understand these things at first; but when Jesus was glorified, then they remembered that these things were written about Him and *that* they had done these things to Him. *John 12:12-16*

GOOD FRIDAY

Good Friday is observed on the Friday before Easter Sunday. On this day Christians commemorate the passion, or suffering, and death on the cross of the Lord, Jesus Christ. Many Christians spend this day in fasting, prayer, repentance, and meditation on the agony and suffering of Christ on the cross. Many churches will have "Good Friday Service"

But they shouted, "Away with Him! Away with Him! Crucify Him!" Pilate said to them, "Crucify your King?" The chief priests answered, "We have no king but Caesar!"

Then he delivered Him over to them to be crucified. And they took Jesus and led [Him] away; so He went out, bearing His own cross, to the spot called The Place of the Skull—in Hebrew it is called Golgotha.

There they crucified Him, and with Him two others—one on both side and Jesus between them.

And Pilate also wrote a title (an inscription on a placard) and put it on the cross. And the writing was:

Jesus the Nazarene, the King of the Jews.

.......He said, It is finished! And He bowed His head and gave up His spirit. **John 19:15-19**

RESURRECTION SUNDAY

On Easter Sunday, Christians celebrate the resurrection of Jesus Christ. Easter happens to be the most attended Sunday morning worship service of the year. A lot of people whether they haven't been to church all year will show up on Easter to give Jesus His props. Because they know God has been good to them and so they will come to give Him His well-deserved respect on Easter morning. Many churches will hold special services on Easter Sunday. Many will bring out extra chairs to accommodate the additional attendees, there will be special songs, and even poems read by children all in celebration of Jesus' resurrection after His crucifixion. Most of these people will dress up for the occasion. As they well should! After all Jesus is King of Kings and how do you come before the King?

Easter Sunday is not a federal holiday; however, churches treat it as if it is because the celebration is about Jesus having come back to life, or being raised from the dead. Jesus paid the penalty for our sin, purchasing for all who believe in Him, eternal life. There is only One Who can forgive our sins. This warrants a significant celebration. It will be a huge celebration with great singing and dancing and of course a wonderfully prepared meal to enjoy afterwards. It's not a federal holiday but even restaurants are also preparing for this day. Some churches refer to this particular Sunday as Resurrection Sunday. There are a couple of reasons for this. One is the origin of the Easter celebration and also because of the commercialization of Easter.

Whether your church calls it Easter Sunday Service, or Resurrection Sunday service I hope you're planning to be there for the celebration. My prayer is you're get up on Easter morning and join with a congregation in giving praise to the King of Kings, the Lord God Almighty, Our Prince of Peace, The Rose of Sharon, The Balm in Gilead, Our Soon Returning King. **Jesus is Lord!** Don't miss the great celebration taking place in churches around the United States on *Resurrection Sunday.*

Only Believe!

For further study of Jesus' death, burial, crucifixion and His resurrection read the following passages: Matthew 27:27-53, Mark 15:16-19, Luke 23:26-24:35; and St. John 19:16-20, 30.

Toni Joy

Confession for the Month of April

Print or write out confession; put where you can see and confess it all month

Make your own confession for this month; write it down and speak it out for the rest of this month

_____

_____

_____

_____

_____

_____

_____

Speak unto all the congregation of the children of Israel, and say unto them, Ye shall be holy: for I the LORD your God am holy. Lev. 19:2

High Maintenance, Part 1

The other day my friend and I were talking about "high-maintenance" people. They sometimes can be more trouble than it's worth in a relationship, This is not to say that that it can't work, but rather that it will either stretch us to our highest potential or it will tear us down to the ground.

High-maintenance: (to me) needy and/or have high expectations in a relationship... It takes more work and care than the average relationship. Usually more than what the average person can give or maintain.

I wondered - *do the average person think God is high-maintenance?*

We read the Old and New Testament, we listen to Pastors preach about who God is and what He expects from us. Then there are the rules and regulations of some churches on what we need to do or be to please them or God.

Is God High Maintenance? Sure He is?

But God is not a high maintenance about what we can achieve in ourselves. He wants us to rise higher, but not in the world, but in Him. God has no expectations that He wants us to achieve in our own ability. He wants us to have it in His ability and power. Maybe this is where the average person misses it. In our weakness we are strong in Christ Jesus. But most are still walking around believing they could never truly be holy. *And when I say "Average", I'm not separating categories of people and saying some can meet God's requirements without the grace of God. No, we all fall short of God's glory. But some of us choose to live by faith more than others. Then He said to them, "Take heed what you hear. With the same measure you use, it will be measured to you; and to you who hear, more will be given - Mark 4;24*

There are more Christians believing that holiness is not achievable, than those that will stretch their faith to living truly... a holy life *(living in the fruit of the spirit)... But the fruit of the Spirit is love, joy, peace, longsuffering, kindness, goodness, faithfulness, gentleness, self-control. Against such there is no law.* **And those who are Christ's have crucified the flesh with its passions and desires. If we live in the Spirit, let us also walk in the Spirit** - *Gal. 5:22,25*

We all have been given a measure of faith. The more we live by faith, the more the *average* person can achieve God's High-Maintenance living.

"High-maintenance living" is for us. For what are we waiting?

*Now to Him who is able to do exceedingly abundantly above all that we ask or think, according to the power that works in us, to Him be glory in the church by Christ Jesus to all generations, forever and ever. Amen." Eph. 3:20,21

For therein is the righteousness of God revealed from faith to faith: as it is written, The just shall live by faith... Rom. 1:17

High Maintenance, Pt· 2

Is God High Maintenance? Why? We can say that He is because His expectations of us is very much higher than what we can achieve in ourselves. Why? Because He wants us to live free from the darkness of this world, not subject to bondage, sickness, and death. He wants us to live prosperous in every area of life. So Jesus gave His life in exchange for ours. It was a high price He paid for us; and yes it is a lot; and yes it will cost us everything; but consider what we're trading: rags to riches, death to life, sickness for divine health, hurt/pain/suffering for love/joy/peace. Given this great cloud of witness, let's step up to a higher way of living. He gave us all the tools to live by - but we got to have faith to work it to grab hold of it and to live a life that is impossible in the world's eyes and in our own ability. It takes faith to walk in the characteristics of God...The Fruit of the Spirit. That's why it's called faith.... you can't see it, you can't feel it, you can't even know it without Jesus Christ. The Word of God says that *faith is the substance of things hoped for, the evidence of things not seen*.

Jesus lived saying those things His Father told Him to say and doing those thing He told Him to do. He is our example.

.... let us run with patience the race that is set before us, Looking unto Jesus the author and finisher of our faith; who for the joy that was set before him endured the cross, despising the shame, and is set down at the right hand of the throne of God

I said all that to say this.... God said "Be ye Holy" as He is Holy. Trust God to walk in a way that's contrary to the way we think, feel, and definitely contrary to the ways of the world. We have to trust that God's ways are better than our ways. The key to life lives on the inside of us. We have to believe that there is more than what we have seen all our lives, what we read in the paper, what we see on the news, how we were raised, and what our family is doing.

Living in the *"Fruit of the Spirit"* we can achieve every expectation or requirement of living a holy life.

We can walk around believing God to do everything. But, just believing isn't enough; we have to walk (act) in it.
If we live in the Spirit, let us also walk in the Spirit. *Gal. 5:22-25*

My Agape Walk Today

Complete this sentence

"I am really Grateful to God

Because ...."

Tell this to someone that

You don't know

✓ <u>I walked in love today</u>

Meditate today on ...

Bring all the tithes into the storehouse,
That there may be food in My house,
And try Me now in this,"
Says the LORD of hosts,
"If I will not open for you the windows of
heaven And pour out for you such blessing
That there will not be room
enough to receive it.
"And I will rebuke the devourer for your sakes,
So that he will not destroy the fruit of your
ground, Nor shall the vine fail to bear fruit for
you in the field," Says the LORD of hosts;
"And all nations will call you blessed,
For you will be a delightful land,"
Says the LORD of hosts.

Malachi 3:10-12

I double dare you to be blessed

Gal 5:22-24 "But the fruit of the Spirit is love, joy, peace, longsuffering, kindness, goodness, faithfulness, gentleness, self-control. Against such there is no law". NKJV

Live In The Fruit - The Unique YOU...

Holiness in not a bunch of things that we do to look righteous, or acts that the church gives to present us as religious.
It is our conduct; how we live our lives every day. And in these everyday attributes is where holiness is. It's living the Fruit of the Spirit.

We might say or think "I don't want to be holy", or "that's a little bit over the edge", or "holiness don't cut it in the real world". We may have to go over the edge for holiness, but it's not that deep.

You are unique (you do know that, right?). You plus (+) God equals (=) **awesome** (the way God intended for it to be). We are a spirit in a natural world. If your life isn't full – check what **spiritual fruit** you are not applying to your **natural being**. Most of us are awake to the natural, but not to the spiritual; however, they were meant to work together.

Let's start to connect the two.
One of the special things about the Fruit of the Spirit is that it's singular; even though there are 9 fruits of the Spirit, they are all connected. When we yield to one the rest tag along because they are one. To make us special, unique, and Christ-like...it's all for one. And when you walk in the Fruit it will change the natural.

Give the world what God created
I want to present each fruit in application to our everyday way of living. It's time to let God out of the box.

"If we <u>live</u> in the Spirit, let us also <u>walk</u> in the Spirit".
Gal 5:25-26

John 15:5 *I am the vine; you are the branches. If a man remains in me and I in him, he will bear much fruit; apart from me you can do nothing.*

Live In The Fruit - The Law
It's more precious than gold

The beginning, who is your Father? Jesus is our DNA that says we are the Children of God. But, even though we are children of God, we still have a choice to walk in the natural or the spiritual realm. Which blood line do we follow? *It depends on where we want to go and with whom.*

We all know the gods of this age (John 8:44, 2 Cor. 4:4): it is doing what we feel like doing, being moved by what you feel. *The works of the flesh are evident, which are: adultery, fornication, uncleanness, lewdness, idolatry, sorcery, hatred, contentions, jealousies, outbursts of wrath, selfish ambitions, dissensions, heresies, envy, murders, drunkenness, revelries, and the like; of which I tell you beforehand, just as I also told you in time past, that those who practice such things will not inherit the kingdom of God. Gal. 5:16-20.*

We all know the Creator of all things (1 John 3:1) who has given us dominion over all things. It is the Fruit of the Spirit that moves us in authority in this natural realm if we walk in it. It is the nature of God in us; our badge that permits entry into the place God has destined for us. Walking by a new law, a new set of rules *get godly results. It makes you invincible.*

It puts us above and not beneath

(Looking at the way the world is today - I thank God for the Fruit of the Spirit - I can't see living in this world without it, *it's more precious than gold*)

Gal 5:22-24 "But the fruit of the Spirit is love, joy, peace, longsuffering, kindness, goodness, faithfulness, gentleness, self-control. **Against such there is no law**".

I have set before you life and death - blessings and curses, you choice

Let's walk in OUR God given authority (It's in our blood). *Find out who you are, what you have, and what you can do – it's*

our inheritance

April 8

Toni Joy

John 3:16 "For God so **loved the world** that He gave His only begotten Son, that whoever believes in Him should not perish but have everlasting life."

Live In The Fruit - *Love*

Who do we value?

God valued us. He gave His only begotten Son for us. Yet we didn't know Him, didn't care, didn't ask for Him, and He still gave. Some of us still don't care. God's love is Agape Love "**Pure, never-ending, never giving up**". This is love; specifically, the kind of love that God wants us to pass on to others. **What?** Value someone that I don't know, that doesn't care about me, that didn't ask me to care about them? **Yes**. **I ask you, how else can the world be saved?**

Maybe we need to change what we value. What if we value people as a whole, regardless of who they are? Love others the way God loves us. Love and enjoy those around us in spite of their faults. This might just destroy prejudices. **Wow, that is the supernatural power of God. Yes, and it's in us.** We should read the love chapter this week (1 Cor. 13). Let us value those we don't like, don't notice, and have high esteem for those that we live with and those who we work with and go to school with. And how about this, lets honor our fellow saints at church. Start a new love walk - *The Agape Walk*. It shows them God whether they receive it or not.

Value everyone you're around!

Homework: pick someone that is hard for you to love or you don't like and begin to value them (some of us have to start with those in our own household) – ask God to help you. Start with the things that are good or lovable about them. **You don't have to be with or hang with someone to value or respect them. Start from the inside and work your way out. Not on your own accord, but the Love of God that's in you.**
It's in you - you may never have paid attention to it.
Remember, don't go by what you think or see.

Toni Joy

James 1:2-4 *My brethren, count it all joy when you fall into various trials, knowing that the testing of your faith produces patience.*

Live In The Fruit - *Joy*

Ride on JOY!!

How do you count it joy? Answer: just like you count your blessings! God is the same, yesterday, today, and forever. Jesus counted on God the Father to raise Him from the dead once He paid the price for us. A debt we could not pay. He rejoiced (joy) and it strengthened Him to endure the cross. We can count on God also! **Joy** will strengthened us also regardless of our circumstance. (Heb. 13:8)

The bible says that the joy of the Lord is our strength. It's trusting God and relying on God being who He says He is and doing what He says He's going to do. So if we believe the Word of God, by faith we rejoice; our joy will rise up and strengthen us. Even when the solution is not yet manifested, your rejoicing insures it; it brings your strength on the scene to see you to the end.

Oh, yes! It will break all the chains of pain and suffering, worry and doubt. Start rejoicing in the promises and joy will be revealed in the morning. You too will be ready to walk on water.

We rejoice by faith because "we know we can count God to be who He says He is".

Praise your way through

Joy is our carrier – our supernatural ride – our chariot

Faith and hope sees the end...Joy takes us to it

Looking unto Jesus, the author and finisher of our faith, who for the joy that was set before Him endured the cross, despising the shame, and has sat down at the right hand of the throne of God. Hebrew 12:2 NKJV

1 Peter 5:7 *Casting all your care upon Him; for He careth for you.*

Live In The Fruit - *Peace*

It Ain't My Job! Believe it or not, there is a time when this is exactly what we should say.

Let it go *and let God*.... I know we all have heard that before. *Peace is giving it to God knowing the matter is solved.* God has delivered us from suffering but we continue to pick it up as if the value is in what He separated us from and not what He separated us unto.

We cannot walk in the peace of God with just letting go; we also have to trust God and allow Him to lead us. As a kid, I never doubted that we would have food on the table and clothes on my back. It wasn't my job; my mom never even talked about it with me. Think about this...

Your child has peace because you carry the burden. Likewise, we have peace because Jesus carried ours.

Prov 3:5-6 Trust in the LORD with all your heart, And lean not on your own understanding; In all your ways acknowledge Him, And He shall direct your paths.

I used to think "I can only trust myself", but it really boils down to this...**we will live by the relationship we have with the world or the relationship we have with God.** *To keep it real... in the world we are out there by ourselves (with no hope). But with God, we are not alone and it ain't our job to* think*, in this relationship... God does the thinking.*

We tend to take on the responsibility of worry and fear (false loyalty to a situation) instead of The trust and loyalty of believing God in the midst of things.

Be anxious for nothing, but in everything by prayer and supplication, with thanksgiving, let your requests be made known to God; and the peace of God, which surpasses all understanding, will guard your hearts and minds through Christ Jesus. Finally, brethren, whatever things are true, whatever things are noble, whatever things are just, whatever things are pure, whatever things are lovely, whatever things are of good report, if there is any virtue and if there is anything praiseworthy--meditate on these things. The things which you learned and received and heard and saw in me, these do, and the God of peace will be with you. Phil 4:6-9

When the entire world around us is in chaos, we have peace in Christ
Cast everything on God – He takes care of it

My Agape Walk Today

Tell a friend

you appreciate

Their friendship

✓ I walked in love today

James 1:2-5 *My brethren, count it all joy when you fall into various trials, knowing that the testing of your faith produces patience. But let patience have its perfect work, that you may be perfect and complete, lacking nothing.*

Live In The Fruit - *Longsuffering*

Perfect is as Perfect does

Can We Really Be Perfect? Are we waiting on it or working on it?
The real work of patience and longsuffering is not giving up nor just waiting; is it listening, waiting and watching to do what God says to do; letting *The Artist better known as God* chisel the perfect us. Most of the time we like to respond to what we think and feel instead of trusting God - and then we really think we are waiting on God to do His part – apart from us.
<u>Waiting in the flesh</u> (world/physical realm) is looking for something to happen to us, being still – doing nothing.
<u>Waiting in the spirit</u> realm is looking for something to happen through us working out our salvation and preparing for the move of God. (Phil. 2:12)
*But let patience have its perfect **work**, that you may be perfect and complete, lacking nothing James. 1:4*

> "Patience / Longsuffering" is a God-inspired energetic resistance to defeat that allow calm and brave endurance – it is change in motion; day by day, step by step, line upon line, precept upon precept (This is from my Spirit Filled Life Bible).

<u>Confession for today:</u> My faith working patience produces change in my life that I may be perfect and complete... <u>lacking nothing.</u>

We want each of you to show this same diligence to the very end, in order to make your hope sure. We do not want you to become lazy, but to imitate those who through faith and patience inherit what has been promised. Heb 6:11-12

Luke 6:35 But love your enemies, do good, and lend, hoping for nothing in return; and your reward will be great, and you will be sons of the Most High. For He is kind to the unthankful and evil.

Live In The Fruit - *Kindness*

Forgive me, forget not - forgive me, forget not – He forgives me and forgets

Have you ever heard someone say "*I forgive but I won't forget*"? I have so many times… it was something about this saying that didn't sit right with me. I wonder is there such a thing as righteous-un-forgiveness. **(Does that even sound like something Jesus would say or do?)**

If God forgave and didn't forget, our redemption would not be complete.

God wants us to forgive one another as He forgave us and casted our sins into the sea of forgetfulness (*Heb. 10:17*). The supernatural power of kindness will cause us to be like God.

Love is 100% *conditional* without the "the Fruit of the Spirit – **kindness**" (Divine Mercy). Kindness gives us a continuous clean slate; *100% unconditional*. I'm not talking about being polite; a sinner can be polite to someone they don't like. Kindness will relieve a suffered wrong. God forgives us of all our sins *and then purifies us from all unrighteousness* (*1 John 1:9*).

Kindness requires us to walk blindly, relying upon God to help us forgive those that have hurt us and to walk in kindness beyond our natural ability.

If there is someone we need to forgive, let's do it right knowing… without Him it is impossible because it is an act of Agape Love. **Some hurts are a matter of the heart that only God can heal regardless of what someone can do to make it up to us, or say to us, or even how much we want to forgive.** Only through the supernatural power of kindness can we forgive *and forget*.

Grace will give you something you don't deserve
Mercy will keep you from getting what you do deserve.
God gave us a **Get Out Of Jail Free** card
and we need to use it every day – *towards others*.
Make sure that nobody pays back wrong for wrong, but always try to be kind to each other and to everyone else. Be joyful always; pray continually; give thanks in all circumstances, for this is God's will for you in Christ Jesus. 1 Thes 5:15-18

Gen 1:31 Then God saw everything that He had made, and indeed it was very good

Live In The Fruit - *Goodness*

He's Got The Whole World In His Hands

(remember that song?). *To receive God's goodness we have to be able to visualize creation. In order to see creation you have to see through God's eyes.*

In today's time creation is hidden. The world would have us to believe that good is in the eye of the beholder as if we define goodness.

Let me correct this kind of thinking the way Jesus did.

There was a certain ruler that called Jesus a good teacher and Jesus corrected him and said none is good but one, God alone (Luke 18:18, 19).

Jesus was revealing to us that the only thing that can be good is what comes from God. Our goodness is wrapped up in God – and God didn't stop His goodness with creation. It continues in us and through us. Look how the world has progressed since creation. It's good until the influence of evil touches it. When we walk in the Spirit, each of us shows God's unique design of His purpose for us. God not only created us, but He has an expected end for us and it's all good (Jer. 29:11).

The Fruit of the Spirit "Goodness" is not just seeing good – it's being good, living good, spreading good. We are carriers of the goodness of God.

Real goodness touches us, only, in a God kind of way.
Our purpose is revealed in God; our destination is revealed in God.
Let's reveal the goodness of God to others by giving them God in us.
Reach out and share with others the goodness of God.
I pray that you may be active in sharing your faith, so that you will have a full understanding of every good thing we have in Christ.
Philemon 6:1

My Agape Walk Today

Fast from

One (1) food choice

today and replace

it with the

phrase

"I am disciplined"

✓ <u>I walked in love today</u>

April 16

Toni Joy

Lam 3:22-23 *Through the Lord's mercies we are not consumed, because His compassions fail not. They are new every morning; Great is Your faithfulness.*

Live In The Fruit - *Faithfulness*

Faith & Trust *are ingredients to Faithfulness*
Without trust you will not act on what you believe and without faith you have no <u>power to trust.</u> <u>**Faithfulness is achieved through a consistent daily act of loyalty.**</u>

Faith is acting on what we believe. **Faithfulness** is holding fast to our faith by bringing it to life in our everyday reality as a whole. **It has everything to do with our life style and way of living every day.** *Do we wake up to start a new day as if it is the first day of our loyalty to God with no doubt - like the zeal of a new love?*

We trust God to do what He says, believe He's able and faithful every day, but are we doing and saying what God tells us? Are we faithful to God? *Are we faithful to our confession? Do we walk the walk and talk the talk when no one is looking? The bigger question is...*

1. **"Can We"**? The supernatural power of God is the force and source working on our behalf; <u>we can count on it</u> *when we show up yielding to the supernatural force of faithfulness*
2. **"Will We"**? Let's take the faith test: Q. what are we faithful to everyday?
(A) Are we faithful to knowing and believing *GOD* is real and *GOD* is faithful?
(B) Are we faithful in living a life of walking by faith and not by sight?
God is going to do His part, but are we? How often is God or the ways of God part of our everyday equation, our daily decisions, or our conversations? Or do we just put God in a box and let Him out on certain days and times when we think it should apply? Everything we say and do should have a spin of God's ways/words around it, supporting it. This week grab hold of something to which to apply faithfulness and release your faith to it every day. Speak it, walk it, talk it, and see what happens. God's faithfulness will ground and empower your faithfulness in turn, building a long-lasting relationship that will never fail. He can trust you with unlimited power; you can trust him to do just what He said He would do. 2 Cor. 1:18-20 *says......* **God is faithful, for all the promises of God in Him are Yes, and in Him Amen** *Don't just say yes - say Yes and Amen!*

Matt 5:5 *Blessed are the meek, for they shall inherit the earth.*

Live In The Fruit - *Gentleness*
The Unwritten Path

The world says that humility (gentleness) is weakness, *but you know, the wisdom of God is foolishness to the world (1 Cor. 3:19).* Humility *is* weakness only if you are beholden to things outside of the will of God. Everything outside of God is subject to failure. *God's the only absolute.*

If you're humbled to God, you will walk in wisdom and strength because you rely on the Word and the power of God. The world doesn't know this because they don't know God. *Have you ever did a trust test with a friend? You stand in front of them and fall back for them to catch you. They might have passed the test but what if they got distracted, sucker-punched, or sneezed; you would hit the floor. God is never distracted!* Nobody has our back the way God has our back. He sees our future where we don't. If we trust Him, He will take us to it. The Word says, **"Yet, because you relied on the LORD, He delivered them into your hand. For the eyes of the LORD run to and fro throughout the whole earth, to show Himself strong on behalf of those whose heart is loyal to Him." (2 Chron 16:8-9)**

Humility towards God see's the weakness of the world, yet it is not concerned only for itself. It sees the need, the mission, the goal and purpose of God and yields to it. It sees the strength/wisdom of God and the weakness/foolishness of pride.

The Spirit of gentleness gets the promotions and the great adventures. They have the success stories. (Num. 12:3)

Moses was called the meekest man of all time and God used him with a task to take His people to a promised land.

Gentleness listens to God instead of limiting themselves *to themselves* or their ego, pride or feelings. They humble themselves to the Creator, instead of to creat**ed** things. They see the need of God and implement it in their life, family, business, ministries, etc. Gentleness (humility) sees what God wants us to see and acts on it. Gentleness is having a pliable heart toward real prosperity and truth which makes us the best candidate to solve any problem.

Being meek and humble takes courage. We trust God to conquer whatever arises to provide the leadership to help others.

To walk in an unwritten path

Brethren, if a man is overtaken in any trespass, you who are spiritual restore such a one in a spirit of gentleness, Gal 6:1

April 18

Toni Joy

1 Peter 1:23 *Having been born again, not of corruptible seed but incorruptible, through the word of God which lives and abides forever.*

Live In The Fruit - *Self Control*

Feed me Seymour

Who are you? Who is the real you? *I'll give you a hint*: when you die, what part lives eternally and what part goes to the dust? The part of you that's dictating your life that you have submitted to do you trust it?

-You are a spirit made in the image of God. You have a soul which consists of the will, the intellect, and the emotions. You live in a body which holds you to this natural realm consisting of the 5 senses.

We are 3-part beings; whichever part we feed the most will be in control.
What you submit too will rule your emotions, your intellect, your will... and your five senses. Your spirit man, the real you, can't be controlled by the world; but, it can step aside and let your soul and body run amok if not fed.

What drives us? What do we crave? What's on our mind most of the day? Answer these questions and we will know whether we, our true self/the spirit man, is in control or out-of-control.

To walk in self-control is to live by faith. Being Spirit led is to live your life walking, talking, hearing, and perceiving through the Word of God as God created you to live it.

When we wake up in the morning, which part of us maps out our day? Is it surrounded by work, worry, money, or faith, trust and hope? What dictates your quality of life? Does the Word of God set your standard or do the lusts of the world set your standard? What rule do you apply when you go through a test, trail, or problems? Do you resort to your training by the Word of God or by the world system?

As Paul said, we are in a race and only one wins; run to win.
Fasting is a good tool we use to gain self-control

Everyone who competes in the games goes into strict training. They do it to get a crown that will not last; but we do it to get a crown that will last forever. Therefore I do not run like a man running aimlessly; I do not fight like a man beating the air. No, I beat my body and make it my slave so that after I have preached to others, I myself will not be disqualified for the prize. 1 Cor 9:25-27

Toni Joy

John 17:14-18 *I have given them Your word; and the world has hated them because they are not of the world, just as I am not of the world. I do not pray that You should take them out of the world, but that You should keep them from the evil one. They are not of the world, just as I am not of the world. Sanctify them by Your truth. Your word is truth.*

Live In The Fruit

Love – Highly regarded **Peace** – secure path & place
Joy – empowered

Longsuffering – Courageous **Kindness** – unmerited favor
Goodness – divine vision

Faithfulness – devoted **Gentleness** – selfless
Self-control – holiness

These fruits are supernatural forces of the very nature and characteristics of God living on the inside of us. You cannot obtain them from the ways of the world. The world only has the appearance of life; but true and real life are of God. It is in the Spirit.

If we take bit-size pieces every-day and allow ourselves to be Spirit-led we could live in the Fruit instead of the world.

Jesus said we are in the world but not of the world. *We decide whose rules we live by. By these decisions, we choose to what we are subject and enslaved.*

If we sow to the flesh, we reap from the flesh; if we sow to the spirit, we reap from the spirit. Whichever you feed, that is what will grow. What you plant, is what you will harvest (Gal. 6:8).

If indeed you have heard Him and have been taught by Him, as the truth is in Jesus: that you put off, concerning your former conduct, the old man which grows corrupt according to the deceitful lusts, and be renewed in the spirit of your mind, and that you put on the new man which was created according to God, in true righteousness and holiness. Ephesians 4:21-24

For in Christ Jesus neither circumcision nor uncircumcision avails anything, but a new creation (A new way of living). Gal 6:15

Meditate today on ...

If then you were raised with Christ,
seek those things which are above, where
Christ is, sitting at the right hand of
God. Set your mind on things above, not
on things on the earth. For you died, and
your life is hidden with Christ in God.
When Christ *who is* our life appears, then
you also will appear with Him in glory.

Col. 3:1-4

If you're trying to live in two
worlds; I know you're tired,
take a break... die and live

My Agape Walk Today

If you wrote

a Psalm,

write down what

a few of the

Verses would say.

✓ <u>I walked in love today</u>

Toni Joy

Deut. 6:8 *And thou shalt teach them diligently unto thy children, and shalt talk of them when thou sittest in thine house, and when thou walkest by the way, and when thou liest down, and when thou risest up. And thou shalt bind them for a sign upon thine hand, and they shall be as frontlets between thine eyes. Thou shalt write them upon the posts of thy house, and on thy gates.*

Special Request

Let's get it started in here!!!
Reading through the bible - there is never a bad time to start.
Somehow I got started in the middle of the year, and that's where it stayed.

Find a spot where you like to read and schedule you some quiet time. We schedule time for other things; every day, every week, or once a month – our spirit is yearning for this time with God.

You can read the bible at the doctor's office, on your lunch hour at work, or even at the park, just make spare time to read. You won't regret it. Once you make that decision it will be easy.

Join me in this quest. Go at your own pace.
For those reading through the bible for the first time:
- Try to read the new and old testament consecutively, like; the new testament in the morning and the old at night, or, the old at lunch and the new after dinner, one week here, one week there, etc.
- Genesis to 2 Kings will flow fine. It will be interesting,
- 1 & 2 Chronicles is more detailed telling about the same as 1 & 2 Kings just specifically about Judah.
- Ezra, Nehemiah, and Esther is the rebuilding of Israel after the exile.
- Job through Song of Solomon is very poetic.
- You have the major and minor prophets; they have stories throughout the Old Testament; they are telling their story at different times.

You don't need time to think about this, just do you?
Let's get it started in here!!!

Esther 4:16 Go gather together all the Jews that are present in Shushan, and fast ye for me, and neither eat, nor drink three days, night or day; I also and my maidens will fast like –wise; and so will I go in unto the king, which is not according to the law; ***and If I perish, I perish***.

The Walk of Fortune

This is a walk that you take risking all to get all. You face your problems head on believing wholly on God. And if God don't move, it's over: but if He does, you coming out on top. Like what the three Hebrew Boys did when they got thrown into the furnace.

From the beginning
-we have Queen Vashti refusing to join the party and be the trophy wife
-we have the King exiling her because his command wasn't met
-we have hatred from Haman wanting to kill all the Jews
-we have Queen Esther fearful of death

Sometimes all it takes is for GOD to get in the mix of a ball of confusion
*Queen Esther fasted

*The King falls in love! *Haman reaps what he sows! *Esther gets courageous! *The Jews are saved! ***What started out as disastrous ends in deliverance.***

Sometimes we find ourselves in situations where the only things we can do (truly the only things we can do) are fast, pray, and believe God to intervene. It is a hopeless feeling to know that a situation is out of control and out of our hands; but we have a God that loves to intervene, show off, show that He loves us, and prove that He loves us. He wants the world to know that there is a God. The more hopeless the situation, the more God can get the Glory. Not that He needs anything, but we do. The world needs to know where the answer is.

This book ended as a true love story, one of hope and prosperity (from fret to fortune).
Our life in God's hand we can take that walk of fortune.

Esther 10:3 *For Mordecai the Jew was next unto king Ahasuerus, and great among the Jews, and accepted of the multitude of his brethren, seeking the wealth of his people, and speaking peace to all his seed.*

Toni Joy

2 Kings 5:11-14 But Naaman became furious, ... I said to myself, 'He will surely come out *to me,* and stand and call on the name of the Lord his God, and wave his hand over the place, and heal the leprosy.' ... So he turned and went away in a rage. And his servants came near and spoke to him, and said, "My father, *if* the prophet had told you *to do* something great, would you not have done *it?* How much more then, when he says to you, 'Wash, and be clean'?" So he went down and dipped seven times in the Jordan, according to the saying of the man of God; and his flesh was restored like the flesh of a little child, and he was clean.

Try It, You'll like it

During Jesus' earthly ministry in his last 3 years when healings were being done there were many ways people received their healing. But we do know one thing they all had in common: it was God's will that ___all___ be healed.
We don't have to wonder about that.
Now He did not do many mighty works there because of their unbelief. Matt. 13:58

The question came up about why some are healed and some are not? What about the children, what about the health in different countries? We talked about sin, un-forgiveness, disobedience, and whether these could sometimes bring hindrances of healings. We also discussed some healings come by faith, some by miracles, some by divine order, some by the prayers of the saints and the laying on of hands.

We don't know all the reasons why things happen the way they do. Sometimes we have to ask ourselves, "are we listening to God or are we missing some wisdom or vital information that stands between us receiving our healing? God is not a respecter of persons. It is God's design that everyone have divine health and be saved. Adam set things in motion that were different orders from what God gave; yet, His mercy and goodness still prevailed. God is God and His Word is true. Jesus died, bore our sins and by His strips we were healed. Not some, but all that accept this saying shall be saved.

Most of us don't question whether Jesus died for the sin of the world. Which means that everyone in the world has the choice to accept Jesus as Lord; but all don't. I don't believe most people will reject healing if God handed it out on a platter. But it is just like that...salvation and healing are handed out on a platter. But, so many of us look into that platter like it has leprosy. If it was a platter of money, we all would grab the plate. If you are sick or wondering about being saved, then picking up the platter can get you saved and healed. Take the risk; take the platter. This is less risky than investing your money. So why not invest some time and faith. Like I said, it can't hurt. *Try it - You'll like it*

Meditate today on ...

Peace I leave with you, My peace I give to you; not as the world gives do I give to you. Let not your heart be troubled, neither let it be afraid.

John 14:27

Why look to a limited world
When you have an unlimited God

My Agape Walk
Today

How Bold Are You

If you don't have a church home

- visit a friend's church·

Call them up and find

out what time church starts·

✓ I walked in love today

Gen. 3:22 And the LORD God said, "The man has now become like one of us, knowing good and evil. *He must not be allowed to reach out his hand and take also from the tree of life and eat, and live forever."*

Good Lookin Out Lord!

Adam & Eve

Sometimes we look at the ways of God and think that He is hard, unloving, not understanding and just wanting to hold Lordship over our head when, in actuality, He is protecting us from a violent and self-destructing environment. Just like we give rules and guidelines to our children; it leads, teaches, and guide them in the ways of life.

It was God's love and guidance that put man over the women and telling the man that he will work for a living, and the woman to desire her husband *(Gen. 316-18)*. **He didn't have to say anything** after Adam eat the fruit. He could have just let him figure it out on his own. Likewise, we don't have to say anything to our children when they act up (some really don't), but why do we? *LOVE*

Prov. 3:12 because the LORD disciplines those he loves, as a father the son he delights in

God taught and prepared them in how to live in unity in a dying and corrupt world and He continues to teach us today.

Let's read the entire bible looking at it from the perspective of LOVE, the love of a father.

The LORD God made garments of skin for Adam and his wife and clothed them. Gen. 3:21

I am thankful that the Lord looked out for me

Heb. 10:37 "For yet a little while, And He who is coming will come and will not tarry.

Ready or Not

Have you ever thought about When Jesus is coming back? Does it bring fear or faith? Are you looking forward to it or do you want Him to wait a while? And then I wonder are we ready? I thought about all the prophesies in the bible that have come to pass. And in the times when they did come to pass, were the people ready? I believe now, as then, some were ready and some were not.

Look at the time of Noah - the time of Moses - The time of Jesus

**For the ones that were waiting on the fulfillment of prophesy it must have been breathtaking to actually see it come to pass.
**On the other hand, for those that were not ready it must have been much fear and anxiety.

I know some of us are saying, "I want to see my kids grow up. I want to enjoy my ideas and dreams." **Ready or not**, He is coming.

Live now! Be blessed. It's a gift from God. But what's coming next is a far greater blessing. **So desire His coming and yet live**.

There is nothing in this world more glorious then what Jesus has planned for us. *He can't come too soon for me.* The best reason we should want Jesus to wait is the only reason I believe He is waiting.... for the world to receive Him. At least those that are **going to be saved**. But I do know that whatever time it is for Him to come, it will be the right time, just as it was in the past.

Let's desire to see Jesus and live while we are waiting. You might as well, because.....

Ready or not····
Just as the sun rises every morning
Jesus is coming

I agree with you Toni Joy, Jesus could return at any time. That's why I practice 1 John 1:9 everyday, several times a day.

"If we confess our sins, he is faithful and just to forgive us our sins, and to cleanse us from all unrighteousness.

I want to be forgiven of my sins every day. I want to be ready when He returns. No man knows the hour the bible says. We don't know the hour, but He certainly left us clues.

Jesus said, *Be ye therefore ready also: for the Son of Man cometh at an hour when ye think not.* Luke 12:40

When the Lord descends from heaven with a shout, with the voice of the archangel, and with the trump of God... I want to be one of the one's caught up in the clouds to meet the Lord in the air. (1Thessalonians 4:16-17)

I don't plan to be and I don't want to be, **left behind**. Yes, yes, Toni Joy, that day is coming. What a rejoicing it will be.

Only Believe!

Meditate today on ...

Be anxious for nothing, but in
everything by prayer and supplication,
with thanksgiving, let your requests
be made known to God; and the
peace of God, which surpasses all
understanding, will guard your hearts
and minds through Christ Jesus.
Phil· 4:6-7

There's a saying;
If you gon worry, don't pray
If you gon pray, don't worry

One way you lose, one way you win
when you do both - you lose all the way around

CONFESSION FOR THE MONTH OF MAY

Print or write out your confession; put it where you can see and confess it all month

Lord I thank you that my life is a
testimony that people can see

Thank you for my mind being
clear, my soul being blessed,
and my body being well·

Thank you for giving me all things
that pertain to life and godliness·

Because you Love me, people see you·
I love you Lord, and thank
you for loving me·

Let your light so shine before men, that they may see your good works and glorify your Father in heaven.

Matt. 5:16

My Agape Walk Today

Buy a cup of

coffee or tea

today for

someone that

<u>You don't know</u>

✓ <u>I walked in love today</u>

Luke 22:44 *And being in anguish, he prayed more earnestly, and his sweat was like drops of blood falling to the ground.*

The Look Of Joy? Part 1

I never thought about what "Joy" looks like until I went through some serious trials that I wasn't sure was going to end. We all assume that we can see joy by - a smile, happiness, laughter, etc. We really can't recognize real joy unless we see it coupled with "***The Night Before Joy***". The scripture says, Jesus endured the cross because of the joy that was set before him.

I questioned so many times "did I lose my joy," but the enemy was trying to steal my joy. Joy lives on the inside of us; it's up to us whether we use it or not. I was determined not to allow my joy to be buried.

As I <u>purposely</u> set out to walk in joy

I found out that it was joy that got me through the hard times. I didn't see it in the middle of the war. It wasn't in the smile and the laughter, but it was there. Joy doesn't start from the outside and flow to the inside; it starts on the inside and work its way outward. What's great about joy is that while it's working on the inside the power of God is strengthening and empowering you to be an unmovable force that creates a praise that knocks down the house. That praise wins the war.

Joy pushes through trouble
Joy see's what God tells you and by faith you are strengthened
Joy pushes you through the barriers.
<u>*Joy - looks like courage*</u>

fixing our eyes on Jesus, the Pioneer and Perfecter of faith. For the joy set before him he endured the cross, scorning its shame, and sat down at the right hand of the throne of God. Consider him who endured such opposition from sinners, so that you will not grow weary and lose heart. Heb. 12:2-3

"Father, if you are willing, take this cup from me; yet not my will, but yours be done." Luke 22:42

My 2 Cents

"This is the day, this is the day that the Lord has made, that the Lord has made, I will rejoice, I will rejoice and be glad in it, and be glad in it. This is the day that the Lord has made, I will rejoice and be glad in it, this is the day, this is the day that the Lord has made".
O'RIORDAN, DOLORES MARY

Several years ago, this was a standard praise song in our church. It was a happy song that made you clap and sing along. The song was written based on Psalm 118:24. Every day we get out of the bed there is something we can rejoice and be glad about.

And then there are those days, weeks, seasons, that a <u>particular</u> something especially **sparks** joy in us. <u>Spark:</u> *a trace of life or vitality, to send forth gleams or flashes*. That **particular** something giving me joy lately is having Friday's as my off day and using those mornings to pull out my kitchen aid mixer and bake something. Those mornings are quiet and peaceful and I appreciate having the time to bake.

<u>Complete this sentence</u>: *The <u>particular</u> something giving me joy right now is_____. Fill in the blank; this will change from time to time.*

Only Believe!

Luke 22:44 *And being in anguish,* **he prayed more earnestly,** *and his sweat was like drops of blood falling to the ground.*

The Look Of Joy? Part 2

Real Joy rejoices in glorious victory. You may have turbulence; joy soothes the turbulence into peace. *The fight is your faith. Do I trust God? It's that trust (faith) that pushes joy. Trust and know that God is there, that He's real, that He knows and that His voice is saying, "remember what I said".* Then you believe.

<u>**Look at how Jesus fought**</u>
And being in anguish, **he prayed more earnestly**, <u>*and his sweat was like drops of blood falling to the ground*</u>
How many of us have anguish so pressing that its sweat is like drops of blood? Joy conquers even this anguish.
What would it take for you to go into more earnest prayer through your turbulence?
<u>*Turning to God in your turbulence produces the force of Joy on the inside of you.*</u>
Have you ever been with someone that gives you favor just because you're with them?
<u>*Now do you see... Joy hangs out with Faith!*</u>
Knowing God and what He placed on the inside of you produces joy.
<u>*Joy*</u>*: Gladness in your inner man. It's a seed in the ground that spouts (grows) pushes through the dirt and produces a harvest. It's fireworks wrapped inside you and is ignited (lighted) by faith. That light (faith) comes from the Word of God and knowing God.*
Faith pushes Joy through!
Get in the ring and sweat the good fight of faith
"Get in there with God"

Toni Joy

<u>Tis the Night Before Joy</u>

*Tis the night before joy and all through the house,
the enemy was stirring, even using the mouse;*

*Everything was tossed
my health, my job, all seemed lost*

*There was fear and trembling
much talk of me stumbling
Hope was seriously fading
My faith was tired even to failing
But deep down inside, what did I see
a glimpse of my victory placed inside of me*

*I could see the way out
Jesus leading me saying –hey, don't doubt*

*He said "rejoice Toni Joy - I got this"
remember, just read over the promise list*

*So in the middle of the night
at my darkest and all time low
by the Joy of the Lord
He strengthened my soul*

*So my joy didn't start by what I could see
but by the Word of God that's inside of me*

*So stop looking to things to make your day
Read the bible daily, let it pave your way*

*Trails and tribulations will hit us all
not your muscles but Joy will break all walls*

*Save your time and money, don't buy into the myth
it's the Joy of the Lord that is your strength*

My 2 Cents

As my husband and I were watching the news report about the manhunt of former LAPD officer Christopher Doner, I mentioned how the anger and rage that we see proliferating in our society reminds me of a scene from the Ghost Busters movie. In Ghost Busters II the ghost busters are striving to keep a particular demonic spirit from being unleashed. This demon is released and it unleashes a spirit of anger and rage over society. In this scene when the spirit releases these emotions violence erupts in the streets; people begin arguing with one another. It becomes chaotic. In my opinion it looks like we're living in a world where a spirit like in the Ghost Busters movie has been unleashed for real. In recent news reports; we're hearing of North Korea defiantly launching unauthorized missiles, meteors falling out of the sky over Russia, the first pope in over 600 years resigns, a lightning bolt hits the Vatican two hours after his resignation, mass shootings over here and over there, unusual weather patterns, storms being referred to as the worst storm in decades" and the list goes on and on. Look at what Jesus said about all of this in Luke 21:25-28 NLT

"And there will be strange events in the skies-signs in the sun, moon, and stars. And down here on earth the nations will be in turmoil, perplexed by the roaring seas and strange tides. The courage of many people will falter because of the fearful fate they see coming upon the earth, because the stability of the very heavens will be broken up. Then everyone will see the Son of Man arrive on the clouds with power and great glory. So when all these things begin to happen, stand straight and look up, for your salvation is near!"

Jesus told us these things would come. Well, they are happening. We're seeing them with our own eyes. He said, we would experience these events before He returns. Watching all of this happening encourages me to move ahead more forcefully with the life I desire to have. I'm one of those people that's still searching, trying, and wanting to experience more of life. I want to try new things, travel more, and see my dreams fulfilled. What about you? Are you still searching, trying, and wanting to experience more of life. Are you believing to get married, to have a child, to go back to school, to start your own business, to buy that new house? Now is the time to move forcefully ahead with your plans. Do you have someone you need to forgive? Do it now. Don't think about it anymore, just do it.

Only Believe!

James 1:2 *My brethren, count it all joy when you fall into various trials...*

Charge Joy

Joy has been on my heart to share with you because we sometimes give "Joy" the shaft (take it for granted). Joy is right up there **IN** the big 3; Love, Joy, and Peace. We won't cast love and peace aside. We continually request them and seek them. When we think about love and peace, we attribute them to God alone.

But, we will throw "Joy" to the curve (in the world) in a quick flash. We don't give the world credit for love and peace, but we will give them the credit for Joy. *You think* maybe we need to take another look at **Joy** and what it means.

Joy is one of the "Fruit of the Spirit". *But the fruit of the Spirit is love, joy, peace, longsuffering, kindness, goodness, faithfulness, gentleness, self-control. Against such there is no law. Galatians 5:22-23*

Every one of these fruit is the character of God. Look at the world, the news; and think about what part of the world has ownership in the fruit. These words are **_"fruit.... of the Spirit"_** not "fruit of the world".

Notes from the "New Spirit Filled Life" bible:
The proper attitude in meeting adversity is to count it all joy, which is not an emotional reaction but a deliberate intelligent appraisal of the situation from God's perspective, viewing trials as a means of moral and spiritual growth. We do not rejoice in the trials themselves, but in their possible results. Testing carries the idea of proving genuineness, Trails serve as a discipline to purge faith of dross, stripping away what is false. Patience is not a passive resignation to adverse circumstances, but a positive steadfastness that bravely endures.
Count (Webster): to add up (sum), to consider.

Consider JOY when you fall......
We can walk out of any situation with Joy...

Mother's Day

On this day we all should take time out of our busy schedules to show our moms how much we love and appreciate the sacrifice they made to give us tender loving care.

As an adult from the time of my first child to now I truly understand all the misconceptions I had growing up (even times as a young adult) of the wisdom and strength my mom had. Sometimes we think they don't care or they are mean because they don't do things the way we want. The many times they didn't let us hurt ourselves and make stupid decisions (and on the other hand, the times she did let us get hurt and make stupid decisions). Now I spend time loving my mom and thanking her for being her. She makes me a stronger mom. I hope that one day my children will know and understand the gift that I bring and that they will grow to be great parents to their children.

Happy Mother's Day.... to all our readers, to their mothers, and their grandmothers. And in remembrance of all of them that has gone on to be with the Lord. We love you and pray that you have a blessed day.

In 1868, Ann Jarvis – mother of Anna Jarvis – created a committee to establish a "Mother's Friendship Day", the purpose of which was "to reunite families that had been divided during the Civil War." Jarvis – who had previously organized "Mother's Day Work Clubs" to improve sanitation and health for both Union and Confederate encampments undergoing a typhoid outbreak – wanted to expand this into an annual memorial for mothers, but she died in 1905 before the celebration became popular. Her daughter continued her mother's efforts.

Mother's Day in the United States is an annual holiday celebrated on the second Sunday in May. Mother's Day recognizes mothers, motherhood and maternal bonds in general, as well the positive contributions that they make to society. Although many Mother's Day celebrations world-wide have quite different origins and traditions, most have now been influenced by the more recent American tradition established by Anna Jarvis, who celebrated it for the first time in 1908, then campaigned to make it an official holiday. On May 9, 1914 President Woodrow Wilson issued a proclamation declaring the first national Mother's Day as a day for American citizens to show the flag in honor of those mothers whose sons had died in war.

In 1934, U.S. President Franklin D. Roosevelt approved a stamp commemorating the holiday.

My Agape Walk Today

Tell someone

that

"Jesus Loves Them"

✓ <u>I walked in love today</u>

Meditate today on ...

For the Son of Man has

come to seek and to save

that which was lost."

Luke 19:10

Add those that you know are

lost to your prayer list, minister

to them. Rejoice in faith

Toni Joy

A Letter to God; I woke up this morning about 4:30 am and said "Good Morning Lord" and just kinda thought about life and happiness, and I had a few questions. So I got my pen and paper and decided to write God a letter. I decided to share this letter because someone might be asking the same questions. And it goes like this...

Dear Lord;

The pursuit of happiness and peace (complete prosperity), is it contingent on *things*, our needs and wants being met? How much of our joy and peace is based on things we can buy? Do "things" give peace and joy? What part does it play and how much?

How do we walk in complete peace and joy when things are not met? People have problems, we have things that go haywire. What about those of us that don't have a job, a home, a car, children that are not saved or in trouble; what about the hearts that are broken, loss of loved ones, the sick, the sorrowful, the shut-in, strongholds, drug addiction, abuse? These are real needs in the world today. But are we putting our needs **before** You; and are we bringing everything we should **to** You?

Is our hope in You. Is our joy and peace in You. I know that walking in the Spirit, the fruit of the Spirit is the key. And, Lord, by no means do I know all the answers; I need you to complete us. And as I'm asking You....I believe this morning I hear You saying, "**Leave all and follow Me. Die with Christ and rise with Christ. Yes, I care about the things you need, and know what they are.**" *"Therefore I tell you, do not worry about your life, what you will eat or drink; or about your body, what you will wear. Is not life more than food, and the body more than clothes? Look at the birds of the air; they do not sow or reap or store away in barns, and yet your heavenly Father feeds them. Are you not much more valuable than they? Can any one of you by worrying add a single hour to your life?*

"And why do you worry about clothes? See how the flowers of the field grow. They do not labor or spin. Yet I tell you that not even Solomon in all his splendor was dressed like one of these. If that is how God clothes the grass of the field, which is here today and tomorrow is thrown into the fire, will he not much more clothe you—you of little faith? So do not worry, saying, 'What shall we eat?' or 'What shall we drink?' or 'What shall we wear?' For the pagans run after all these things, and your heavenly Father knows that you need them. But seek first his kingdom and his righteousness, and all these things will be given to you as well. Therefore do not worry about tomorrow, for tomorrow will worry about itself. Each day has enough trouble of its own. Matt. 6:25-34

Continued tomorrow – meditate on this scripture for today.

Continued..... *A Letter to God;*

As I was talking to God and asking all these questions
– He was answering me, with His Word and in my spirit,
Ministering to me – confirming to me that *"**All is well, His Word is true**"*. Being reminded that all things work out for the good for those that love God.

In my heart I know that the answer is the Word of God - The whole Word - the Bible. The Spirit of God living on the inside of us. It comes to us like flashes. All of God's Words coming together a verse here and a miracle there. It's us living every day with God and God with us. It's all of God: Father, Son, and Holy Spirit wrapped in all of us (spirit, soul, and body).

So we have to ask ourselves - how much do we want to die to self, and live in Christ? Our worries, sorrows, troubles are not supposed to be trophies for us to carry as if this proves we are alive. It proves we are here on earth. It up to us to prove that God is too! ***Our life is in God by letting God be God in us***.

These things I have spoken unto you, that in me ye might have peace. In the world ye shall have tribulation: but be of good cheer; I have overcome the world. John 16:33

**Talk to Him as much as possible.
Write your own letter to God and hear Him answer.**

Confession for today

*Lord I will not worry about anything; my source of everything is in you, my family is in your hands, my job is in your hands; you are my life; even my sanity is in you – **You are my Peace***

My Agape Walk Today

Fast from One (1) form of

Communication today

(texting, Facebook, instant message,

Twitter, phone, e-mail, etc·)

replace it with the phrase

"I am disciplined"

✓ <u>I walked in love today</u>

2 Tim. 1:6 Therefore I remind you to stir up the gift of God which is in you... *through the laying on of my hands. For God has not given us a spirit of fear, but of power and of love and of a sound mind.*

I'm So Excited

Are we supposed to eagerly serve the Lord by running into the house of God to see what we can do? This reminds me of a song we use to sing a long time ago.

<u>I was glad when they said unto me, let us go into the house of the Lord</u>

But I hear people now trying to find ways to have service in their own house to keep from going to church (that kind of thinking is all about us and not about God - bringing God on our level of thinking and not reaching towards God) - can anyone phantom how deceptive this is? We say, "do I have to go to bible study, do I have to go to church, why do I have to get these kids ready for church?" If you know like I do, you would be running them to church. They will be 16, and 18, and young adults, and grown folks in a minute. I think they can use the help, even if we don't think we do. I actually heard someone say the other day, sadly, "I guess the only thing I can do is pray". ***I was like, wow – honey... "We get to pray".***

Let's get excited to serve God, to pray, to lay hands on the sick, etc.

Let's wake up in the morning asking God about the day, go through the day looking for God to move, go to bed at night getting prepared for tomorrow. We prepare for work and other activities, how much more should we prepare our life for God's use?

Let's allow God to be our source of needs and wants. If we believe that God will supply our every need then we should be eager to do whatever He tells us to do, when, where, and how. **God wants us to put ourselves on the line as He has put Himself on the line**.

Let's be eager to serve God, His Way...<u>Get Excited!</u>

After removing Saul, he made David their king. God testified concerning him: 'I have found David son of Jesse, a man after my own heart; he will do everything I want him to do. Acts 13:22

I have no problem with having church in our homes if we're called by God to teach, preach, etc. and we are under a Pastoral covering ourselves; these gifts were given to men for the edifying of the saints, not a calling to just you and yours. Now if it's just our family, of course we should have devotion at home, we should teach our family the Word of God; but it <u>should</u> <u>not</u> replace church.

My 2Cents

Well, that's interesting Toni Joy, I got up this morning thinking along the same lines. I was thinking about how it appears people have so many excuses now as to why they can't make it to church during the week for bible study or on Sunday's for worship service. What's that really about? I agree with you, some of it is selfishness; more about them than about God. But, as I was thinking about this I was thinking about this scripture...."*Now the Holy Spirit tells us clearly that in the last times some will turn away from what we believe...*" 1st Timothy 4:1 NLT So, God has already told us this would happen during the end times.

I think this subject is on a lot of church folks' mind lately. We're looking around us and finding many people not running into the church doors as they used to. I believe (and this is my opinion) we just might be looking at that falling away happening right before our very eyes. The scripture I quoted above continues like this..."*they will follow lying spirits...*" Now I do remember when I was young and growing up in the Methodist Church in the church bulletin every week there was a list called the *"Sick & Shut-In"*. These were church members that were in some capacity unable to physically attend church. We were supposed to pray for them, go by and visit with them, send cards, or call them. Their consistent absence in church was legit.

Consider this...who would motivate us or encourage us to not go to church?

It's certainly not The Holy Spirit. We don't get that kind of encouragement from Him. Whatever, the reasons we continually not go to Church has to be looked at a bit more carefully. The bible say's in the last days it's possible for God's own people to be fooled. References **Mark 13:20; 22, Matthew 24:24.** The bible teaches, the devil is conning, crafty, and subtle.

It's so easy to get out of the habit of going to mid-week bible study and even Sunday services. All you have to do is miss a few times, get comfortable with it; and bam, there you have it. And so many say, why bother getting dressed and driving when I can watch church on my computer, my I Pad, my tablet, my T.V., or listen to it on the radio? We should preach the Gospel of Jesus Christ through every available means, but it's not intended to offer an on-going alternative to live worship in the House of God.

Meeting together at the church house is scriptural and the will of God for us (Heb. 10:25). For me personally it's scary watching so many confessing Christians comfortable with not going to church regularly. The trap is truly easy to fall into. We all should pray that we will not fall into this trap. We need The Holy Spirit to keep us. It could happen to any of us. Only Believe!

My 2 Cents

I wonder how of many you might be feeling the way I've been feeling lately about the news reports. Whew! I think I'm a little fed up with listening to the news. Right now, I feel like I just can't take any more bad news. I'm reminded of a line from the movie ***The Wiz;*** in that movie the wicked witch said, ***"don't bring me no bad news."***

I believe I have reached my tipping point in listening to the constant reporting of bad news. I arrived at that point when I heard the reports about the three young women rescued from being held captive in the house in Cleveland. That news was grievous and exhausting. I didn't want to hear all the ugly details. You just knew they were going to pick this story apart as they do. So whenever I ran across a report about that situation, I purposely didn't read it. I didn't follow the story. I decided right then when that story broke that it was time for me to take a sabbatical from bad news. It appears there has been an escalation of wickedness. I don't believe our minds were designed to continually take in information that grieves and stresses us over a long period of time. In *2 Timothy 2:13, Paul said, "But evil men and impostors will grow worse and worse".* It certainly looks like the reports we hear now have become far more horrendous than in the past?

Because of technology, news is more accessible from around the world. Now we are constantly bombarded with all sorts of gruesome news reports. I wonder if even those that report the news sometimes feel overwhelmed by the type of things they have to report. **Do I have any witnesses, that sometimes we should take a break from the bad news?**

Well, I'm going to leave you with some good news. ***"These things I have spoken to you, that in Me you may have peace. In the world you will have tribulation: but be of good cheer, I have overcome the world."*** St. John 16:33

I saw an interesting news article on *The Today Show* yesterday. In Ethiopia there is a new school run by *Belachew Girma*. He is given the title "Laughter Therapist". In this school he teaches "How to Laugh to a Better Life." He is supposedly the *World Laughter Master*. He says he teaches his students how to laugh for your health, how to laugh and look on the bright side of life despite one's problems. He also conducts seminars. He conducted one here in the United States in 2011. His subject when he conducts the seminars is "How to Change Yourself and the World with Laughter."

A cheerful heart is good medicine, but a broken spirit saps a person's strength. Proverbs 17:22 NLT.

Only Believe!

Meditate today on ...

The LORD *is* gracious and full of compassion,
Slow to anger and great in mercy·
The LORD *is* good to all,
And His tender mercies are over
all His works·
Ps· 145:8-9

Hallelujah, I love the way God loves
Go through the day knowing & receiving
His grace and mercy, goodness and kindness

Deut. 6:25 *And it shall be our righteousness, if we observe to do all these commandments before the* LORD *our God, as he hath commanded us.*

Together Forever

I'm sorry to say that most people think that the Old Testament has passed away, **_but nay, no, and double no_**. In order to know God like we should, we need to know the God of yesterday. *He is the same yesterday, today, and forever-Heb. 13:8.* One example that excites me is the grace and mercy that God had for the Israelites (over and over); He was so faithful and forgiving. That gives much hope for me personally and for the world because sin is not even sin anymore. Most people are doing their own thing. They have allowed the majority to rule and not God.

Same God – different times – one story – one book – one B.I.B.L.E

Today, the Ten Commandments are all wrapped up into one:

Owe no one anything except to love one another, for he who loves another has fulfilled the law. For the commandments, "You shall not commit adultery," "You shall not murder," "You shall not steal," "You shall not bear false witness," "You shall not covet," and if there is any other commandment, are all summed up in this saying, namely, "You shall love your neighbor as yourself." Romans 13:8-9

The best connecter of all is in Hebrews 11:40 (from the Message Bible). Have you seen the movie "Jerry Maguire"? This scripture reminds me of the part when he looked at her and said "You Complete Me". The Commandment to love completes us **_in faith_**.

Between Abraham, Noah, Moses and many others, even though their lives of faith were exemplary, God had a better plan for us...that their faith and our faith would come together to make one completed whole. Their lives of faith are not complete apart from ours. Heb. 11:40

My favorite scripture in Deuteronomy

Love the LORD your God with all your heart and with all your soul and with all your strength. These commandments that I give you today are to be on your hearts. Impress them on your children. Talk about them when you sit at home and when you walk along the road, when you lie down and when you get up. Tie them as symbols on your hands and bind them on your foreheads. Write them on the doorframes of your houses and on your gates. Deut. 6:5-9 .... Behavior for the true fanatic

My Agape Walk Today

You just got up;

Jesus walks in the room –

What would

He tell you

To do today!

Do it!

✓ <u>I walked in love today</u>

My 2 Cents

Overworked. Overwhelmed. Overstimulated. We live such busy lives. I often wonder how much of our business is actually the will of God for our lives?

I have come to the conclusion that it is the will of God for us to live much more simplified than what we do. Our schedules hold so many to-do's that we seemingly can never find the time to do them. Have you ever felt like you needed to just slow down and enjoy your life, your friends, and your family? Do you sometimes feel like if one more project gets added to your list of projects you are going to scream?

Busy, busy, busy, way too busy. Got to exercise, got to work, got to do family, got to cook, got to shop for the food to cook, got to houseclean, commitments. How do we slow down and simplify? *That Is The Million Dollar Question. The answer is*: We have the potential and ability to slow down. It's a matter of purpose, determination and prioritizing which is what I did last Saturday. I made a decision I would slow down on that day and do basically nothing. I whipped out my patio swing cushions, dusted them off and sat them in the swing. I got in my car went to the store got some fixings for a good sundae (made with frozen yogurt of course). Pulled out a novel and sat on my patio swing for hours.

It felt good. It can be done. It was so refreshing I marched into my office on Monday and put my vacation days on the calendar to be taken in a couple of weeks. Our lives are way too jam-packed; purpose in your heart to slow it down. I'm issuing a challenge as Toni Joy did. I challenge you to purpose to find a day soon to do nothing but relax. As my spiritual daughter Tonya say's all the time, "Do You Boo!" Only Believe!

Meditate today on ...

*Bless the LORD, O my soul: and all that
is within me, bless his holy name.*

*Bless the LORD, O my soul, and
forget not all his benefits:*

*Who forgiveth all thine iniquities;
who healeth all thy diseases;*

*Who redeemeth thy life from destruction; who
crowneth thee with lovingkindness and tender mercies;*

*Who satisfies your mouth with good things, So
that your youth is renewed like the eagle's.*

Ps. 103:1-5

Now make it personal;
*Who forgiveth all my iniquities; who healeth all my
diseases; Who redeemeth my life from destruction;
who crowneth me with lovingkindness and tender
mercies; Who satisfies my mouth with good things,
So that my youth is renewed like the eagle's.*

I'm blessed

Memorial Day

Excerpt taken from Wikipedia

Memorial Day is a US federal holiday which is celebrated every year on the last Monday of May. It's a day of remembering the men and women who died while serving in the United States Armed Forces. Formerly known as **Decoration Day**, it originated after the American Civil War to commemorate the Union and Confederate soldiers who died in the Civil War. By the 20th century, Memorial Day had been extended to honor all Americans who have died while in the military service. It typically marks the start of the summer vacation season, while Labor Day marks its end.

Memorial Day is not to be confused with Veterans Day; Memorial Day is a day of remembering the men and women who died while serving, while Veterans Day celebrates the service of all U.S. military veterans.

The practice of decorating soldiers' graves with flowers is an ancient custom. Soldiers' graves were decorated in the U.S. before and during the American Civil War. A claim was made in 1906 that the first Civil War soldier's grave ever decorated was in Warrenton, Virginia, on June 3, 1861, implying the first Memorial Day occurred there.

Read much more at: http://en.wikipedia.org/wiki/Memorial_Day

Salute... *to those men and woman that gave their lives to serve our nation.*

Toni Joy

Exod. 7:7 "And Moses was eighty years old and Aaron was eighty three when they spoke to Pharaoh."

How do you want to go?

I am truly amazed at the life and death of Moses. We are talking about a man that made a major mistake, left everything he knew, then years later came back to lead the people of Israel out of bondage (at the age of 80). This is what was said at his death at 120 years old, **"And Moses was a hundred and twenty years old when he died; his eye was not dim, nor his natural force abated."** Duet. 34:7

It is never too late to get it together. I don't care what we go through in life, we can pull it together and start again. I am 50 years old and have to begin again. Yes it's hard, but nothing is impossible with God.

Some start over by choice, but some have no choice (the important thing is that we start over). Some don't take the opportunity. They settle into a lower level living justifying it with little reasons and some with really good reasons for not trying to reach their goals and dreams. Even the best of reasons is not good enough for those of us covered by the Blood of Jesus. In the world, we can come up with some really good barriers and strongholds that keep us down and make being down look good. The Israelites wanted to run back to Egypt whenever trouble came remembering the good things and not the bad. But, there were so many times even God wanted to leave the Israelites alone, but didn't. If He didn't leave them then, before Christ, He won't leave us now *In Christ*! Being down was not the disappointment with God, wanting to stay there was. Let a new way of living emerge. Give yourself permission to prosper in-spite of the way we feel or think; or even how we got there.

Let the Life of Moses inspire us to go forward in courage!
No man shall be able to stand before you all the days of your life; as I was with Moses, so I will be with you. I will not leave you nor forsake you. Joshua 1:5

James 1:2 Consider it pure joy, my brothers and sisters, whenever you face trials of many kinds...

Optimist or Pessimist

What do you see when the daily cares of life hit you in the face? Do you see the *issue/problem/trouble* or do you see the *goal/answer/solution*?

As humans, it's our nature to see the problem; but, as believers it's our nature to see the answer. As we pray the Word of God, it always sees our ability, direction, or need/wants. The other morning as I was praying I wasn't really feeling it. My body just wanted to go back to sleep, but I knew I needed to pray. After a few I thank you Lord, I truly thanked the Lord that when He see me He sees Jesus. I'm glad He didn't see the tired old me pathetically trying to wake up. Then I realized that seeing things the way God sees them is how we are supposed to see things through the eyes of Jesus. And when we don't we are really being a pessimist.

Optimist: a belief that good ultimately prevails; looking at the positive side of things
Pessimist: a belief that evil outweighs the good; looking at the negative side of things

Faith makes you an optimist no matter where you find yourself. Faith always sees us through; faith sees what God sees.

Have the God kind of faith... For assuredly, I say to you, whoever says to this mountain, 'Be removed and be cast into the sea,' and does not doubt in his heart, but believes that those things he says will be done, he will have whatever he says. Mark 11:23

In talking to the ladies at Naomi's Nest I posed this question, *"If your child ran into the house crying and their knee was bleeding, what would be the first thing you would do?"* One lady said, "I would ask her what happened?" And another lady said, "My first instinct would be to take care of her knee". Jesus didn't ask what happened, He didn't ask for a critical report; He just healed, delivered, and solved the problem. Yes, we do need to repent, but get in front of the issue and not behind it.

Jesus asked, "_What do you want me to do for you?_"
Not "_what happened to you?_"

My 2 Cents

Last week, I talked about the need for a little R&R (Rest and Relaxation). I mentioned the words: **Overworked, Overwhelmed, Overstimulated**.
This week I want to add three more words to that list: Fatigued, Exhausted, Stressed.

What is Relaxation?
Basic definition: The process in which the tension among all the muscles in the body is absent. It's also defined as a state of mind in which stressors, negative self-talk, and other worries are eliminated from the mind.

As one popular female T.V actor says, *"I want to go there."* Yes, with a quickness. So relaxation is both a mental state of mind and a physical state.

Here are a few tips for some precious downtime. (1). If you don't have the money for a vacation right now, have a staycation instead. A staycation is a stay at home vacation where the focus is on resting. (2). Get outside and into nature. Take a walk, ride a bike, walk the dog, or go sit by the water. The fresh air, flowers, grass, and trees can have a calming effect. (3). Let your mind wander and dream. (4). Take a long warm bath complete with something beautifully scented and music that inspires you. This is a good way to rinse stress away. (5). Turn off the television, the computer, and other items that are distracting and enjoy a time of solitude.

It's important that we take time for ourselves daily. A medical stress management team wrote, "Common signs of stress are Mood Swings, Mental Exhaustion, the Inability to Concentrate, Insomnia, and Memory Retention Problems". Did you see yourself in that list? It's time to come away from the hustle and bustle. *Only Believe!*

Toni Joy

Matt. 9:13 *But go and learn what this means: 'I desire mercy and not sacrifice.' For I did not come to call the righteous, but sinners, to repentance.*

So What

Sometimes I think about how the Devil fools us so many times and steals our blessings by throwing our past in our face or telling us that we are not worthy to be blessed, we did too much too long, we hurt too many people, etc.

The devil came to steal, kill, and destroy; but we know that, don't we? - don't we! Regardless of how much we're aware of that, we still allow the devil access to our feelings and thoughts. **Jesus kept things so simple and sweet....**

"SO WHAT"

He proved that by dying on the cross in-spite of us saying "Crucify Him" - He said, "So What." (He knew who was behind it.)

He told Peter that he was going to deny Him three times, but He said, "So What." (He knew who was behind it.)

The men in the town brought a woman to him and said they caught her in the very act of adultery and He said,
"So What." (He knew who was behind it.)

He told the thief next to Him on the cross that he would be in heaven with Him, and knowing his crimes... said
"So What." (He knew who was behind it.)

He knew when we lied, cheated, stole, killed, gossiped, hated, etc. "So What." (He knew who was behind it.)

So the next time you're tempted to be moved by what you feel or think about being ashamed, unworthy, unrighteous...say, "So What?!?" Jesus said it so why can't we because **WE** know who is behind it.

Say SO WHAT and put the devil to shame.
If you and I don't start putting him to shame, who will?
(I'm not talking about the "So What" to keep sinning - but the "So What" to letting the past get in your way or the "So What" and stop letting sin keep you in sin.)

John 4:1-42 (The woman at the well) After you read this, think of how many times Jesus had to say "So What" before this woman stopped with the excuses and got the message. If that woman can say *So What*; then I know we can.

My Agape Walk Today

How Bold Are You

Invite a friend that don't go to church or have a church home to Visit your church Sunday.
Call them up today.

✓ _I walked in love today_

Joshua 1:8 *This Book of the Law shall not depart from your mouth, but you shall meditate in it day and night that you may observe to do according all that is written in it. For then you will make your way prosperous, and then you will have good success.*

Unreasonably Committed

I beseech you therefore, brethren, by the mercies of God, that ye present your bodies a living sacrifice, holy, acceptable unto God, which is your **reasonable service**. Rom. 12:1

If this is reasonably committed, what is unreasonably committed?
Going beyond <u>what we think it is</u> to be committed
What God thinks is reasonable…is unreasonable to most

Trust in the LORD with all thine heart; and lean not unto thine own understanding. In all thy ways acknowledge him, and he shall direct thy paths. Be not wise in thine own eyes. Prov. 3:5-6

We had a movie night at church one day and after the movie My Pastors shared the call of God on their life to win the world to Christ. They were very serious about getting the Word of God in our hearts and minds. Their last thought to us was *"What do you think it would be like if we committed to memorizing the whole bible and how that would change things today"*.

Joshua spoke to the Israelites about their commitment to God and their faithfulness when he said,

"Choose you this day whom you will serve, but as for me and my house, We will serve the Lord·"

We're almost half way through the year. Do you remember some of your New Year's resolutions? Finish the rest of the year with a bang! If you're not charged up – get charged up. **<u>Get in the Word of God</u>**.

Be Unreasonably Committed

My son, give attention to my words; Incline your ear to my sayings. Do not let them depart from your eyes; Keep them in the midst of your heart; For they are life to those who find them, And health to all their flesh. Keep your heart with all diligence, For out of it spring the issues of life. **Prov. 4:20-23**

My 2 Cents

I'm still thinking about the subject of time management (not wasting time). I picked up a book titled, **How Did I Get So Busy?** As I read the introduction it read like the author personally knew about my life. One of the first questions she ask in the book is; **"Do you find yourself rushing from one activity to the next?"** Of course!!!! Here's another question the author ask that resonated with me, **"Is your social life disappearing because you don't have time for friends and fun?"** I have not been spending time with my friends as I normally would. I'm hating that too. I miss them. I haven't read the book yet just the introduction, but because the author captured my attention with those first few questions, I'll read the book.

I believe God has a plan and a purpose for each of us. I'm also certain that plan and purpose can be accomplished. It's up to us to manage our time and resources wisely in order to successfully fulfill our purpose.

The book of Ecclesiastes in the Old Testament says, **"There is a time for everything, a season for every activity under heaven"**. God has given each of us 24 hours in a day. Every day we wake up we're allowed to choose how to utilize those 24 hours. Those 24 hours are a gift. If we don't have a plan **each day** how to best use those hours, we can and will end up squandering time away. We have to make a shift and do some things differently if we are really going to pursue our purpose. When you think about it; do you know anybody that set out to be a failure in life? Probably not. Most people want to be successful at something. But, it's how we use our time that makes the difference. As one of my favorite bible teachers said, **"You can sit on the front porch in a rocking chair all day long saying I wish I had a million dollars. Wishing it is not going to make it happen"**. Getting up and doing something about the pursuit of our dreams will make it happen. Prioritizing is important. I am convinced we are just too busy. But, what are we busy doing exactly? Are we busy for the sake of being busy? If our busy lifestyles have become overwhelming and it's not getting us where we want to be, it's time to stop the madness.

Only Believe!

Meditate today on ...

Owe no one anything except to love one another, for he who loves another has fulfilled the law

Rom· 13:8

Forgive everyone today;

Including yourself

Feel free to fulfill the law

Live Life Loving

CONFESSION FOR THE MONTH OF JUNE

Print or write out a confession; put it where you can see and confess it all month.

There is something to be said every day; and I will speak those things which are good, kind, lovely, and edifying to the other person.
I say the things that my heavenly Father instruct me to say
I do the things that my heavenly Father instruct me to do

At the end of this day, it will be said...
"well done, good and faithful servant"

"His master replied, 'Well done, good and faithful servant! You have been faithful with a few things; I will put you in charge of many things. Come and share your master's happiness!' Matt. 25:23

My Agape Walk Today

Tell something that

Jesus did for you

To someone that

<u>You don't know</u>

✓ <u>I walked in love today</u>

<u>A Thought about Change,</u> Part 1

**To everything there is a season, and a time to every purpose under the heaven. Ecclesiastes 3:1
He hath made everything beautiful in his time: Ecclesiastes 3:11a**

I read a book by Spencer Johnson M.D. called "Who Moved My Cheese", and it inspired me to share my thoughts on "Change". I recommend this book for you to read. I have read it many times.

Many of us at this very moment find ourselves in the midst of transition. Our attitude will shape how we enter this transition period and how successfully we maneuver through it.

Some of us, when change comes and catches us off guard, the first thing we do is run off with our hands up, screaming and yelling. I can hear some of y'all laughing cause you know it's true. When really, what we should do is take the time to process it properly before we respond.

Only Believe!

I want to take some time to talk about change because it's something each and every one of us have in common. I doesn't matter who you are or where you come from....

You will experience Change

Meditate today on ...

For though we walk in the flesh, we do not
war according to the flesh. For the weapons
of our warfare are not carnal but mighty
in God for pulling down strongholds, casting
down arguments and every high thing that
exalts itself against the knowledge of God,
bringing every thought into captivity to the
obedience of Christ, and being ready to punish
all disobedience when your obedience is fulfilled.

2Cor. 10:3-6

We have the power to keep or release a thought

Wow, that's freedom

Go figure

A Thought about Change, Part 2

In all your ways know, recognize, and acknowledge Him, and He will direct and make straight and plain your path. **Proverbs 3:6 The Amplified Bible**

Maze: a confusing network of intercommunicating paths or passages; a labyrinth. A state of bewilderment, confusion, or perplexity.

Our path never has to be confusing nor perplexing; however, often it is. Which direction to turn, which decision is the right decision, to say yes or no, for many, conjure fear and confusion. But according to Proverbs 3:6 we need not fear when change comes, nor when the time comes to make the big decision. We can look to God and acknowledge him, recognize Him in all of our plans and He'll point to the path we must take. Ahhh, but the dilemma lies in trusting Him to direct us and have control over our lives. That fearful maze of life has no control over us when we let Him in and *allow* His direction.

I don't want to stop changing and learning. Life can be a wonderful adventure. It's our decision. As Benjamin Franklin said, "many men die at 25 and aren't buried until they are 75". Some people stop living, growing, changing and learning. They become stagnated. When doors were open for change, some shut the door on it. Some open doors are your heavenly Father wanting to bless you. "...behold, I have set before thee an open door, and no man can shut it:" Revelation 3:8 *Only Believe!*

Toni Joy

*There is such peace that comes with trusting God,
especially when it comes when you're in a maze.
We can breathe again and have the awesomeness to
"See the Salvation of the Lord".*

I always pictured when Moses was caught between the Egyptians and The Red Sea he told the Israelites, "Stand still and see the salvation of the Lord!" Then he lifted his rod and the waters were separated. I love that, I love that. **WE CAN STAND STILL AND SEE THE SALVATION OF THE LORD**. That's what trusting God is all about.... *Maze? What maze?*

That's where I go when caught between a rock and a hard place. My 2Cents started with a scripture trust in the Lord.... and as we trust the Lord;

Do not be anxious about anything, but in every situation, by prayer and petition, with thanksgiving, present your requests to God. And the peace of God, which <u>transcends all understanding</u>, will guard your hearts and your minds in Christ Jesus. Phil. 4: 6-7

My Agape Walk
Today

Pick a person
To be kind to
"ALL DAY"
Don't make it an easy pick

✓ <u>I walked in love today</u>

A Thought about Change, Part 3

You, Lord are the light that keeps me safe. I am not afraid of anyone. You protect me, and I have no fears. Trust the Lord! Be brave and strong and trust the Lord. Psalm 27:1, 14

"...You protect me, and I have no fears." The scripture above indicates we **should not** be afraid of anyone. Trust the Lord and be brave. God told Joshua, "Have not I commanded you? Be strong, vigorous, and very courageous. Be not afraid, neither be dismayed, for the Lord your God is with you wherever you go." Joshua 1: 9. I believe God is commanding that very thing of you and me today. We're to be strong, be courageous. No matter the changes we're facing and no matter who is trying to get in the way of our change, God is with us. We've got to see change in a different light. Here is one way to view change, *"If you're gonna make a change, you're gonna have to operate from a new belief that says life happens not to me, but for me."* Tony Robbins.

When change happens, let's not take the easy way out; by running. Nope, let's stand and go looking for our dreams and goals.

Every day, allow life to surprise you with different kinds of obstacles. Don't get stuck on the same ways and things, but don't lose sight of your dreams and goals.

To be continued.... *Only Believe!*

A Thought about Change, Part 4

For My thoughts are not your thoughts, neither are your ways My ways, says the Lord. For as the heavens are higher than the earth, so are My ways higher than your ways and My thoughts than your thoughts. **Isaiah 53:8-9** AMP

Continued... As different as we are, every morning most of us put on our jogging suits and running shoes, leave our homes, race out into the maze looking for our goals, using simple trial-and-error methods of completing our tasks, remembering what road works and which ones didn't.

On the other hand, sometimes we allow powerful beliefs and emotions to cloud the way. It makes life in this maze more complicated and challenging.

What's interesting is, sometimes our approach is simple. If we don't find what we need, we just seek another avenue without complaining or going through changes. We don't waste time grieving over the loss of yesterday's tasks. We just move on making decisions quickly.

On the other hand, we can rely on not-so-simple thinking. We use lessons from past experiences, intelligent and sophisticated thinking, and our beliefs and emotions. Oh boy, you know we have a problem when we are relying on own abilities and then our emotions kick into gear.

A lady that I know recently encountered a problem with paying her utilities. She shuts her lights and gas off for the summer. Somebody disrupted her goal; literally, someone stole money from her. I respect how she handled it. She forgave, fasted, and prayed for guidance and wisdom. She knew and believed the above verse, that He would lead her down the path to a new direction of completing her goal. The process of seeking **His ways** in this matter required that she go through a maze of organizations and people to get her utilities back on; but, they will be back on this week. She allowed Him to guide her steps, leading her to this one and that one until she found the right way (a way of getting the bill paid).

There is always new ways! **When your way has been moved who do your first response most resemble**? Yours or the Lord's?

Only Believe!

Meditate today on ...

When I consider Your heavens, the work
of Your fingers,
The moon and the stars, which You have
ordained,
What is man that You are mindful
of him,
And the son of man that You visit him?

Ps. 8:3-4

Lord thank you
Tell Him what you're thankful for...

A Thought about Change, Part 5

That men may know that thou, whose name alone is Je-Ho'Vah, art the most high over all the earth. Psalm 83:18 KJV
And Abraham lifted up his eyes, and looked and behold behind him a ram caught in a thicket by his horns: And Abraham went and took the ram, and offered him up for a burnt offering in the stead of his son. *And Abraham called the name of that place Je-ho-vah-jireh: as it is said to this day, In the mount of the Lord it shall be seen. Genesis 22:13-14*
(Je-ho-vah-jireh, "the Lord will provide")

Continued... As in life, sometimes we find that our whole plan has to change. Sometimes we're not surprised we notice them small hints every day and prepare for the inevitable and know instinctively what to do. We put on new shoes and go in a new direction.

On the other hand, sometimes we don't pay attention to the small changes that had been taking place each day; we take for granted that things will be the same. And to our surprise – boom - the ground is pulled from under us. We put our hands on our hips, and turn red. We yell and scream, and holler.

Who is responsible for this? This isn't fair!

We're not ready for change. We don't want to deal with what we have to face; then we tune everything out.

How many times have we behaved like this when our plans have disappeared? Whether the move was subtle or abrupt how many times have we not immediately turned to Jehovah? I would like to tell you every time change came into my life I responded with ease. Uh, no, I haven't always instinctively turned to Jehovah-jireh first. Even though, Philippians 4:19 (my God shall supply all my needs...) was one of the first scriptures I memorized. When our plans go hay-wire, Jehovah is there to meet the need. *Only Believe!*

Ahhh, My 2Cents hit a nerve on this one···

I don't believe I knew until this moment that I was acting like child a very short while back; I am still mending the wounds from it. But the key here is ***I am moving on…***I picked myself up (with help from The Holy Spirit) and stopped screaming, *"this isn't fair"*.

(Sometimes we change our owe plans by the decisions we make and regret it (and God knew it). <u>Still move on – this is a must</u>)

But I am so glad at this revelation of stupidity that I didn't stay there. I learned a good lesson and it made me more aware of being in a position to hear God's direction in my life. But it's a little more than that for me. What's more important to me now is God's direction in my life *and **His presence moment by moment***. The end will be there… and I will thoroughly enjoy His guiding. This will leave very little room to *cry and stomp*.

When God says jump - Let's say "How High"

I wanted to share what my father thought was important to note while in recovery; it may help someone that doesn't know what to do with shame, resentment, guilt, etc. I'm not sure if this was in a book or his own thoughts; but they became personal to him.

Road to Serenity

No room in my life for shame;

Don't try to fix it, get rid of it.

Guilt can be fixed;

Apologize, pay restitution, etc.

Keep awareness up (impossible when high)

Resentments cannot be a part of my life;

It's a number one destroyer,

Sabotages my spirituality.

Remember to be thankful

In memory of Willard (Pete) Patterson

Father's Day

To all our father's and grandfather's; you are the firm foundation of the family – may God continue to be the motivating force that drives you to be our hero's and leaders.

Father's Day was founded in Spokane, Washington at the YMCA in 1910 by Sonora Smart Dodd, who was born in Arkansas. Its first celebration was in the Spokane YMCA on June 19, 1910. Her father, the Civil War veteran William Jackson Smart was a single parent who raised his six children there. After hearing a sermon about Jarvis' Mother's Day in 1909, she told her pastor that fathers should have a similar holiday honoring them. Although she initially suggested June 5th, her father's birthday, the pastors did not have enough time to prepare their sermons and the celebration was deferred to the third Sunday of June.

After much work and a lot of time

In 1966, President Lyndon B. Johnson issued the first presidential proclamation honoring fathers, designating the third Sunday in June as Father's Day. Six years later, the day was made a permanent national holiday when President Richard Nixon signed it into law in 1972.

Happy Father's Day to the Father of Father's
Our Heavenly Father –The Father of Creation
My Father and Yours

A Thought about Change, Part 6

No, dear friends, I am not all I should be, but I am focusing all my energies on this one thing: Forgetting the past and looking forward to what lies ahead. Philippians 3:13 NLT

When change happens...We process it differently. Some will get on with it, recognize things change, and concede that it's time for us to change as well.

On the other hand some of us are still trying to understand how things got away from us. We are amazed and upset that this happened. I am of the mind that all of us can be a little bit of both ways. Some changes stump us, paralyze us, and behoove us. Some changes we just know were inevitable; so, move on. As the character Vi Rose from "Joyful Noise" said, "sometimes change can just take a big chunk out of our behinds." I do have to admit, I have experienced changes that made me feel like somebody took a big chunk out my behind. LOL! My husband belonged to a gym that he visited three times a week faithfully. He made friends there, was comfortable there and enjoyed his visits. He purchased a lifetime membership. His three times a week visits went on for several years. One day my husband went for his workout and was told the **GYM WAS CLOSING PERMANENTLY.** Guess who he acted like when he related the news to me. <u>**BOTH**</u>. First I got the "ah man" reaction for a few weeks. He was mad. He shouted about his lifetime membership that he wouldn't get a chance to continue to utilize. He fumed about how unfair it was. Then after a few weeks he decided he'd had enough of fuming about it. He pouted until even he got tired of it. Finally he started acting like he would handle it with ease. He went gym shopping. He found nothing that compared to what he had before, the pool and sauna. But he was willing to compromise. He used visitor passes to other gyms, he ask buddies of his did they find a new gym. He was determined to find a new gym. He didn't appreciate his gym closing down. But he decided to move on. He is currently still gym shopping. I am just grateful he is releasing the past and looking forward to what lies ahead of him in this regard. Sometimes we are forced to change and that's not always bad. Because if we don't change we can become extinct. *It's best we search out the changes ahead of time and hurry into action, rather than get locked in and be left behind.* Letting go can be difficult. I can attest to that. But we have to release the past and go in a new direction. **I'm in the 'let's get a new way going' mode. How about y'all?** *Only Believe!*

No, dear friends, I am not all I should be, but I am focusing all my energies on this one thing: Forgetting the past and looking forward to what lies ahead. ***Philippians 3:13 NLT***

The beginning scripture is one that should be an active ingredient in our daily walk;

Pressing ahead to win in Christ is a forever changing life style.

Change is not a choice
But how you flow with change is

So don't get extinct on us - be ready for the "Let's get a new way going"

I'm not sure about all of you out there, but I enjoyed ***My 2Cents*** perspective on *A Thought about Change·*

Not only did it help me understand some positions I had been in, but the ones I'm in now -
we all have decisions to make at different times in our life.

We are not through yet·····

My Agape Walk Today

Fast from One (1)
"Word" you always
say and replace
it with the phrase
"I am disciplined"

✓ <u>I walked in love today</u>

I have given them the glory that you gave me, that they may be one as we are one – I in them and you in me – so that they may be brought to complete unity. Then the world will know that you sent me and have loved them even as you have loved me –John 17:22-23

All You Need Is LOVE, Walk in Love

For God so loved the world that he gave his one and only Son, that whoever believes in Him shall not perish but have eternal life. For God did not send his Son into the world to condemn the world, but to save the world through Him -John 3:16-17

How's your love walk today? Is the motive behind everything you do governed by love?

I believe that if love is in the fore-front of our thinking and the foundation of our being, we would open up the true potential of our gift and purpose in life. We were created for a reason. I believe that through love, we will find that reason. We have to know how to work this love. Love is an action word. We can say, "I love you". We can feel loved; but until it is acted out, it will not produce fruit. For God so loved the world that He gave. If we are following God, we will find that Love is the only cure.

I know we say that it's hard to show love in some situations, but we are to love anyway. We can do it in Christ! Because when we are born again, we have the Love of God living on the inside of us. God is our example that love prevails. God loved us when we weren't even looking for Him. He loved us when we shouted, "Crucify Him". He still loves us today... He continually pours His grace and mercy on us. His love never ends.

Continue with today's devotion on the next page

God's expression of "**Agape**" love is pure love to His Son and all mankind. It is the nature of God; **God is Love**

<u>In Vines:</u> *Christian love is the fruit of His Spirit in us. Christian love, whether exercised toward the brethren, or toward men, generally, is not an impulse from the feelings, it does not always run with the natural inclinations, nor does it spend itself only upon those for whom, some affinity is discovered. Love seeks the welfare of all.*

God's perfect will for us is to walk daily in the fruit of the Spirit

But the fruit of the Spirit is love, joy, peace, forbearance, kindness, goodness, faithfulness, gentleness and self-control. Against such things there is no law. Those who belong to Christ Jesus have crucified the flesh with its passions and desires. Since we live by the Spirit, let us keep in step with the Spirit. Gal. 5:22-25

Every day we must walk on purpose in love towards our family, friends, and all those that come in our path. This shows the love of God towards others and towards ourselves. Walking in the Fruit of the Spirit frees us from the flesh and the sin of it....*walk by the Spirit, and you will not gratify the desires of the flesh. Gal 5:16*

The bible says that love covers a multitude of sins. Isn't that what we want from God? And that's what God want us to give others. Are we walking in love today?

<u>It wouldn't be complete if I didn't mention Eph. 6...</u>
Husbands.... do you love your wife as Christ loves the Church, *daily*?
Wives... are you loving your husband as you love the Lord, *daily*?
If not, let's begin today

I am not writing you a new command but one we have had from the beginning. I ask that we love one another. And this is love: that we walk in obedience to his commands. As you have heard from the beginning, his command is that you
walk in love *1 John 1:5-6*

My 2 Cents

I have a question for you today. Do you believe in this scripture? *Hitherto have ye asked nothing in my name: ask, and ye shall receive, that your joy may be full. John 16:24 KJV*

Do you believe this scripture indicates we can ask God for our hearts desires in Jesus Name and He would grant that prayer request because He wants our joy to be full?

Do you believe it's an indication that no matter how big the request or how impossible it seems to us, we can request it to be done in our life if it lines up with His plan and will for us no matter how big it is?

Do you believe that scripture is an indication that God wants us to be full of joy as we go through life? So, therefore, ask Him in prayer for things that would bring delight to us as long as it's His will and plan?

When I read that scripture it makes me think of this scripture; *The thief cometh not, but for to steal, and to kill, and to destroy: I am come that they might have life, and that they might have it more abundantly.* John 10:10

I believe today, Our Heavenly Fathers wants us to ask Him for those things that would bring joy. Do you believe He wants to bless you (empower you to prosper)?

Only Believe!

The Fight of Faith – 1Timothy 6:12

I had the opportunity to talk with a young man regarding his career challenges. He's in his late 20's working full time while also working on his Master's Degree. He's well liked everywhere he goes. He was like that even as a kid. One of the executives at his place of employment has taken a liking to him and is interested in promoting him to a management position.

This executive followed through on his word and got the process of interviewing started. During the period of his interviews the young man got a new supervisor. This new supervisor is the fly in the ointment, the problem, the hindrance, the obstacle. The day I spoke with him, he was despondent, disappointed, talking defeated. Ecclesiastes 5:3 (AMP) - *For a dream comes with much business and painful efforts.* He views this new supervisor - who has been giving him a hard time and even gave him a bad referral to the executive - as standing in the way of his promotion. He also viewed this new supervisor as the victor.

Making this brief: I shared with him that some things in life are worth fighting for. A career change can be one of those fights. So, I told him fight for this new position. Don't fight the supervisor, don't disrespect him or his position. But, stand his ground, still believe in the promotion, still expect it. Even though it becomes difficult and it appears that it's not gonna happen, don't be so quick to claim defeat.

Fight the good fight of faith! Obstacles come. It happens to us all; however, it doesn't mean we give up and quit. We keep fighting. There are things in life worth the fight: marriages, career moves, health, relationships. The list is long.

Yet amid all these things we are more than conquerors and gain a surpassing victory through Him Who loved us. Romans 8:37

Only Believe!

My Agape Walk Today

Have a nice

conversation with

someone you

have not talked

to before

✓ *I walked in love today*

Judges 4:4 "And Deborah, a prophetess, the wife of Lapidoth, <u>**she**</u> judged Israel at that time.

Women Rule!

Have you ever heard someone insinuate that Woman should not be in leadership roles? "God can do what God wants to do!!!! Sometimes we need to quit speaking in the Name of God - Thus says the Lord - about something we think we know.

This is an Old Testament truth about **God's people**. *A woman ruled...*··

I was going to keep reading and not talk about this, but I couldn't help myself. I even had to stop my son and tell him, "Don't ever let someone tell you that God can't use women to do the work of God", and read him this story.

I don't know if God used Deborah because a man wasn't available – *if that helps you, let it be*, **God uses women and still does**. God *really* can do what God wants to do. And if I were you, I wouldn't try to figure out the motives or reasoning of God other than to say it's because He loves us. There are many other woman that God used (Old and New Testament). God also used women in-between-the-lines throughout the bible. Just to name a few: Rehab, Esther, Ruth. During the judging of Deborah, He used Jael's wife (from the people of Moses' father-in-law) to kill Sisera that escaped the pursuit of Deborah and Barak. <u>When Sisera ran, he went into the tent of Jael's wife to hide</u>: *"then Jael Heber's wife took a nail of the tent, and took a hammer in her hand, and went softly unto him, and smote the nail into his temples, and fastened it into the ground; for he was fast asleep and weary. So he died."* Judges 4:21

Be very careful when you say what God won't do. Let's not get our thinking and beliefs mixed up with God's way of doing things. We don't want to stop God from doing a miracle in <u>our</u> life.

And the land had rest forth years. Judges 5:31

Love IN Action

There is nothing that can compare to watching love in demonstration to encourage us. I want to share with you two recent instances of love displayed that really touched my heart. As I share with you, these scriptures are ringing true in my heart --*Be devoted to one another in brotherly love. Honor one another above yourselves.* (*Romans 12:10 NIV*) 1st John 3:16-18 says, *This is how we know what love is: Jesus Christ laid down his life for us. And we ought to lay down our lives for our brothers. Dear children, let us not love with words or tongue but with actions and in truth.*

The first instance, one of the ladies in our congregation is facing a serious physical challenge. I tearfully watched as she was called to the front of the church and all the women of the church came forward to present her with cards in which they had written words of encouragement and pledging their support. They hugged her and prayed over her. Several of us cried as much as she did; I was one of them. I was touched to witness their outpouring of love. It just reminds us we're not alone. People do care! Jesus isn't walking the earth in the flesh -- He's walking through us. He's touching lives through us, He's comforting through us, and He loves through you and me.

The second instance, one of my buddies has a birthday coming up. I called to kid her about it. I ask what she would do to celebrate. She said, she had no plans. Her husband said in the background, "Would you talk to my wife please and find out what she wants for her birthday; she won't tell me anything." So I begin to throw out ideas. She wasn't interested in any of them, until I threw out the words MASSAGE, SPA. I had her attention. I told her let me call you back shortly. I went online and pulled up *Tamara Spa in Farmington Hills* and took a look at their packages. It's her birthday; it should be a package right. I chose one of the packages that included everything. The private aromatherapy steam bath, hot rocks massage, the Lavender facial with cucumber eye treatment, hand and foot wax, lunch, manicure/pedicure. You get the picture. I called Tamara and made an appointment for her birthday. I then called her back to speak with her husband. I shared with him that I had already asked for an appointment for his wife. What he said next is what touched my heart. He didn't ask what it cost. He said, **"Is this the best package they offer, this is my wife, I want her to have the best."**

And the word of God says, "Husbands love your wife". The man did not inquire about the cost. I love it when a man loves his woman! My buddy expressed how pleased she was that I took the time to do this for her. I just take pleasure in knowing she married a man that loves her. *Only Believe!*

Meditate today on ...

Then Peter came to Him and said, "Lord, how often shall my brother sin against me, and I forgive him? Up to seven times?"

Jesus said to him, "I do not say to you, up to seven times, but up to seventy times seven·

Matt· 18:21-22

It's what God does for us, thank the Lord

Matt. 13:25-26 *But while men slept, his enemy came and sowed tares among the wheat, and went his way. But when the blade was sprung up, and brought forth fruit, then appeared the tares also.*

If it looks like a duck and it quacks like a duck It's a duck - or is it? Part 1 of 3

I was praying and meditating one morning about my past, present, and future - and I started thanking the Lord for being saved. Then I pondered about some of the things I thought was normal (coming from the world's "point of view") that some saved people think is normal also. I started praying for the Lord to open our eyes to the difference between what's normal to God and what's normal in the world (weed and wheat). Jesus spoke about us being in this world, yet we are not of this world (John 17:14).

If you read the whole account of this parable, the servant asked the owner "Do you want me to pull up the weeds that grow with the wheat"? The owner said "No, you might up-root the wheat with the weeds". Jesus said at the end time they will be separated.

While I was meditating I understood this parable somewhat, but I wondered, if the rapture happened tomorrow, how many of us may not get noticed? *Do we think a little different*? Let this confession be our own:

I am God's special person, set apart for His use AND I LOOK LIKE IT

1 Peter 2:9-10 *But you are a chosen generation, a royal priesthood, a holy nation, His own special people, that you may proclaim the praises of Him who called you out of darkness into His marvelous light; who once were not a people but are now the people of God, who had not obtained mercy but now have obtained mercy.*

Matt 13:30 Let both grow together until the harvest, and at the time of harvest I will say to the reapers, "First gather together the tares and bind them in bundles to burn them, but gather the wheat into my barn."

If it looks like a duck and it quacks like a duck It's a duck - or is it? Part 2 of 3

Take notice to the birds of the air. They share the same space, but over the years, they still look different, have different goals, purposes, characteristics, etc.

Now take notice to us - there *should* only be two distinct differences: saved and unsaved. But as we grow up together sharing the same space are we to share the same goals, the same purposes, and the same characteristics?

After someone spends time with us, what do they know about us that we didn't say? Do we look like a saint or a sinner? A sinner dressed like a saint or a saint dressed like a sinner, or do we show our true likeness? And I'm not talking just about the outer appearance.

I am a friend of God, He knows my name...we have the same thing in mind.

[One day] the evil spirit answered them, "Jesus I know, and I know about Paul, but who are you?" Acts 19:15

Acts 19:15-16 *And the evil spirit answered and said, "Jesus I know, and Paul I know; but who are you?" Then the man in whom the evil spirit was leaped on them, overpowered them, and prevailed against them, so that they fled out of that house naked and wounded.*

If it looks like a duck and it quacks like a duck It's a duck - or is it? Part 3 of 3

There were certain Jews that were into witchcraft that saw Paul do miracles in the Name of Jesus, so they decided to use the name of Jesus themselves on a demon possessed man. *Demons know the real thing when they see it.* One of the bible translations says "one day the evil spirit asked...."

This is a good reason to **not** worry or be jealous of those that seem to be so blessed and yet we know they are wicked. They will be asked if their works are from an evil spirit or God Himself. Real love will cause us to pray for them. It is God's will that none should perish and all come to repentance; this also should be our mind.

Everything in the dark will eventually be exposed. In time, our evil will find us out, or our good will find us out. Sometimes we live our lives like we have time to get saved, time to fix a wrong, time to change, time to live by faith. Even in faith we really don't know when Jesus is coming back. Jesus said only the Father knows the end time (Matt. 24:34-37). We should live each day as if <u>Today is the Day</u>. *Fix a wrong today, get saved today, change today, and live by faith today.*

Let our walk and our talk reveal who we are so that when Jesus comes He will find us ready and without blemish.

Luke 12:42-43 And the Lord said, "Who then is that faithful and wise steward, whom his master will make ruler over his household, to give them their portion of food in due season? Blessed is that servant whom his master will find so doing when he comes."

My Agape Walk Today

How Bold Are You

Think about getting

a journal and talk to God.

allow Him to talk to you.

Write your goals

and dreams.

✓ <u>I walked in love today</u>

Ruth 3:3-4 Therefore wash yourself and anoint yourself, put on your best garment and go down to the threshing floor; but do not make yourself known to the man until he has finished eating and drinking. Then it shall be, when he lies down, that you shall notice the place where he lies; and you shall go in, uncover his feet, and lie down; and he will tell you what you should do.

Who found Who

I always hear "The man has to find the woman, we are not to pursue the man". This interpretation came from Proverbs 18:22 *He who finds a wife finds a good thing, and obtains favor from the LORD. Good interpretation…Amen.*

Ruth went to his field to glean. Ruth followed Naomi's instructions on "How to get a Man". But also...

It was Boaz field. He also gave instructions (twice). And she yielded to them.

…Stay this night, and in the morning it shall be that if he will perform the duty of a close relative for you – good; let him do it. But if he does not want to perform the duty for you, then I will perform the duty for you. As the Lord lives! Lie down until morning. Ruth 3:12-13

Now I know that some of you will wonder about a move like this. So here you go…. *And now, my daughter, do not fear. I will do for you all that you request, for all the people of my town know that you are a virtuous woman. Ruth 3:11*

This is my view to "Who finds Who".
It is the Lord's doing. I believe that if _WE_ (both parties-male and female) are where the Lord wants us to be, doing what the Lord wants us to do, we will be at the right place, at the right time, doing the right thing. God moves on both the man and the woman.

Let God decide the matter of Who Found Who.

Your job is to be *where God wants you to be* and to *yield to the leading of Holy Spirit in your everyday walk.*

Who found Who in the Cinderella story?

1Sam. 16:7 ...for the LORD seeth not as man seeth; for man looketh on the outward appearance, but the LORD looketh on the heart.

Cinderella "man" in the background

Samuel asked to see Jesse's sons because God told him that He had chosen one of them to be the king. Jesse brought out Abinadab; it wasn't him. Then Shammah; the Lord had not chosen him. Then seven of his other sons; the Lord had not chosen these. Samuel asked are there any other sons? **Jesse casually mentioned David not considering him as a choice of the Lord; it was that son, David, which the Lord had chosen to be king**.

This reminds me of Cinderella because the step mom had dismissed her as a choice for the king. How many of us are in the background being dismissed, not even being considered as the choice for President, CEO, Mom of the Year, the kid that will turn out being the successful one, or the one that God will call out to be a Pastor, Lawyer, Teacher; the one that will come out of jail and completely turn his life around?

Aren't we glad that God sees the heart and that it is God that saves, that forgives?
Let God do the choosing, there is room for everyone.

But we also have to seek the heart of God and not of man. Believe God to get us the promotion, to take care of our needs, to be the source of our lives. If we follow the life of David we will find that David trusted God and not man. *The Lord that delivered me out of the paw of the lion, and out of the paw of the bear, he will deliver me out of the hand of this Philistine. And Saul said unto David, go, and the Lord be with thee.* 1 Sam. 17:37

I would rather be a Cinderella in the background and trust God than a man out front being known by all man – trusting in man.

*After <u>removing Saul</u>, he made David their king. God testified concerning him: 'I have found David son of Jesse, a **man after** my **own heart**; he will do everything I want him to do.* Acts 13:22

CONFESSION FOR THE MONTH OF JULY

Print or write out confession; put where you can see and confess it all month

Make your own confession for this month; write it down and speak it out for the rest of this month

_____

_____

_____

_____

_____

_____

Toni Joy

......for he is Lord of lords, and King of kings: and they that are with him are called, and chosen, and faithful. Revelations 17:14

King of Kings

Over the years of the relationship that I have with God the Father, Jesus as Lord, and Holy Spirit as the leading force in my life, I have come to understand more. Namely, I am nowhere near the level of quality care that God gives. A close approximation of this love is that of a loving parent; except God does it with perfection. The Lord has got me through many hard times. There is nothing I can say to really convey the **_quality_** of understanding necessary for **you** to trust God because the testimony is my personal life, my things He did for me daily that I can't always put into words. He doesn't just show us from time to time to remind me that He cares; but all the time. He wants to fellowship with us daily.

We have people in our lives that we can go back through the years and they were always there for us. We know them...We've grown and toiled together. How much more glorious the relationship with God Almighty would be? A relationship that we can 100% trust.

In a time of need, He is my Lord, my help, my lawyer, my doctor, my confidant. He is also our peace and joy. Yes He Is All That AND... What's more is He has given us Holy Spirit who dwells in us continually. Holy Spirit is our A*dvocate, Comforter, Helper and Guide. He carries me through all things, tells me all things, and warns me of all things by revealing all things. **He is everything we need.**

There are many times I don't understand some of things I'm being lead to do, or say as I'm in the midst of it, but I understand He **is** leading and I trust Him as my daily bread. In that daily care is love, joy, peace, goodness, kindness, patience, self-control. Many times we don't *feel* it; yet, we grow to know it.

Build a relationship with Him now. Set time aside to get in the Word, to pray, to meditate on Him. We want to grow up with God, not just to know Him like an associate (someone you haphazardly know).

He is the Kings of kings, Lord of lords - He is everything we need

Know therefore that the Lord thy God, he is God, the faithful God, which keepeth covenant and mercy with them that love him and keep his commandments to a thousand generations. Deut. 7:9

Toni Joy

2 Thes 3:13-15 *But ye, brethren, be not weary in well doing. And if any man obey not our word by this epistle, note that man, and have no company with him, that he may be ashamed. Yet count him not as an enemy, but admonish him as a brother.*

Is your faithfulness too much for some?

Is our devotion too much for our friends, co-workers, families, spouse, and children? Do you think sometimes we feel pressured to suppress our faith? Are we watering down the truth for the sake of company? I know I've told my children many times that it's better to be alone than to be with the wrong crowd. It's easier said than done, but the outcome is worth its weight in gold.

Ultimately we have to consider who we are trying to please. What is the bottom line? Where do we want to end up? When we find ourselves in a place where we are wondering if living by faith or living by what we see is better for us, we need to check **our** hearts because we may have been dealing with a problem or situation too long and may be on the wrong road. Let's question our own sincerity of our time with God. We need to know that it is an inward problem and need to look there first. Even if the devil/others initiated all the problems, it ends with us. The decisions we make are key. It is a trick of our own mind to think that anything is better without God or God's way of doing things.

It might be a simple matter; but regardless, let's stop, listen, and regroup. God loves us and wants us to **enjoy life!** All of us... yes even you... and yes even me.

Let's live the sweet life...

...lean not on your own understanding; In all your ways acknowledge Him, and He shall direct your paths. Prov.3:5-6

Whatever choices we make, others are following us whether we are compromising or standing our ground in faith. **Loving our friends and family is putting God's Word first whether they like it or not**

And we know that in all things God works for the good of those who love him... Rom. 8:28

4th of July
Independence Day

On this day in 1776, the Declaration of Independence was approved by the Continental Congress, setting the 13 colonies on the road to freedom as a sovereign nation. As always, this most American of holidays will be marked by parades, fireworks and backyard barbecues across the country.

Let's also celebrate another Independence Day; which is a different day for each of us, yet we all celebrate the same freedom...being born again into the Family of God. So as we celebrate the independence of America, let's remember our deliverance from the darkness of this world system.

Giving thanks unto the Father, which hath made us meet to be partakers of the inheritance of the saints in light:

Who hath delivered us from the power of darkness, and hath translated us into the kingdom of his dear Son:

In whom we have redemption through his blood, even the forgiveness of sins... Col. 1:12-14

My Agape Walk Today

Shake hands

with someone

today that

You don't know

Introduce Yourself

✓ I walked in love today

John 9:7 *After saying this, he spit on the ground, made some mud with the saliva, and put it on the man's eyes. "Go," he told him, "wash in the Pool of Siloam" (this word means "Sent"). So the man went and washed, and came home seeing.*

Tender Loving Care

As I was reading the passage above (*Turn to it and read 9:1-6 to get the full picture*), I pictured when my kids were younger and I would see them fall, run outside, pick them up, brush the dirt off their knees, I would take a cloth, wet it with my mouth and wipe the scrapes off their knees.

I understand the compassion Jesus felt as He spit on the ground and wiped the blind man's eyes. I see the love that Jesus has for us as He had for this man. He focused on that man - His hurt.

Jesus had compassion on them and touched their eyes. Immediately they received their sight and followed him. (Matt. 20:34)
When Jesus came out and saw a large crowd, he had compassion on them, because they were like sheep without a shepherd. So he began teaching them many things. (Mark 6:34)

That compassion continues through us....

We are to be drawn to help people. I pray many times for the Lord to give me boldness to walk in the Love of God towards the world. This love is not just for pastors and ministers. Believe it or not, other than TV and Radio, as laymen we have more access to the world than our pastors and teachers. So when we hear people putting down pastors and churches - guess what - they are talking about us too.

We shouldn't hold our love only for our children and family.
We are to share it with the world.
And he stretched forth his hand toward his disciples, and said, Behold my mother and my brethren! (Matt. 12:47-50)
So the next time we have the opportunity to show the world God, (metaphorically speaking) spit on the ground and dive in to heal the wound.
Therefore, as God's chosen people, holy and dearly loved, clothe yourselves with compassion, kindness, humility, gentleness and patience. Col. 3:12
Suffering for Doing Good, finally, all of you, be like-minded, be sympathetic, love one another, be compassionate and humble. 1 Pet. 3:8

Sister Toni Joy said, "the next time we have the opportunity to show the world God...dive in to heal the wound." When I read that, it reminded me of the news story about the 68 year old bullied bus monitor, **Karen Klein**. She was verbally abused and tormented on a school bus by a group of students. The story went viral. The video was everywhere. **Max Sidirow** of Toronto Canada, saw the video and launched a fundraising drive online to help Karen. He felt compassion for her. His intentions with the fundraiser was to raise enough money to send her on a good vacation. However, people gave way beyond his expectations. Through the fundraiser, Karen received $703,873. I would call that "diving in to heal the wound". Karen has been quoted as saying, she is overwhelmed with the outpouring of support from the public. She said, people that she didn't know told her they loved her. If you ask me, $703,873 is showing a whole lot of love.

Keep in mind this money did not come from a group of churches; neither were all of these people Christians (I'm sure some were). For the most part these were every day, ordinary people, seeking to heal someone else's wounds. Thank You God for giving us the ability to experience and express the emotion of love.

My little children, let us not love in word or in tongue, but in deed and in truth. 1 John 3:18 NKJV**.** There are those times when we must express our love through action not just with our mouths.

Only Believe!

Meditate today on ...

For out of the abundance of the heart the
mouth speaks· A good man out of the good
treasure of his heart brings forth good things,
and an evil man out of the evil treasure brings
forth evil things· But I say to you that for
every idle word men may speak, they will
give account of it in the Day of Judgment·
For by your words you will be justified, and
by your words you will be condemned·"

Matt· 12:34:37

Don't just watch what you say –
listen to yourself, it's who you are·

Matt 16:13-15 *He asked His disciples, saying, "Who do men say that I, the Son of Man, am?" So they said, "Some say John the Baptist, some Elijah, and others Jeremiah or one of the prophets." He said to them, "But who do you say that I am?"*

Who is God and where is He? Part 1

Where do we look for God and who do we say He is? Some people plan to see Him at church, at a certain place, to act a certain way. Some people try God and when He lets them down or disappoints them, they walk away like there really isn't a God.

Some of the Jews were looking for a god to deliver them physically; they were looking for a king to take the throne. Could you imagine the disappointment they had in Jesus when he was taken captive? They wanted to believe; they hoped even to the end, but He didn't line up. In their eyes, He was just a man. He didn't do what they wanted him to do. Consequently, they *crucified Him.*

Like back then and even now some believe God was/is supposed to prove Himself on our level of expectation of what a god is supposed to be and do. When we get disappointed should we re-evaluate God's position or ours?

We must believe God **at His word**; the Word is not supposed to line up with what **we** think. The change must take place with **us**, not God.

God wants to be more than just what we think; the bible says that those who worship God must worship Him in Spirit and in Truth *(not in our understanding).*

John 4:21-26 *Jesus said to her, "Woman, believe Me, the hour is coming when you will neither on this mountain, nor in Jerusalem, worship the Father. You worship what you do not know; we know what we worship, for salvation is of the Jews. But the hour is coming, and now is, when the true worshipers will worship the Father in spirit and truth; for the Father is seeking such to worship Him. God is Spirit, and those who worship Him must worship in spirit and truth." The woman said to Him, "I know that Messiah is coming" (who is called Christ). "When He comes, He will tell us all things." Jesus said to her, "I who speak to you am He."*

Num. 13:30...*Caleb said "Let us go up at once and take possession, for we are well able to overcome it ...but the men that had gone with him said "we are not able to go up against the people, for they are stronger than we "There we saw the giants (the descendants of Anak came from the giants); and we were like grasshoppers in our own sight, and so we were in their sight."*

Who is God and where is He? Part 2
In Egypt - When the Israelites left Egypt they had to go through the wilderness to get to the Promised Land.
If we follow our vision or purpose, we are going into the wilderness;
<u>We can be Joshua and Caleb</u> or we can be the thousands of others that died, settled and made their home in the wilderness.

We can look good and still have a relationship with God *while we are in the wilderness*. Sometimes the wilderness can make us forget our vision and purpose and who God really is and can be in our lives. Then we settle for what the world says good and great are. In all of this, God still fed them manna and took care of them.

Trying to achieve our dreams (our calling in life, being who God says that we are, and walking in the fruit of the Spirit) will cause the devil to put so much pressure on us that we will reach out for anything to pull us out. The world will show us a fake flower to smell, and with the fear and pain that is in front of us, we won't notice that it's fake. It can hit us so hard that we will grab it to relieve the pain. That fake flower will sometimes be sin or a mirage directing us where to go. This is why the Israelites looked back to Egypt thinking slavery was looking good. But don't judge them; our slavery will look good too but that we know the truth.

But our vision and purpose can be a rope around our waist that pulls us out of the quicksand. But we have to recognize that it is quicksand – _not letting go of our hope_ will keep our eyes open.

Cont. on next page

Cont.

You can pass out, cry, lose some of the battles, wear out the shoes on your feet, lose some friends, make mistakes, and fall flat on your face. Don't stop calling on the Name of Jesus, hearing the Word of God, or having that one person you know can pray you through to talk to you and pray with you.

God is in the wilderness with you

All of the Israelites *were in the wilderness*. Don't think for a minute that Moses, Caleb, Joshua, Aaron, Miriam, and many others were not there with them (*for 40 years – ouch, they were there*). Yet this group continued the vision and their hope in God. Moses handed the scepter to Joshua – Joshua and Caleb brought the family of God out. Let's bring out our family. Who are we going to give the scepter to if we don't get out?

Never lose your vision or purpose. Never forget who God is and where. Get in the Word! When it *seems* like it is not helping, pray... when praying *seems* like it is not helping, pray in the Spirit.... when that *seems* like it is not helping, Keep doing it - it only seems like it's not helping.

23rd Psalms

The LORD is my shepherd; I shall not want. He makes me to lie down in green pastures; He leads me beside the still waters.
He restores my soul;
He leads me in the paths of righteousness For His name's sake. Yea, though I walk through the valley of the shadow of death,
I will fear no evil; For You are with me;
Your rod and Your staff, they comfort me.
You prepare a table before me in the presence of my enemies; You anoint my head with oil;
My cup runs over.
Surely goodness and mercy shall follow me all the days of my life; And I will dwell in the house of the LORD Forever.

God IS amazing

My Agape Walk Today

Call someone

And give them

A scripture.

Life them up with

words of joy.

✓ <u>I walked in love today</u>

Matt. 7:21 *Therefore whosoever heareth these sayings of mine, and doeth them, I will liken him unto a wise man, which built his house upon a rock:*

"Founded" On A Rock

Today at church - I was sitting there and the title of what was pressed on my mind to write about came to me; "Founded" On A Rock. Then the Pastor said "The title to my message is - Founded on a Rock. *Did he just hear my thought?*

I dealt with some serious things this week and as I meditated on the things going on around me I wondered how I was handling it and how people around me were handling it. I thought about my foundation. Was I ready for this, prepared to handle the things that were arising? I still don't think I know the full answer to these questions. But I'm glad that I thought about it because we have to know that it is sometimes a process to get through situations. And it's never too late to check your foundation to make sure that you are relying on Christ at every turn.

One of the ways of knowing if your foundation is firm is assess what was your first response? <u>*What was the first thing you looked to for help? Or the first thing you said?*</u> *Did you call on God? Did faith stick out? Which kingdom did you rely on?*

There will be times that our foundation will be tested or tried. If it hadn't yet, it will be. This is not a prediction of doom, but a promise. In James 1, it says "to count it all joy **when** you fall into divers temptations...... not **if** you fall into....

When situations hit home - just in case we miss the mark, set goals and boundaries, tighten up the weapons of warfare (Eph. 6), check our life of prayer, tithing, giving, and walk of love. I know it's a lot, but take it one day at a time. We are not in this alone. We have the help of Holy Spirit. During these trying times we need to ensure that we are dying to self and living In Christ.

Founded on a Rock - <u>*What will happen when yours is shaken?*</u>
Know ye not that they which run in a race run all, but one receiveth the prize? So run, that ye may obtain. And every man that striveth for the mastery is temperate in all things. Now they do it to obtain a corruptible crown; but we an incorruptible. I therefore so run, not as uncertainly; so fight I, not as one that beateth the air: But I keep under my body, and bring it into subjection: lest that by any means, when I have preached to others, I myself should be a castaway. 1 Cor. 9:24-27

I want to inspire you with a portion of one of my favorite poems. I hope it encourages you when you're going through test and trials. In 1989 I was given my first real opportunity to speak in a public arena; I recited this poem because it meant a lot to me. When I was finished reciting, I went back to my seat and sat down. I felt the poem didn't need my editorial comments. To my astonishment; I received great applause.

<u>*Don't Quit*</u>

When things go wrong, as they sometimes will,
When the road you're trudging seems all up hill,
When the funds are low and the debts are high,
And you want to smile, but you have to sigh,
When care is pressing you down a bit,
Rest, if you must, but don't you quit.

Life is queer with its twist and turns,
As everyone of us sometimes learns,
And many a failure turns about,
When he might have won had he stuck it out;
Don't give up though the pace seems slow-
You may succeed with another blow.

Success is failure turned inside out-
The silver tint of the clouds of doubt,
And you never can tell how close you are,
It may be near when it seems so far,
So stick to the fight when you're hardest hit-
It's when things seem worst that you must not quit.

Author Unknown

Only Believe!

Meditate today on ...

Again I say to you that if two of you agree on earth concerning anything that they ask, it will be done for them by My Father in heaven. For where two or three are gathered together in My name, I am there in the midst of them."

Matt. 18:19-20

Keep good company, be blessed. Partner with those that know the Word of God

John 1:4 *In Him was life, and the life was the light of men.*

The Gift of Life

The gift of life is a very special gift that only comes from God. This particular gift is called the light of men.

Light: Illumination, glow, beam, radiance

And the light shines in the darkness. John 1:5

Q. How do we bring the light to shine (or turn it on) and will it bring us out of dark places?

*Picture yourself in a dark room and light a match that illuminates that room. Now picture yourself in a dark situation, or a position out of which you can't see your way. Jesus in you, the Word in you, the God in you are the illuminations in that situation or position. Focus on the light in you and you **will see** your way out. **BELIEVE THIS***

....follow the light (I just wanted to say that)

We know who we are In Christ...we are the light of the world. Jesus was a gift to the world. He left us as the gift to the world. When people see us they should see Jesus; they should see the light.

So let our light shine
We should be the light in any dark situation: give life to dead things, be the perfect problem solver, the right medicine, the up-lifter of souls, the great inventor, the perfect parent, the best friend, the great companion.

While I am in the world, I am the light of the world." John 9:5
(Now) - YOU are the light of the world. Matt 5:14

My Agape Walk Today

Fast from One (1)
phrase you always
say and replace
it with the
phrase "I am
disciplined"

✓ <u>I walked in love today</u>

John 11:50 *Nor consider that it is expedient for us, that one man should die for the people, and that the whole nation perish not.*

The Passion of Christ

He that committeth sin is of the devil; for the devil sinneth from the beginning. For this purpose the Son of God was manifested, that he might destroy the works of the devil. 1 John 3:8

Have you ever heard at the end of a powerful statement of sincerity "**With a Passion**"? I know you heard this one: *"I hate him with a passion"*. **God has passion... "For God so loved the world that He sent His only begotten Son". He loved us with a passion. Jesus has passion... "I have come that you may have life and life more abundantly". He died with passion. He rose with Passion.**

Jesus' passion was to give life and destroy the works of the enemy. If we are not careful we can neglect the very purpose of God. It is the reason He gave His life for us. It is through the **passion of salvation** that we are to live). And for this reason...

The world need to see the "passion" of Christ; "He went about doing good and healing all that was sick".

Do people see passion in us - Can we say "I love God... with a passion"? This passion is a verb; an action word. Does our passion have works that follow?

Let us be like Paul, that our life will not be lived in vain. *"But by the grace of God I am what I am: and his grace which was bestowed upon me was not in vain; but I laboured more abundantly than they all: yet not I, but the grace of God which was with me." 1 Cor. 15:10*

For though we walk in the flesh, we do not war after the flesh: (For the weapons of our warfare are not carnal, but mighty through God to the pulling down of strong holds;) Casting down imaginations, and every high thing that exalteth itself against the knowledge of God, and bringing into captivity every thought to the obedience of Christ;

And having in a readiness to revenge all disobedience, when your obedience is fulfilled. Are we living "With A PASSION?"

"**Live with Passion**". How can I tell if I am living passionately or not, or feel passionately about anything?

The Random House College Dictionary, defines Passion - **any powerful or compelling emotion or feeling. Strong affection; love. A strong or extravagant fondness, enthusiasm, or desire for anything**.

What do we feel powerful or compelling emotions about? What do we have strong affection or love towards? Or what are we extravagantly enthusiastic or fond about? Whatever, that person, place, or thing is, we can say we are passionate about it.

When I think about passion demonstrated (of course other than Jesus Christ) I think about the entertainment business. They certainly come across as passionate.

What about you? What are you passionate about? What in your lives can people point to and say you appear to be passionate about that? Is there any one thing that you are extravagantly enthusiastic about? There is one thing today that I have strong affection and love towards...my Lord and Savior Jesus Christ. I hope I am living passionately for Him. After all He came that I might have life and have it more abundantly. And the mind blowing thing about it is He gave His life for me.

Yes, I hope He sees me as living passionately for Him. If not, *I* **_must_ _step up my game_**. *Only Believe!*

Meditate today on ...

And my God shall supply all your need according to His riches in glory by Christ Jesus· Now to our God and Father be glory forever and ever· Amen

Phil· 4:19

God wants to bless us
And His riches are endless

July 20

Toni Joy

Luke 5:16 *So He Himself often withdrew into the wilderness and prayed.*

Person to Person

Prayer... We have knowledge, we have the Word, we have faith

Why pray?

It's where we win the battle. It's where we release the power. It's the exchange of agreement and fellowship. It's open, personal, and present communication and help with and from God. It's everywhere anytime help from on High.

When this communication is open, not only can you talk to God, but God can talk to you. You're intimate with the Father. He can share with you and trust you. Yes, even when you mess up, repent and talk to Dad.

It helps to stay humble and pray in all situations, not forgetting that it is God working in us and not "we" ourselves. It gives God permission to step in whenever He wants. How? We must allow Him to change our direction, decision, and desire, at a moment's notice for our good. I truly believe there are many things that God is working on our behalf: things we don't know that surrounds all situations, things that we don't need to know until the moment we need to know it so that we don't have time to mess it up with our ways or thoughts. **Prayer is our secret weapon that the enemy can't touch like the red shoes in the Wizard Of Oz.**

When we pray, we build a personal relationship with God; we become friends. We are able to conquer all things because God and His ways become more real than what we see, hear, and feel. **_He already knows; so talk to Him_**

"Because he loves me," says the LORD, "I will rescue him; I will protect him, for he acknowledges my name. He will call upon me, and I will answer him; I will be with him in trouble, I will deliver him and honor him. With long life will I satisfy him and show him my salvation." Ps 91:14-16

My Agape Walk
Today

Tell someone that

you are a

Child of God -

Someone that don't

know you are;

today

✓ <u>I walked in love today</u>

Matt. 6:19-21 "Do not lay up for yourselves treasures on earth, where moth and rust destroy and where thieves break in and steal; But lay up for yourselves treasures in heaven, where neither moth nor rust doth corrupt, and where thieves do not break through nor steal: For where your treasure is, there will your heart be also.

If I Die Before I Wake
Now I lay me down to sleep, I pray the Lord my soul to keep,
If I shall die before I wake, <u>I pray the Lord my soul to take. Amen.</u>
Written by: Joseph Addison, in the year 1711
It's the day before <u>YOUR</u> last day on earth, and only you know it (and you couldn't tell anyone), and you had all day to think about how you were going to deal with your last day on earth: What would you think about, what would you consider – What would you do?

I was talking to someone the other day; they were questioning some serious decisions they had to make. I told him that he only had this one lifetime here. Then I had to think about that myself. I had a few decisions of my own. **Was I going to make these decisions based on things I see and hear or on heavenly things?**

After thinking about this for a minute, it came to me that there are too many scriptures on the here and now governing what we see, what we feel, what we think but hummmm, what are they based on? Holy Spirit is here to help us with the here and now. God created us (Spirit, Soul, and Body), and there are promises and provisions for it all. So if you want the most out of life, consider the Word of God for your life. I would hope it will be the answer Jesus gave.....

"Thy will be done" – He let God have the DAY

Our life is precious. Let's not take it for granted. Live each day as if it were our last. <u>So as we ponder our thoughts of the question above, think about this scripture:</u>

But seek ye first the kingdom of God, and his righteousness; and all these things shall be added unto you. Take therefore no thought for the morrow: for the morrow shall take thought for the things of itself. Sufficient unto the day is the evil thereof. **Matt. 6:33-34**

Good question Sister Toni Joy. That's serious pondering and processing.

If it were the day before my last day on earth and I knew it, what would I do? I'm sure one of the first things on my schedule that day would be getting in contact with everyone I love and everyone that's impacted my life in a positive way. I would contact them to share my gratitude and love for knowing them. I would want to make sure they knew how much I love and appreciate them. Then I would do several things; (1) eat all the cakes, cookies, pies, ice cream and quality chocolate candy I can possibly shove into my mouth, (2) go down my bucket list (yes, I have a bucket list) and cross off as many things as I could do that day, (3) I would do one of the things most people don't like me to do-- and that is I WOULD SING ALL THE SONGS I LIKE REALLY, REALLY, REALLY LOUD.

Every day is a gift from God;
I should be doing all the things I mentioned above now. Can y'all hear me?

SINGING? CAUSE I'M SINGING LOOOOUUDDD. I'M SINGING "... this is my story, this is my song, praising my Savior all the day long." "Blessed Assurance, Jesus is mine....." Y'all go ahead and sing the rest of it for me. Sing it LOUD! *Only Believe!*

Meditate today on ...

If you are willing and obedient,
You shall eat the
good of the land;
Isa· 1:19

The only thing between
you and eating the
good of the land is
YOU

There is nothing to lose and everything
to gain - The Land is God's

Attitude...

Attitude determines the size of our dreams and influences our determination when we face obstacles. People don't have dominion over our attitude. Dream stealers and naysayers can surround us with their negativity, but it's up to us to decide how we are going to process the negativity.

To continue to move forward we have to choose to control our attitude and not surrender it to someone else. No one else can make us angry; we make ourselves angry when we surrender control of our attitude. Don't surrender. No matter how persuasive they are in hindering you and setting stumbling blocks in your path, don't surrender your attitude.

Don't fail the test. Don't believe their report of you. We must guard against losing control. Our attitude is an asset which must be protected. At all cost when in pursuit of our dream, vision, and goals we have to keep a positive attitude. Possessing a right attitude is vital to our success. We have to possess a positive attitude about ourselves regardless of what others say or do.

Only Believe!

John 2:5 His mother said to the servants, "<u>**Do whatever he tells you**</u>."

Just Do it - IS IT THAT SIMPLE....?

I'm excited to think that it is. I heard someone say that the hardest thing is making the decision. I believe that it is, because once we make the decision to believe- we know what to do and where to go. Even though the process, after the decision is made, may not be easy – but **the faith is there.** Instead of fighting a losing battle, we are fighting a winning battle. **Fight the good fight of faith... 1 Tim. 6:12**

Let's look at faith........

Sometimes faith doesn't make sense; let's be real. We may even want to believe, but sometimes faith means to be on an island all by yourself waiting on a boat with no bottom (well, that's the picture looking from the outside in). Believe it or not - that's actually how people will see you. ***On a boat with no bottom!*** Mary (Jesus' Mother) knows that ride; she knew that the quest that Jesus was going to give them was going to put them on that lonely island with a bottomless boat. So she told them "Whatever He tells you - DO IT".
"Fill the jars with water"... ***"Now draw some out and take it to the master of the banquet."*** ... ***<u>They did so</u>, and the master of the banquet tasted the water that had been turned into wine.....***
We get instructions like this - and we also need to ***DO IT***. We need to stop thinking so hard, waiting until we understand it or agree (*or feel it*), and just ***DO IT***.

God has our best interest in mine. It's not for HIM, it is for us. We need. We need to stop worrying about what someone else is going to get out of it or how we look, and start knowing like we know, like we know, and again - <u>***like we know***</u>, that it is for us and our interest to just DO IT. What would it do for us to just love, to just not worry, to just give, to just........... WOW; maybe go where we want to go, have what we want to have, be who we need to be... Think about it.

**"As the heavens are higher than the earth, so are my ways higher than your ways and my thoughts than your thoughts.
*Just Do It!***

My 2 Cents

Recently, I encountered a situation in which I had to "just do it." Do what? Do what He says! What the Word of God says! I did not want to just do it. A few days ago, I had the unfortunate experience of a loud confrontation. A stranger started belligerently yelling at me about something I said to him. I mean, this guy was so belligerent that he was spitting and foaming at the mouth.

At first, it startled me. And then my flesh rose up. I felt the heat rising from my feet. And it was not a hot flash either. The more he yelled and spat, the angrier I was getting. I'm thinking to myself, "I'm gonna go toe-to-toe with this guy". I was getting ready to let him have a piece of my mind. This was not gonna be pretty. I can hear y'all now. No, I don't cuss. But, I was getting ready to give him one of those good ole nice-nasty Christian telling offs.

And then something quicken on the inside of me. I suddenly remembered Whose I am, and Who I represent. I recalled my Savior's words. *"Turn the other cheek"*. I knew what I had to do. I made myself, "just do it". I-turned-and-walked- away! And then my husband walked up and approached the man, who begin yelling at him. But, my husband spoke immediately to the man's pain. He said, to the man, I see your pain. He begin to speak to him prophetically. The man was hurting, not physically, but he had some issues he was dealing with and was just mad at everybody period. My husband's calmness and loving demeanor completely calmed him down. He listened to everything my husband said, and afterward told my husband he wanted to visit our church.

Short and sweet; *just do it*. Now you see, I was considering letting loose on a man that wasn't angry with me at all. He was just angry. What I said to him was neither insulting nor wrong. He needed to be touched, to be ministered to. Regardless of a wrong suffered, love! Jesus said, *love your enemies*. Sometimes that means turn the other cheek and walk away. Also consider **The Law of the Garbage Truck by David J. Pollay.** In his book he says "many people are like garbage trucks. They run around full of garbage, full of frustration, full of anger, and full of disappointment. As their garbage piles up, they look for a place to dump it. And if you let them they will dump on you, don't take it personally." Just walk away. *Only Believe!*

Meditate today on ...

Because you have made the LORD, *who is my refuge,*
Even the Most High, your dwelling place,
No evil shall befall you,
Nor shall any plague come near your dwelling;
For He shall give His angels charge over you,
To keep you in all your ways·
In *their* hands they shall bear you up,
Lest you dash your foot against a stone·
Ps· 91: 9-12

You have Angels watching over you,
to keep you from stumbling –
they guide your steps·

2 Cor 13:4-5 *Examine yourselves as to whether you are in the faith. Test yourselves. Do you not know yourselves, that Jesus Christ is in you?--unless indeed you are disqualified.*

Are we graded on a curve?

When we set our standards, do we go by the majority (what most people do)? How much do we care about going against the grain?

The majorities do not set the rule;
> **The Word of God *is what it is*. Luke 6:38**
> **How we measure it, is what we meet**

Take for instance "sin", in the world – some sins are not sin anymore; some sins have become a way of life and have become an exception to the rule (like fornication, homosexuality, adultery, murder, etc.)

We were created to live above the norm – we were born again to have an abundant life (John 10:10). But it's going to cost us, even though Jesus paid the price we have to change our major and course in life. We have to walk by faith and not by sight. We will have to lose the world or lose Christ. The rule has changed. Meaning, the rule the world has for life's issues is usually judged by the majority or a vote; not so in the kingdom of God. *The Word of God is what it is, <u>still</u>* which is to our advantage because after all these years **not one thing or person has come up with a better plan for life than God's**.

Read the text book (the B-I-B-L-E).

When we choose to be like everyone else or anyone else verses being spirit led, we miss the mark, we miss the grade, we miss the reward.

Let's walk by a higher standard of living (Grade "A" Christians)
The just shall life by faith

Study to shew thyself approved unto God, a workman that needeth not to be ashamed, rightly dividing the word of truth. 2 Tim 2:15

Ps. 23:4 *Yea, though I walk through the valley of the shadow of death, I will fear no evil; For You are with me; Your rod and Your staff, they comfort me.*

"In The Valley"

There are no perfect people; and as long as we are human – that means me and you, and we will go through valleys....

We will always have valleys; there is nowhere we can go without them. **But we are not to park in the valley.** Don't believe the lies that Satan tells like that God is not with us in the valley. **The truth is the only way out is with God; so you better know He's with you.**

Keep dreaming, praying, praising, speaking the Word, and following The Holy Spirit. As we go thru test and trails, go from faith to faith, glory to glory. Every move we make has a conquering that's needed.

You see, the valley is in the mist of our route to our dreams and goals. We live in a world that was created for us, but an alien landed, took hold, and sprouted a valley. If we hang out in the mist too long, we think like the alien, look like the alien - and worst of all, we will make it our home, with the alien.

Many of us park in the valley listening to the lies of this world. The world is full of false promises and fake mirages of success. We get blinded by the lust of the flesh and we forget who holds the true promises... **If only we can make the kingdom of God more real than the world in which we see....**

The Just shall live by faith

If you dare to dream, to hope, to want to succeed in life I dare you to live by faith. Without faith, it's like going into a fight without your boxing gloves.

As we go through life, and the valley, and the mist - Take your back pack of faith in God and His promises. Fill the pack full of your hopes and dreams). Don't go in empty and needy or you will look to the mirage. Know who you are in Christ. But most of all....

Know that God is with you

....no harm will overtake you, no disaster will come near your tent. For he will command his angels concerning you to guard you in all your ways.
Ps. 91:9-11

My 2Cents

The Lord is my shepherd; I shall not want. He maketh me to lie down in green pastures: he leadeth me beside the still waters. He restoreth my soul...Psalm 23:1-3a

He restoreth our souls: the mind, the will, the emotions, and the intellect. Sometimes we need rest and restoring for our mind, will, emotions, intellect.

<u>Restore:</u> to bring back to health, soundness, or vigor. Jesus said,

Come to me, all you who labor and are heavy-laden and overburdened, and I will cause you to rest. (I will ease and relieve and refresh your souls). **Matthew 11:28 Amplified Bible**

Do you need an easing, relieving, or refreshing for your soul - your mind, your emotions? Go to Him! Hallelujah! Nuff said. *Only Believe!*

CONFESSION FOR THE MONTH OF AUGUST

Print or write out your confession; put it where you can see and confess it all month

This is the day that the Lord has made, I will rejoice and be glad in it.

I am prepared for the upcoming fiscal year. I am focused and excited about my future plans. Plans to prosper and succeed.

I am sober and have a sound mind Therefore, I am a blessing going everywhere for good things to happen

Sing to the LORD, bless His name;
Proclaim the good news of His salvation from day to day.
Ps. 96:2

Ezra 4:2 *they came to Zerubbabel and to the heads of the families and said, "Let us help you build because, like you, we seek your God and have been sacrificing to him since the time of Esarhaddon king of Assyria, who brought us here."*

Mixed Drinks

Zerubbabel knew what he was doing to deny their neighbors in the building of the temple:

> *But Zerubbabel, Joshua and the rest of the heads of the families of Israel answered,*
> *"You have no part with us in building a temple to our God.*
> *We alone will build it for the LORD, the God of Israel*

There are times when we have to separate ourselves from the world when it comes to the foundational or shall I say *the structure* of our lives and ministries. We are in this world but not of this world which means the Word and Wisdom of God should pattern our lives; not what makes sense to the world.

God says to not be unequally yoked, to set our minds on heavenly things, to not get our counsel from the ungodly, etc. The two don't mix. In Matt. 6:24 it says we cannot serve God and mammoth; we will love one and hate the other. It's a sneaky drink; it doesn't hit you at once, but it will sneak up on you. All kinds of accidents will happen. You will wake up with a hangover.

You may start out building alone, but God knows when we need help and who to send. Don't mix the anointing with those that don't have a clue. Don't mix your drink, it looks good, feels good, but it will make you sick.

There is only one way to drink and drive
Jesus said to them, "Very truly I tell you, unless you eat the flesh of the Son of Man and drink his blood, you have no life in you
For my flesh is real food and my blood is real drink. John 6:53-55

My Agape Walk Today

Go "out of your way"
to say something
nice today to
someone that
<u>You don't know</u>

✓ <u>I walked in love today</u>

August 4

Toni Joy

Luke 1:6 *And they were both righteous before God, walking in all the commandments and ordinances of the Lord blameless.*

<u>Keep On Living</u>
God will bless others just to get a blessing through to you!

I couldn't help thinking as I set out to read the book of Luke, that Zacharias and Elizabeth was blessed with a mission to bring forth the forerunner for Jesus Christ (John the Baptist).

How 'bout that? I remember years ago when the saints use to have a saying "**God will open doors, and bless others just to get your blessing to you**". If He wants to promote you, if need be, He will promote six others just to get you your promotion.

See, God doesn't want us working like the devil; stepping on people's toes, putting people down - just to bring us up.... God said vengeance is His - so it's not our job to take care of that. We are to bless and receive blessings...

God will shower his blessings on others just to show His love to us. People all around us are blessed just because we are. So don't be afraid to love your enemies or be a blessing when there isn't even a reason to be blessing - **we are being like God**. Sometimes we don't know why things are being done the way they are. So let's not get in the way of the plan of God, nor stop the plan of God.

Let's not question who, when, where, and how - Just be a blessing.... That's living.... and then some

Just keep on living - we will see the Glory of God.

God is in control - So don't get weary of well doing
Just keep on living... <u>that promotion is coming, that promise is coming, that deliverance is coming, that house is coming,</u>

Luke 1:7 *And they had no child, because that Elisabeth was barren, and they both were now well stricken in years.*

Luke 1:13 *But the angel said unto him, Fear not, Zacharias: for thy prayer is heard; <u>and thy wife Elisabeth shall bear thee a son, and thou shalt call his name John</u>*

My 2Cents

Other's blessings can impact our lives. I was recently a recipient of one of those types of blessings. A couple of Sundays ago, I walked up to one of the ladies after worship service and sincerely complimented her on her dress. She said the dress was gifted to her. She went on to say, although, she liked the dress it did nothing for her. She looked at me and said, "a dress like this is better suited to a figure like yours." She went on to say, "You can have it." I didn't try to act humble or anything and say, oh no, that's o.k. I said, really, well, thank you very much. **I received that blessing**. Bless His Holy Name!!!

Another time, I was out shopping with a friend and we were both admiring a necklace-earring set. I went on and purchased something else but she purchased the set. When we got in the car after shopping at several other stores, she handed the bag with the necklace set to me and said, "I changed my mind, here you take it." See, y'all I know when to humble myself and when to just RECEIVE THE BLESSINGS. Bless His Holy Name!!! Sometimes we buy things thinking it's for us; and find out a short time later it's better suited for another person. Many times I've purchased things for myself and ended up giving it to someone else. I can tell you with conviction you'll know when it's not for you and who to give it to.

I will cause you to become the father of a great nation. I will bless you and make you famous, and I *will make you a blessing to others*. Genesis 12:2 NLT *"I will make you a blessing"*. You and I are blessed to be a blessing and to receive blessings as well. I underlined the **receive** part because some of us are more comfortable **being** the blessing. I use to be like that loooonnnggg years ago. I've since received revelation of the Word of God... *"give and it shall be given."* As the song goes - **"go get yo blessing."** It's not gonna fall out the sky. God uses people!!! (By the way, if you haven't cleaned out your clothes closet in a while now would be a good time to start giving away some of those pretty clothes you haven't worn at all or in a while.) *Only Believe!*

Meditate today on ...

Be sober, be vigilant; because your adversary the devil walks about like a roaring lion, seeking whom he may devour.

1Pet. 5:8

The thief does not come except to steal, and to kill, and to destroy. I have come that they may have life, and that they may have it more abundantly.
John 10:10

He is like a roaring lion, He is a fake, so don't be fooled. He looks for your worse day So don't give him one,

Give your life to Christ

Ps 37:25 I was young and now I am old, yet I have never seen the righteous forsaken

"Eye On The Sparrow"

We sometimes overlook or take for granted God's care of us. I believe if we live knowing that the Lord is watching over us we would have a lot more faith, and would allow God to move in more areas of our life than He does. For example: If we believe that God will warn us of danger or surprise attacks of the enemy, we would believe that He would also give us direction on our job, marriage, promotions, finances, and over all our well-being. That belief would cause us to be more blessed and at peace knowing that our lives are in good hands.

If He helps on one end, He will help us on all.

Confession of a long-lived life

All my life the Lord watched over me, even on things I didn't know, He knew and took care of it (whether I realized it or not at the time). Even His Angels watched over me. I made up in my mind; no, more so in my heart, because my mind may fail me that I will never worry about what will happen to me when I can't care for myself. If God helped me when I could do for me, He will help me when I can't. God cared for me when I was young and I didn't know anything about the level of my ignorance, or the levels of His unfailing mercy or grace. Now, I know He can care for me in my old age. Even if my mind forgets Him, He will not forget me. If He didn't leave me then, why would He now?

I am determined and have no doubt that I will dwell in the house of the Lord forever. When I'm asleep - when I'm awake, when I'm wrong - when I'm right, when I'm hot and when I'm not, when I'm persecuted and when I'm favored, when I'm crying and when I'm laughing, when I win and when I lose, when I'm hurt and when I'm well, when I'm sad and when I'm glad, No matter where, when, or how I am, the Lord is with me!

"Never will I leave you; never will I forsake you."
So we say with confidence; "The Lord is my helper; I will not be afraid, What can man do to me?" Heb 13:5-6

My Agape Walk Today

Lift up your
spirit today by
calling someone
and give a testimony
of how
"Good God Is"·

✓ <u>I walked in love today</u>

2 Corinthians 9:7 *Every man according as he purposeth in his heart, so let him give; not grudgingly, or of necessity: for God loveth a cheerful giver.*

There Is A Difference

There is a difference between **Giving** and **Tithing.**

**Giving is doing what you want and tithing is 10%.
Giving is from the kindness of your heart and tithing is obedience to the Lord's heart.**

Even though there is a different, we tend to only do one or the other. **Why? It's not like** drinking and driving.
It's like paying the gas and electric bill, eating and tipping, feeling good and smiling, working and getting a check.

~~~~~~~~~~~~~~~~~~

We tithe and give in the worldly system. Let's, for the fun of it, look at tithing in the world as taxes.
(In the kingdom of God, tithing is 10%)
What is the percentage of taxes? Wow, I don't even want to go there.

~~~~~~~~~~~~~~~~~~

Giving and Tithing are matters of the heart (spiritual laws carried out in the natural realm - God doing His thing with His creation). There is the "principle of taking" in the world and the "principle of giving" in the Kingdom of God - these principles are laws that work for the enforcer whether saint or sinner.

So should we pay taxes, tithe, and give?
And Jesus answering said unto them, Render to Caesar the things that are Caesar's, and to God the things that are God's. And they marveled at him.
Mark 12:17

August 10

My 2 Cents

For all the animals of the forest are mine, and I own the cattle on a thousand hills. Every bird of the mountains and all the animals of the field belong to me. If I were hungry, I would not mention it to you, for all the world is mine and everything in it. Psalm 50:10-12 NLT

God owns all of it! He said, "All the world is mine and everything in it." We are simply stewards. It's not ours anyway; we just think and act like it is. So, the first portion of our income belongs to Him according to Malachi 3:8-12. That first portion is 10% of what He has blessed to come into our hands. Don't forget the giving part is in there too. God's blessings come to those who live in obedience to Him. Here are a just a few reasons we should obey Him in tithing and giving:

1. To prove His faithfulness - He told us to prove Him, see won't He open the windows of heaven...
2. To honor Him
3. To support the work of spreading the Gospel
4. To claim the promise of Luke 6:38 "give and it will be given..."
5. To enjoy the windows of heaven blessings
6. To expect His provision - He provides for His children

Only Believe!

Meditate today on ...

Do you not know that those who run in a race all run, but one receives the prize? Run in such a way that you may obtain it. And everyone who competes for the prize is temperate in all things. Now they do it to obtain a perishable crown, but we for an imperishable crown. Therefore I run thus: not with uncertainty. Thus I fight: not as one who beats the air. But I discipline my body and bring it into subjection, lest, when I have preached to others, I myself should become disqualified.

1 Cor. 9:25

Prepare yourself to walk in Christ
Practice the Word, everyday

August 12

Toni Joy

Job 42:1-6
Then Job answered the LORD and said: "I know that You can do everything, And that no purpose of Yours can be withheld from You. You asked, 'Who is this who hides counsel without knowledge?' Therefore I have uttered what I did not understand, Things too wonderful for me, which I did not know.
Listen, please, and let me speak; you said, 'I will question you, and you shall answer Me.'
"I have heard of You by the hearing of the ear,
But now my eye sees You. *Therefore I abhor myself, And repent in dust and ashes."*

Know it for Yourself

Job said "Through hearsay I have misunderstood You, now I know for myself", then he repented for his ignorance. I wonder about those of us in the church, if the things we speak are by our own thoughts or by the Word of God. Sometimes we can miss it by humanizing the Word of God. One thing is for sure, we will miss it by speaking and believing things that we hear from others especially the ones that know so much and haven't studied for themselves. You know the ones that can tell you what the bible says and haven't read it. By this we have reduced the Word of God to gossip.

Job 1:8 ...**"Have you considered My servant Job, that there is none like him on the earth, a blameless and upright man, one who fears God and shuns evil?"**

Can we stand up to Job's quality of living? And to think he had to repent for his assumption of God. If someone like Job can miss it, we better get humble really quick. We have to ask ourselves "Where did we get our truth from?"

Let's speak the Word of God; that we have studied ourselves and if we quote someone – find scriptural reference for it

And the LORD restored Job's losses when he prayed for his friends. Indeed the LORD gave Job twice as much as he had before. Job 42:10

My Agape Walk Today

End every sentence
with the words
"Thank You"
except when
It really doesn't
apply

✓ I walked in love today

Luke 4:41 *And devils also came out of many, crying out, and saying, Thou art Christ the Son of God. And he rebuking them suffered them not to speak: for they knew that He was Christ.*

Call It Like It Is - Part 1

Now if the demons can call it like it is, JESUS, so can we.
The thing is; *Jesus had power over the demons; we have that power. Jesus walked about healing and delivering. Why don't we?*

We can, but first we have to *Call it like it is*. We have to acknowledge sin, sickness, weights, strongholds, demons, bad habits, lust, perversion, ugliness, etc.

If we don't Call it like it is - it will remain, like it is·

How many things are there in our lives that we have been trying to get rid of, or change? Some things are straight-up demonic, but some are the simple things we know, like overeating. Food don't just happen to be in front of us and we just happen to eat it (like Aaron said to Moses "It just came out the fire"). Whether it's lust, greediness, an over active - under active gland, or stress, we have to attack it from the root. Call it like it is and start dealing with it, before IT finishes dealing with us. **Don't let another day go by the same way!!!** Sometimes it's hard or painful to deal with the truth. In actuality, truth is with God. It's hard or painful sometimes to deal with a lie - that's where the devil come in and push. He doesn't want us to deal with the truth. I think about Jack Nichols in the movie *A Few Good Men*, "**You can't the handle the truth!**". **Well, it was already handled In Christ Jesus.**

"I have told you these things, so that in me you may have peace. In this world you will have trouble. But take heart! I have overcome the world." John 16:33

There were many times that Jesus told his disciples to "be not afraid". There is only one thing to be afraid of and that is of going to hell - **and that's not going to happen. This too has be handled**. So be bold, be strong, and be very courageous;

I make a decree today, to Call it like it is.
Look at it face to face, put it under my feet.

2 Cor 10:3-6 *For though we walk in the flesh, we do not war after the flesh. For the weapons of our warfare are not carnal, but mighty through God to the pulling down of strong holds. Casting down imaginations, and every high thing that exalteth itself against the knowledge of God, and bringing into captivity every thought to the obedience of Christ; and having in a readiness to revenge all disobedience, when your obedience is fulfilled.*

Call It Like It Is - Part 2

In Mark 5:1-13, we see Jesus dealing with a demonic spirit in a man. Jesus addressed the demon and told it to leave.

The first thing we always do; is look at the person. But if we look behind the person, we may see the real problem. Sometimes the problem is satan himself, and sometimes it's as simple as not liking someone; it could be a spirit of jealously. Jealously, hatred, envy, are attributes of satan. It was that spirit itself in satan that made him exalt himself above God and be cast out of heaven.

Rebuke evil by the power of God - Jesus defeated the enemy in his own house. ***We have to on-purpose speak to the problem.*** There are two things that we have that will immediately cause evil to loosen its grip on us: prayer and the Word of God. Deal with the problem by the power of God and the man by the love of God. The Word of God is powerful, stronger than a two edged sword. See the problem like it is – for what it is, and use the Word of God on the problem...

In the Name of Jesus, I demand by the power of God that this thing be removed·
Get your thoughts in line with the Word of God
See it, call it, do it· Jesus did·····

My 2Cents

Stand truth in the face and stare it down. Jesus said, we shall know the truth and it SHALL make us free. How about it? Want to be free today? There is an old saying, "tell the truth and shame the devil". I find that saying hilarious because how can the devil know any shame? Shame the devil? Oh yeah, he would laugh in your face. Now confront him with truth like Jesus did in the wilderness and you'll get some respect. He'll even leave you for a season like he did Jesus.

Everybody respects truth; even demons fear and tremble at the word of God. We might not like it, but we have to respect the truth when confronted with it. Jesus put the word on the devil. Every time the devil said something to Jesus, Jesus came right back with the truth of the word of God. You know how they say "call a spade a spade" and "if it quacks like a duck, it's a duck." Seek the truth, speak the truth, walk in the truth of the word of God and be free.

Wherefore putting away lying, speak every man truth with his neighbor: Ephesians 5:25

For I rejoiced greatly when brethren came and testified of the truth that is in you, just as you walk in truth. I have no greater joy than to hear that my children walk in truth. 3 John 3 **Only Believe!**

Meditate today on ...

Death and life are in the power of the tongue,

Prov· 18:21

Speak life

If you have a bible...Read Ps. 24

"Read your Bible Day"

I like this Psalm because it makes a powerful statement, explains the statement; then asks us a question. Why are we asked this question? Because once we answer it, we are held accountable to the knowledge of it. God wants us to know this. We have to own it. He wants us to generously receive His blessings. Know this for sure.

Want to know what I'm talking about? Read Ps. 24

The earth is the Lord's and the fullness thereof (then it explains what the fullness thereof consist of):
1) the world   2) and they that dwell therein

I love the next few verses (Amp. Version)
Vs. 4 The one that has clean hands and a pure heart, who has not lifted himself up to falsehood or to what is false, nor sworn deceitfully.
Vs. 5 we, that dwell therein, that belong to the Lord, shall receive the blessings from the Lord, and righteousness from the God of His salvation (Jesus).
Vs. 6 *Therefore, seek the Lord (This is the generation of those who seek Him [who inquire of and for Him and of necessity require Him], who seek Your face, [O God of] Jacob.* **Selah** *[pause, and think of that]!)*

NOTICE: We all know that we belong to the Lord. Maybe sometimes we forget that the world does too.....If this is so.....
Vs. 7 Lift up your heads, and be lifted up, you age-abiding (everlasting) doors, that the King of glory may come in.
Selah means... pause and think of that.

Think about this (The earth is the Lord's and the fullness thereof) when you wake up in the morning, as you are going through your day, when you lay down to sleep at night. Seek God and He will come in. *Seek God and He will come in. Seek God and He will come in. Seek God and He will come in.* **Selah... pause and think of that.**
Still have your bible... Read Matt. 6:26-33

Meditate today on ...

And in that day you will ask Me nothing. Most assuredly, I say to you, whatever you ask the Father in My name He will give you. Until now you have asked nothing in My name. Ask, and you will receive, that your joy may be full.

John 16:23-24

Ready, set, NOW; ASK

My Agape Walk
Today

In <u>every</u> <u>situation</u> <u>Today</u>,

ask yourself

"What would

Jesus Do"

Then do that.

✓ <u>I walked in love today</u>

Romans 8:2 *For the **law** of the Spirit of life in Christ Jesus has made me free from the **law** of sin and death.*

Get Out Of Jail Free Card

What is the *"Law"* of the Spirit of Life in Christ Jesus?

For those of us that believe the Word of God, the life is The Word of God, the law is the Fruit of the Spirit (the Word of God put it like this):

*But the fruit of the Spirit is love, joy, peace, longsuffering, kindness, goodness, faithfulness, gentleness, self-control. **Against such there is no law.***
Which means if we want to walk in the best quality of Life, the Spirit of life in Christ Jesus is the law to which we yield.
Are we willing to walk that walk? Are we willing to trust God to do something so different from the ways of the world?
We believe the Word of God; we know that it has power. We say, "God is Good", and we sing;
Jesus loves me this I know, for the bible tells me so.

But saying this and singing it isn't enough. We have to be bigger and braver than just knowing and believing. Real faith is acting on what we say and believe and sing *every day.*

Of what are we scared? Being different? Letting go of *Good Sins like:* anger, jealousy, strife, un-forgiveness, gossip, poverty, sickness, guilt, or envy. Oh yeah, we think some of these are things to which we have a right.

Let's trust God and be like Jesus

Can we leave sin? And receive a gift?
Leave the devil and receive the free gift of Life

It's our Get Out Of Jail Free Card

The thief does not come except to steal, and to kill, and to destroy. I have come that they may have life, and that they may have it more abundantly.
John 10:10

Toni Joy

Ps. 19:14 *Let the words of my mouth, and the meditation of my heart, be acceptable in thy sight, O Lord, my strength, and my redeemer.*

Take It To The Grave

We used to have old sayings that sound good - but are not. Some are disguised as describing our feelings or just a phrase. Words that some use every day, innocently, such as cursing the Name of God and others or "This is killing me", or "If it kills me". I'm sure we can think of many more. We curse ourselves with our own words.

Sometimes we live by a promise to die daily and we have no idea that we curse ourselves with this covenant of secrecy that keeps us from being free.

We have hidden things in our heart: un-forgiveness, shame, regret, hate, resentment, jealousy, evil intentions, malice, self-loathing and unworthiness.

We vow to take this to the grave with us. But why give some things to God and hide other things that we feel nothing can be done about. We say we trust God, but do we? Have we let go of the deep things in our heart? In actuality, we are not hiding it from God - He knows everything. We are just blocking our blessing and the blessing of those that God has given us to be a blessing too. God wants us free from the bondages of hurt, pain, and sin. *Please give it to God, He's not just the God of our little boo boos. He is the God of Life. Do you really think Jesus went to the cross just to put a Band-Aid on us? To just give us a car, a house, or riches?*

Come onnnnn..... I know IT is heavy, been there, done that, may not be finished. Be free of IT, let IT go.
It might hurt to let it go, but IT is killing you to keep it.

Come unto me, all ye that labour and are heavy laden, and I will give you rest. Take my yoke upon you, and learn of me; for I am meek and lowly in heart: and ye shall find rest unto your souls. For my yoke is easy, and my burden is light. Matt. 11:28-30

Get in your prayer closet and get free of things that hold us. God cares about the condition of your heart.

Keep (guard) thy heart with all diligence;
for out of it are the issues of life. Proverbs 4:23

Taking secrets to the grave? Some secrets we need to take to The Lord in prayer and get rid of them.

Especially those infamous "deathbed confessions" that some folk reveal to family members as they lay near death. I heard one elderly woman tell about her husband sharing secrets as he lay dying on his hospital bed. She said, he confessed to an affair with one of her friends. She said, if he had not already been with one foot in the grave she would have made sure he made it all the way dead.

There are a lot of secret things in our hearts that in order to live a life free of the heaviness of these secrets we really should seek to release them to God. According to Psalm 44:21, He already knows the secret things of our hearts. We might not feel safe revealing the secret things of our heart to others, but we're safe with Him. Hebrews 4:13 says, *And there is no creature hidden from His sight, but all things are naked and open to the eyes of Him to whom we must give account.* The day is going to come that you're going to have to talk to Him about it anyway; so we might as well give it up now in order to live as freely as He has designed us to live. Jesus came that we might have life and have it more abundantly. It's not His will for us to be in bondage by holding damaging things in our hearts. *Create in me a clean heart, O God, and renew a steadfast spirit within me.* Psalm 51:10

Only Believe!

Meditate today on ...

Therefore I say to you, whatever things you ask when you pray, believe that you receive them, and you will have them.

"And whenever you stand praying, if you have anything against anyone, forgive him, that your Father in heaven may also forgive you your trespasses. But if you do not forgive, neither will your Father in heaven forgive your trespasses

Mark 11:24-26

The righteousness with God is through the forgiveness of sins; Un-forgiveness blocks that connection. It's not worth it.

My Agape Walk Today

How Bold Are You

Make a plan today to set

time aside to read

through the bible

- day by day

Genesis to Revelations.

✓ I walked in love today

Toni Joy

Psalm 121

I will lift up my eyes to the hills— From whence comes my help?
My help comes from the LORD, Who made heaven and earth.
He will not allow your foot to be moved;
He who keeps you will not slumber.
Behold, He who keeps Israel Shall neither slumber nor sleep.
The LORD is your keeper;
The LORD is your shade at your right hand.
The sun shall not strike you by day,
Nor the moon by night.
The LORD shall preserve you from all evil;
He shall preserve your soul.
The LORD shall preserve your going out and your coming in
From this time forth, and even forevermore.

The Third Person

There are so many choices in life, stages in life, changes in life; there is no way to know the best choice other than to involve the supernatural, all-powerful, all knowing Holy Spirit.

In things we experience and have not experienced, learned through books or taught by our parents, or just think we know, we still need the help of Holy Spirit. There is no situation alike and no-one that knows the answer to everything correctly without God giving it to him. I know this because each of us are creatively different which makes every situation creatively different especially once we touch it. I don't think there is an exact replica of and flower; surely there are no replicas of a child of God.

But God knows everything and is everywhere

Know the right decision, the perfect direction, The Holy Spirit.

But the Helper, the Holy Spirit, whom the Father will send in My name, He will teach you all things, and bring to your remembrance all things that I said to you. Peace I leave with you, My peace I give to you; not as the world gives do I give to you. Let not your heart be troubled, neither let it be afraid.
John 14:26-27
"Me, Myself, and The Third Person – Holy Spirit"

Toni Joy

Phil. 4:8-9 *Finally, brothers and sisters, whatever is true, whatever is noble, whatever is right, whatever is pure, whatever is lovely, whatever is admirable - if anything is excellent or praiseworthy - think about such things. Whatever you have learned or received or heard from me, or seen in me—put it into practice. And the God of peace will be with you.*

Speak Up For Yourself -Talk Life

**We talk about the way we feel, the way we think,
we talk about the past, about the future
but how often do we talk about who we are in Christ?**

Sometimes we wake up in the morning motivated by what we dream, what we ate last night, or what we went to sleep thinking about - love, peace, joy, loneliness, regret, anger, confusion, hurt, familiar things/ feelings/thoughts. We have to **say** *"No" to allowing wrong thoughts and feelings to pave the way for our day, and allow love, joy, and peace to rule our hearts and minds. We have to continually come to the conclusion that what we say is what we will have.* We may go through a spell every now and then being overwhelmed by what we think and feel. Just re-group, talk yourself out, quickly). We should know what we're going to say regardless of the errand thoughts. We replace those thoughts with these words: I am the righteousness of God. I am in love with God and He is in love with me. I am blessed, highly favored, and more than a conqueror. I am forgiven and redeemed. I am not alone. All my needs are met in Christ Jesus. I am obedient to the Word of God; I am Holy Spirit led. Money Cometh to me. All the time, I am walking in prosperity. I am healed; I am living in divine health. I am living in love, joy, peace, kindness, goodness, gentleness, self-control, patience, faithfulness...

WE HAVE TO SPEAK UP...
My Kids are blessed; my family is blessed. We are covered by the blood of Jesus. I cast down every imagination that comes against the knowledge of God. I submit myself to the Word of God, to the leading of Holy Spirit. I walk in the fruit of the Spirit.

Let go of what we see and "Speak Up" about the truth

"Talk Up" **- Life and Death are in the Power of the Tongue** Prov. 18:21

Meditate today on ...

But even if our gospel is veiled, it is veiled to
those who are perishing, whose minds the god
of this age has blinded, who do not believe, lest
the light of the gospel of the glory of Christ,
who is the image of God, should shine on them·
For we do not preach ourselves, but Christ Jesus
the Lord, and ourselves your bondservants for
Jesus' sake· For it is the God who commanded
light to shine out of darkness, who has shone in
our hearts to give the light of the knowledge of
the glory of God in the face of Jesus Christ·

2 Cor· 4:3-6

Pray that the veil be removed from your loved
ones eyes - That they receive Jesus as their

Lord and Savior

August 29

My 2 Cents

Professor Joseph Ferrari of DePaul University Chicago found that **20%** of the world's population is *chronic* procrastinators. Also discovered through extensive research were these chilling facts: Procrastinators are *less wealthy*, *less healthy* and *less happy* than those who don't delay.

With all that we see happening around us every day--seemly to me those things are screaming, STOP WASTING TIME!! As I read the headlines I sense an urgency to fulfill my purpose, my hopes and dreams. I was talking with a friend on Saturday. She said that she finds herself striving more than ever to pursue her goals. We were discussing how it appears we're busier than in years past, and we haven't taken the time to get together for lunch or go to a movie together like we used to. Mainly because we're both focused on life pursuits. I suggested to her that we buy a timer and time ourselves doing different tasks during the day so that we can better control our time.

How many of us can testify to what she said? We put off doing something we intended to do that day, because we got caught up with other things and what we intended to do gets pushed back another day. Or if you're like me that something else gets pushed to next week, sometimes it ends up pushed aside to next month; then you look up, it's six months later and you are just getting around to it. Better management of time is the key.

Psalm 90:12 (TLB) says, "Teach us to number our days and recognize how few they are; help us to spend them as we should." Love this scripture.

Second Corinthians 6:1 (The Message) says, "...we beg you, please don't squander one bit of this marvelous life God has given us." Don't squander **your time because your time is your life. If you waste your time, you waste your life.**

I believe I've definitely done some squandering in the past. But, I repent and turn from it. **As Sweet Brown said, "Ain't nobody got time fa dat."**

"Procrastination is the bad habit of putting off until the day after tomorrow what should have been done the day before yesterday." – Napoleon Hill

"Somebody should tell us, right at the start of our lives that we are dying. Then we might live life to the limit, every minute of every day. Do it, I say! Whatever you want to do, do it now! There are only so many tomorrows." - Pope Paul VI *Only Believe!*

Psalm 78 *Yet he was merciful; he forgave their iniquities and did not destroy them. Time after time he restrained his anger and did not stir up his full wrath.* ***He remembered that they were but flesh, a passing breeze that does not return.*** *How often they rebelled against him in the wilderness and grieved him in the wasteland! Again and again they put God to the test; they vexed the Holy One of Israel. They did not remember his power— the day he redeemed them from the oppressor, the day he displayed his signs in Egypt, his wonders in the region of Zoan. But he brought his people out like a flock; he led them like sheep through the wilderness. He guided them safely, so they were unafraid; but the sea engulfed their enemies.*

But God, again

I was about to have a pity party the other day facing our inability to make ends meet. Have you ever had one of those days when you can't reach the mark and everything is going wrong?

As always I look to the Word and prayer to find out how I'm supposed to be feeling, thinking, and acting for the situation, the moment. This time I was moved by...

He remembered that they were but flesh, a passing breeze that does not return.

As God would put it "I have to do this by the integrity of my heart and guide them with my skillfulness of hands". He was speaking of David, but it was the anointing of God that empowered David to lead.

So when we have a pity party we are allowing our feelings and the situation to rule us and we limit God to guide us. Are we really saying, "God can't or won't do it"?

God went with us to the north and south, east and west, following us to bless us – to forgive us. Read all of Psalms 78 (and this is the short version of the lengths He went to forgive us, to reach us). God continually forgave them over and over and over. ***If He did it for them, he will do it for us.***

Meditate today on ...

I beseech you therefore, brethren, by the mercies of God, that you present your bodies a living sacrifice, holy, acceptable to God, which is your reasonable service. And do not be conformed to this world, but be transformed by the renewing of your mind, that you may prove what is that good and acceptable and perfect will of God. For I say, through the grace given to me, to everyone who is among you, not to think of himself more highly than he ought to think, but to think soberly, as God has dealt to each one a measure of faith.

Rom. 12:1-3

CONFESSION FOR THE MONTH OF SEPTEMBER

Print or write out your confession; put it where you can see and confess it all month

I plead the blood of Jesus over the children in my house, the children in my family, the children in my neighborhood, the children in the city; that they are protected from the negative influences of the world – that Angels are covering them from head to toe to keep them from harm – that the saints of God are continually around them day and night, at school and at play.
Give them the desire to want good grades and be wise in all they do.
Thank you Lord for giving me wisdom on how to train them up in the way they should go.

It takes "Thy" kingdom to raise a child

Labor Day

The first Labor Day holiday was celebrated on Tuesday, September 5, 1882, in New York City, in accordance with the plans of the Central Labor Union. The Central Labor Union held its second Labor Day holiday just a year later, on September 5, 1883.

In 1884 the first Monday in September was selected as the holiday, as originally proposed, and the Central Labor Union urged similar organizations in other cities to follow the example of New York and celebrate a "workingman's holiday" on that date. The idea spread with the growth of labor organizations, and in 1885 Labor Day was celebrated in many industrial centers of the country.

The character of the Labor Day celebration has undergone a change in recent years, especially in large industrial centers where mass displays and huge parades have proved a problem. This change, however, is more a shift in emphasis and medium of expression. Labor Day addresses by leading union officials, industrialists, educators, clerics and government officials are given wide coverage in newspapers, radio, and television.

The vital force of labor added materially to the highest standard of living, the greatest production the world has ever known, and has brought us closer to the realization of our traditional ideals of economic and political democracy. It is appropriate, therefore, that the nation pay tribute on Labor Day to the creator of so much of the nation's strength, freedom, and leadership
— *the American worker.*

Darlita (Dee Dee)

"A Last Minute Life"

Ephesians 2:10 *For we are his workmanship, created in Christ Jesus for good works, which God prepared beforehand, that we should walk in them.*

Have you ever felt that things in your life happen at the last minute? You wake up rushing because you overslept. You pick up fast food and spend more money eating out because there is no time to cook. The bills that have mounted were due weeks ago and you are paying it on the last day of the shut-off notice. Your kids project for school you knew about three weeks ago, yet you find yourself burning the midnight oil in an effort to turn it in on time with the hope of them getting a minimum of a B due to lack of preparation. Hence **"A Last Minute Life"** - I know because I lived this way for a decade of my life.

I was going to Church and praying but I was not fully taking advantage of God's provisions for my life, His Word. Fortunately, a friend invited me with her to join a women's bible study on Exodus and Leviticus. Through this study I learned that nothing God does is last minute. Remember God prepared Noah and his family to build the Ark before the flood. Prior to God bringing his people out of Egypt he began their preparation. He prepped Moses as their deliverer and told him that He would be with him. After He delivered them from Egypt He continued his preparation for their life through His words which were detailed instructions to live by. Although Jesus died for our sins God prepared him well before his death. Hmmm I thought Nothing God does is last minute so why am I living "A Last Minute Life". God revealed to me through prayer that it was because although I was going to church and bible study I was not spending my time listening to Him. If I were not listening then He could not adequately prepare me for the life He wanted me to live; a rich, fulfilled, happy and holy life.

I began doing my devotion daily, studying more and applying God's word and most importantly, listening during my time with Him. My last minute life literally turned into one that was being planned, not rushed. I started shaping up and living the life God wanted me to have. My daughters projects were not being turned in late but she received extra points for turning it in early. My gas was not being turned off because I did not make the payment before the shutoff date. I was not oversleeping. My youngest daughter arrived at school on time. I was literally cooking 3-5 healthy meals in one day then spreading them out during the week. I was saving money by not eating fast food. And, the stress of a last minute life was lifted; I could feel the yoke breaking. Clarity of mind was present, not a haze of anxiousness and rushing to and fro without seeing any positive results.

I will confess that there are times when I seem to want to slip back into that old pattern - then I am reminded, Nothing God does is last minute!

So if I remain following Him and keep his words, I won't lead

"A last minute life but A Well Planned Life"

Clean it up WEEK
Project Week

There are so many things that need to be done in the house that it would take more time in the day, which we don't have, to get it all done. So this week I propose a project called "Clean it up WEEK"; where we take one thing at a time each day this week.

I don't want to tackle the obvious things that we do every day, but the things that we look at and say "I'll get that later". Like clean the microwave, get a spider web out the corner, clean the woodworks, the chandelier, that one window you look out and see that same spot all the time, etc.

Whether it's a big thing or a little thing; every day this week we are going to just do it – get it done. By the end of the week – we would have done those things that we always put off for another day.

Cleanliness is next to Godliness
I don't think this is in the bible, but it sounds good.

Meditate today on ...

The word is near you, in your mouth and in your heart" (that is, the word of faith which we preach): that if you confess with your mouth the Lord Jesus and believe in your heart that God has raised Him from the dead, you will be saved· For with the heart one believes unto righteousness, and with the mouth confession is made unto salvation· For the Scripture says, "Whoever believes on Him will not be put to shame·" For there is no distinction between Jew and Greek, for the same Lord over all is rich to all who call upon Him· For "whoever" calls on the name of the LORD shall be saved
Rom· 10:8-12

From the best to the worst, the richest to the poorest - He loves us all

Toni Joy

Matt 26:41 *Watch and pray, that ye enter not into temptation: the spirit indeed is willing, but the flesh is weak.*

Step out of the box

Praying is just about everything to me – whether it's at church, home, on my knees, walking, running, in passing, at work, at play... *you get the picture.* Talking to God is vitally important to our lives.

But, I believe there are times in our lives where is seems we can't fast, we can't pray, and it feels like we are caught up in strongholds that we can't loose – we are at a loss for words. Things have us so down that we can't see our way up. There are things we just can't seem to get to; no different than the things we can't let go, like smoking, drinking, gambling, cursing, etc.

Have you ever got so furious or at your wit's end and still didn't have the answer?

To the other side!

Don't stop talking to God. Keep taking that ax to the tree... It will come down. It's just like the scripture says; the spirit is willing but the flesh is weak. Let's not use this as an excuse to fail but to push past the flesh; *step out of the box – to the other side; from our way to God's way, from our side to God's side, from our thoughts to God's thoughts, from death to life – Jesus gave us the way.*

God said "do not worry" (read Matt. 6:25-34 to find out how.)

For everyone who asks receives, and he who seeks finds, and to him who knocks it will be opened.

Matt 7:8

We have help – receive it

Casting all your care upon Him, for He cares for you. 1 Pet. 5:7
"Because he has set his love upon Me, therefore I will deliver him;
I will set him on high, because he has known My name.
He shall call upon Me, and I will answer him;
I will be with him in trouble; I will deliver him and honor him.
With long life I will satisfy him, And show him My salvation." Ps. 91:14-16

September 7

Toni Joy

James 4:7 *Therefore submit to God. Resist the devil and he will flee from you.*

DIVE IN <u>In James 1:8 its says to draw near to God and He will draw near to us</u>. One thing though, we can do all the resisting we want to, but if we neglect the drawing near to God - we lack the power to resist.

Now - After we've drawn near, *do we really resist?*.
The power is in submitting to God

Jesus did; Jesus was led into the wilderness to be tempted. Three times the devil tempted Him; each time He submitted to God and resisted the temptation. The devil gave up. (Matt. 4:1-17). And yes, they were real temptations: 1) He was hungry, 2) He was the Son of God, and 3) He very much wanted to take the world out of the devil's hands *and escape the cross. Remember His prayer – "and He fell on His face, and prayed, saying, 'O My Father, if it is possible, let this cup pass from Me; nevertheless, not as I will, but as You will." Matt. 26:39*

Do you see the submission to God? Do you see the resistance?
Draw near / Resist, they go hand in hand together

The devil is not going to let go easily, just because you're saved or you love God. Who can love God more than Jesus - and that didn't stop the devil. Jesus resisted 3 times before the devil quit. So we ask ourselves, do we really resist? When we draw near to God, the Power is there. We may have to submit numerous times. The devil cannot overpower us with God. And the devil knows the difference. ***And the evil spirit answered and said, "Jesus I know, and Paul I know; but who are you?" Acts 19:15***

We have the help. ***The secret is that we have to get in a position (submission to God) in order to access the help.*** On may ask how do you submit? How do you do it?" Answer: I just jump in by faith. We have to trust God to walk in the wilderness knowing that God is on our side. Jesus went into the wilderness and came out completely ready for His calling. *From that time Jesus began to preach and to say, "Repent, for the kingdom of heaven is at hand." Matt. 4:17*

So what do you think will happen when we come out the wilderness?

Dive into God, resist the devil and he will flee!

Heb. 5:12-13 *In fact, though by this time you ought to be teachers, you need someone to teach you the elementary truths of God's word all over again. You need milk, not solid food! Anyone who lives on milk, being still an infant, is not acquainted with the teaching about righteousness.*

Disturbed **So what am I disturbed about?**

I know we're human. I know we make mistakes. I know we're not perfect; I'm a perfect example of *not being perfect*. But I find myself looking at the world and some of the Christians in it, and saying to the top of my lungs,

> ***"Our Goal is not to understand that we are not perfect, but to understand that we can do all things through Christ who strengthens us."***

We lean on "*not being perfect* or *being human*" wayyyy too much. I have heard that saying wayyyy too much as an excuse of accepting a lower standard of life. Have we forgotten that God created us, and then brought us back redeemed from a fallen state?

What do God tell us to consider when we look at ourselves? Look at The Message bible" interpretation of Matt. 63:34...

[People who don't know God and the way he works fuss over these things, but you know both God and how he works. Steep your life in God-reality, God-initiative, God-provisions. Don't worry about missing out. You'll find all your everyday human concerns will be met. "Give your entire attention to what God is doing right now, and don't get worked up about what may or may not happen tomorrow. God will help you deal with whatever hard things come up when the time comes.]

It couldn't have been said any better than this - this needs a hallelujah, amen...

I have the opportunity of working in a non-Christian atmosphere where I get to watch people be who there are, even Christians. Where do we start and stop listening to God about our conduct? I like the idea of being the light in a dark place. Just because we're in the world, we don't have to act like the world. We're not just Christians in church.

... Solid food is for those who are grown up. They have trained themselves with a lot of practice. They can tell the difference between good and evil. Heb. 5:14

Meditate today on ...

And these signs will follow those who
believe: In My name they will cast
out demons; they will speak with new
tongues; they will take up serpents; and
if they drink anything deadly, it will
by no means hurt them; they will lay
hands on the sick, and they will recover

Mark 16:16-18

We have the power
Let's get busy; look around, they need us

Perpetually Busy: That's exactly what I have experienced.

Perpetually: continuing or continued without intermission or interruption; ceaseless. Continuing or lasting for an indefinite long time.

Busy: actively and attentively engaged in work or a pastime. (2) full of activity, (3) having a lot of things to do.

Do you find yourself continuing without interruption, full of activity, or having a lot of things to do? I have! I quit. I'm working at a cease and decease of that nonsense. It's something unnatural about always having your plate full; always having something to do or someplace to go. Don't you find that unbalanced?

I know I've been on the subject of time (time management) lately. It's what is on my heart right now. I'll move on from this subject shortly. It's good to know my recent writings about time and time management is helping at least one of the readers. I spoke with Nina a faithful reader of Agape Weekly. She expressed to me that she and her husband have implemented a few new things in their schedule after reading these articles about time management.

Being more conscience of how I spend my time is changing my life for the better. I am using the timer and that is working tremendously for me. I would go as far as to say buying those timers was a smart move for me. However, the one I purchased for my office broke the first day of use. Ugh! But, it works so well for me at home I'm going to buy another one for my office.

How many of you agree with me, that being perpetually busy is not the smartest thing to do? *Only Believe!*

Toni Joy

John 14:23 Jesus answered and said to him, "If anyone loves Me, he will keep My word; and My Father will love him, and We will come to him and make Our home with him.

Close Encounters

When I got saved I remember the first *"divine encounter"* that I experienced was Love and Joy. I was at a point in life where I felt complete despair (a failure). A friend had been inviting me to church. The night before I agreed to go to church in the morning I remember only deciding to go, just to get out the house. I didn't know that it was God who I needed. **Keep inviting people to church and ministering to them. They really don't know. I never would have went if she had stopped asking me.**

I listened to the Words of God and was mesmerized. At the end of service I didn't even want to leave church; I didn't want to go back to my world. I thought that if I left church, that the love and joy I had at that moment would stay in that building and I would walk right back into the despair I felt just a few hours before. A touch from the Lord can change your life in a moment - forever. My friend finally got me to leave. I'm sure we were the last ones to leave church. The moment I left the church doors, the Love of God engulfed me – it was no longer me, but Christ in me.

Every time I meditate on that moment, I am strengthened by the Joy and Love of God; I could conquer anything. My world was changed in a moment. I saw everything differently. My despair changed to hope, my whole outlook on life was through the eyes of God.

So now - whenever you feel faint or you forget who you are in Christ
(if you feel stuck or lost)
Think back to your first encounter with God - remember who HE is, then remember who YOU are
Remember your first love
that if you confess with your mouth the Lord Jesus and believe in your heart that God has raised Him from the dead, you will be saved. **Rom. 10:9**

Luke 14:27 *And whoever does not bear his cross and come after Me cannot be My disciple.*

Count the Cost - read Luke 14:26-35

I was in awe how these scriptures blended together. Putting God First, hating your family, and counting the cost. I used to have to separate these verses for me to get an understanding out of them.

One day I was facing a problem, so I starting bombarding my mind with the Word of God, so that the world wouldn't have a chance to give me advice. The Lord just opened my eyes to Luke 14.

Jesus is not asking you to hate your mother and father. As a matter of fact, if you love anyone you will put Jesus first. *Jesus is telling us that if we love anyone, want to win in anything, succeed or help others and ourselves, we would put Him first.* He created us, gave us life – without that life in us we are nothing. Some decisions are hard and some are hurting, but we have to see the big picture and count the cost. Jesus said that He is **The Way, The Truth, and the Life**.

He says that if the salt has lost its flavor it is good for nothing, fit for nothing, to be thrown away.

Let's count the cost of our salvation, our family, prosperity. Whatever problems we are having – count the cost first before we lose something. It could be a job, your family, a friend, your life.

This is what the Lord has to say about us, it applies to family **Whoever seeks to save his life will lose it, and whoever loses his life will preserve it.** *I tell you, in that night there will be two men in one bed: the one will be taken and the other will be left. Two women will be grinding together: the one will be taken and the other left. Two men will be in the field: the one will be taken and the other left.* **Luke 17:34-36**

My Agape Walk Today

<u>Do not</u>
Say the words
"Never
Or Can't"
Today
If you do, repent out loud

✓ <u>I walked in love today</u>

Meditate today on ...

Be strong and of good courage
Only be strong and very courageous
Have I not commanded you? Be
strong and of good courage
Only be strong and of good courage
that you may observe to do according
to all the law which Moses My servant
commanded you; do not turn from it
to the right hand or to the left, that
you may prosper wherever you go.
Do not be afraid, nor be dismayed,
for the LORD your God is with you
wherever you go.

What is the Lord stressing to us? Joshua 1

Isa. 58:12 *Those from among you shall build the old waste places; You shall raise up the foundations of many generations; And you shall be called the Repairer of the Breach, The Restorer of Streets to Dwell In.*

Delight Yourself

As I was reading Isaiah 58, I imagined myself in a position to be called "The Repairer of the Breach". Wow, why not? This is how the Lord says to delight ourselves in Him. Sometimes in the world to delight yourself is to be selfish; but in the kingdom of God, to delight yourself is to be self-less.

"If you turn away your foot from the Sabbath, From doing your pleasure on My holy day, And call the Sabbath a delight, The holy day of the Lord honorable, And shall honor Him, not doing your own ways, Nor finding your own pleasure, Nor speaking your own words,
Then you shall delight yourself in the Lord. Isa. 58:13-14

Why do I find this so liberating and delightful? It is so tiresome and heavy to always think "Me". We think it's rewarding because we think we are gaining, but in actuality we are getting more caught up in self. We need this, we need that, we need more, got to have this... it never ends.

To me, for God to delight us and to give us the desires of our heart means complete satisfaction to receive the Kingdom of God, and HIM, His righteousness. This speaks such joy and soundness; like a breath of fresh air or lying down in green pastures. No worries, no bondage, no lack. Let's free ourselves and find out what delighting ourselves really is. We may just find ourselves helping others and solving problems in our household, our community, our church, our schools, and the work place. *Is that delight?* Cont. next page

Cont.

"If you take away the yoke from your midst, the pointing of the finger, and speaking wickedness, If you extend your soul to the hungry And satisfy the afflicted soul, Then your light shall dawn in the darkness, And your darkness shall be as the noonday.
The Lord will guide you continually, And satisfy your soul in drought, And strengthen your bones; You shall be like a watered garden, And like a spring of water, whose waters do not fail.
Those from among you Shall build the old waste places; You shall raise up the foundations of many generations;
*And you shall be called **the Repairer of the Breach, The Restorer of Streets to Dwell In.***

This is **"Hall of Fame kinda stuff"** - we can do this y'all. I can't sing, dance, or act. I'm not a doctor, a lawyer, or politician; but I can do all things through Christ who strengthens me. We can be self-less; and even if you can dance, sing, act, or you're a doctor, lawyer, teacher what is the most important job in the world? Jesus died to give this to us and I think we ought to do it. I'm serious;

The clock is ticking
If you want to be blessed, forward selflessness to everyone you know
Isn't this what we receive every day in emails (these chain letters – I don't like them)?
But this is my chain letter.
<u>If you want to be blessed -</u> pass selflessness on - Delight Yourself in the Lord - Be a repairer of the breach

Delight yourself also in the Lord,
And He shall give you the desires of your heart.
Ps. 37:4

1 Thess. 5:17 Pray without ceasing...

Talk to God, All the time

The Lord tells us to talk to Him all the time. I bet you're asking 'where in the bible does it say that?' It's everywhere - everywhere you see "Pray". Prayer is communication with God. Speaking of the verse above (***pray without ceasing)***, I find myself praying while I'm working, shopping, cooking, at the gym, etc. One particular day, I was taking a break at work and as I was walking to the break room thinking about how the things of God are foolishness to the world (particularly thinking about how it looked walking and praying). Then I looked around and everyone was walking and talking (by themselves).

> **...They were on cell phones with ear plugs**
> *... hey, I didn't look crazy anymore*

I can talk to God all I want too, anywhere, and anytime – and I would fit right in.

For those of us that don't want to look different, you can talk to God now; you just have to work on not looking pious - and don't look up in the air (He's closer than you think).

> *There is a* ***great*** ***big*** ***reason*** *to talk to God about everything...*
> ***He can talk to you about everything***
> *so I would say....*

It's a Good time to talk to God

James 1:5 *If any of you lacks wisdom, let him ask of God, who gives to all liberally and without reproach, and it will be given to him.*

Meditate today on ...

My son, give attention to my words;
Incline your ear to my sayings·
Do not let them depart from your eyes;
Keep them in the midst of your heart;
For they are life to those who find them,
And health to all their flesh·
Keep your heart with all diligence,
For out of it *spring* the issues of life
Prov· 4:20-23

The Word of God is truth
Life depends on it

September 18

Toni Joy

Isaiah 36:21 *But they held their peace, and answered him not a word: for the Kings commandment was, saying, "**Do not answer him**."*

Peace, Be Still

During this period of time in Isa. 36 when Hezekiah was King over Judah, a great King, King Assyria came against Judah. This King sent messengers to the people of Judah questioning the protection of their God and King, and telling them to just surrender. Basically telling them that he was greater than their God and King. He threw the King's' mistakes up in his face and asked, "Is this the God and Man you want to serve"?

Then the commander stood and called out in Hebrew, "Hear the words of the great king, the king of Assyria! This is what the king says: Do not let Hezekiah deceive you. He cannot deliver you! Do not let Hezekiah persuade you to trust in the LORD when he says, 'The LORD will surely deliver us; this city will not be given into the hand of the king of Assyria.' "Do not listen to Hezekiah. This is what the king of Assyria says: Make peace with me and come out to me. Then each of you will eat fruit from your own vine and fig tree and drink water from your own cistern. Isa. 36:14-15

The people of Judah and King Hezekiah were very scared, but the King called for the prophet...he inquired of the Lord.

What I want you to see is in the midst of *all the fear and failure* - they obeyed the King and kept quiet. ***They held their peace****. They inquired of the Lord.* And Isaiah said to them, *Thus you shall say to your master, Thus says the LORD: "Do not be afraid of the words which you have heard, with which the servants of the king of Assyria have blasphemed Me. Surely I will send a spirit upon him, and he shall hear a rumor and return to his own land; and I will cause him to fall by the sword in his own land." Isa. 37:6*

When all we see is defeat and obstacles against us be still, be quiet. Find what the Lord wants you to do and say concerning the matter. Don't let the deceitful promises of the world or the cunning enemy come in and tell you things that will take you out of the will of the Lord by making the promises of the world more believable than the promises of God. The devil will throw our own lack of faith and failures in our face and blame God for everything. Don't let him do it. Remember, the devils a liar.

Hold your tongue; allow the manifestation of God come to pass.

My Agape Walk Today

End every sentence
with the words
"God Bless You"
except when It really
doesn't apply

✓ _I walked in love today_

Meditate today on ...

Do not lay up for yourselves treasures on earth, where moth and rust destroy and where thieves break in and steal; but lay up for yourselves treasures in heaven, where neither moth nor rust destroys and where thieves do not break in and steal· For where your treasure is, there your heart will be also·

Matt· 6:19-21

Live your life building the kingdom of God here on earth·
The true riches are "In Christ"

September 21

Toni Joy

Clean it up Day

Project Help

Clean up someone else's house

One day this week, pick someone that you know needs help with cleaning or fixing something at their home, and volunteer to help them.

I remember years ago when my sister didn't have any kids and I had 3 she use to call me and ask what day she could come over and help me clean up the house. That was such a blessing to me. Hey... she hasn't done that in so long, let me call her (just kidding). I am going to call her – it's my turn to help her.

Join me in this "help someone this week" project. Make the plan today

Caring is Helping

Toni Joy

Prov. 3:5 *Trust in the LORD with all your heart and lean not on your own understanding;*

Let's Test it Out
<u>What happens when we ignore our own thinking and go with God's?</u>

The world puts all the answers in front of us, what we should do and be; yet, God wants us to ignore it and trust Him.

Daniel, Shadrach, Meshach, and Abednego decided not to eat of all the King's delicacies and eat just veggies. The chief of the eunuchs said, "why should I agree to this and present you to the King looking worst then the others?" So the chief agree to test their eating diet for 10 days; *at the end of the ten days they looked healthier and better nourished than any of the young men who ate the royal food.* **Dan. 1:15**

The stewards allowed the delicacies to be taken away from them. The choice they made gave them wisdom and knowledge above everyone else. *To these four young men, God gave knowledge and understanding of all kinds of literature and learning. And Daniel could understand visions and dreams of all kinds.* Dan. 1:17

What do you think will happen when we turn our backs on the wisdom of the world? We would walk in wisdom and knowledge just like Daniel and the three Hebrew boys. We think (in this day and time) that it would be much harder to follow God today than it was for them. Not so. The more peer pressure is turned up, don't you think God can turn up the volume also? They had religion then; so do we. They had sin and rebellion then; so do we. They had peer pressure, financial pressure then as we do now. It was just as hard or easy back then to serve God as it is now. We have the Spirit of God living on the inside of us; they went by raw faith with no *inside Holy Spirit* help.

I'm going to be one of the Hebrew boys, "who wants to play" and test this thing out with me? Yeah, let's fast for 10 days and see if we look better and feel better, Let God direct our lives for a while and see the wisdom and understanding of life that precedes us. *I double dare you to fast....*

....then we would be able to go through a fiery furnace too

Therefore, I urge you, brothers and sisters, in view of God's mercy, to offer your bodies as a living sacrifice, holy and pleasing to God—this is your true and proper worship. Do not conform to the pattern of this world, but be transformed by the renewing of your mind. Then you will be able to test and approve what God's will is-his good, pleasing and perfect will. **Rom. 12:1-2**

My 2 Cents

I carry a 5x7 leather journal in my purse. I use this journal to jot down ideas, inspirations etc. Yesterday, as I was flipping through the journal I came across an inspiring story that I had torn out of a book and taped into this journal. These stories, notes, ideas, hopes, and dreams – as I read them over and over - keep me going.

I've had this journal since 2009, I'm very selective about what I put in it. What I put in this particular journal has to speak to me in some way.

By nature I am a dreamer. I have a tendency to dream about how I would like things to be or how I would do things if I had the resources. I dream about doing things way outside of my bank account. One of my favorite scriptures in the bible is **Mark 10:27... with men it is impossible, but not with God: for with God all things are possible.**

For my birthday a few years ago, I was presented with a beautifully embroidered wall hanging with this scripture.

Maybe you should get a Journal

I am so glad, though it might be impossible for us; never with God is it impossible. I believe in the impossible.

Only Believe!

Meditate today on ...

Therefore <u>submit</u> to God. Resist the devil
and he will flee from you. Draw near
to God and He will draw near to you.

James 4:7

The devil is a defeated foe. Get
behind God and the devil won't see
you. He will see Jesus and run.

My Agape Walk Today

Everything that
bothers you today;
write it down (really)
and give it to God.
"Poof" – it's not your problem now.

✓ <u>I walked in love today</u>

2 King 13:15-19 *Elisha said, "Get a bow and some arrows," and he did so. "Take the bow in your hands," he said to the king of Israel. When he had taken it, Elisha put his hands on the king's hands. "Open the east window," he said, and he opened it. "Shoot!" Elisha said, and he shot. "The Lord's arrow of victory, the arrow of victory over Aram!" Elisha declared. "You will completely destroy the Arameans at Aphek."Then he said, "Take the arrows," and the king took them. Elisha told him, "Strike the ground." He struck it three times and stopped. The man of God was angry with him and said, "You should have struck the ground five or six times; then you would have defeated Aram and completely destroyed it. But now you will defeat it only three times."*

Don't Stop

In the above verse, Elisha (before he was about to die) said to the king "Get a bow and **some** arrows" and shoot the ground. As we see, he only shot 3 arrows and Elisha was angry because he didn't venture out more. Elisha was throwing out the blessing - but the King stopped short.

Have you ever had an urgency, got God involved, had a perfect plan or goal and as you neared the end and everything looked bright and promising you start slacking on the plan or goal? *I have. I felt the need to start a reading study to strengthen myself in a particular area. As things got better I started drifting away from my plan. It would be months later that I saw that same weakness; it dawned on me that I stopped my study plan. I learned that I need to go the distance, stay focused, and see God's thoughts and ideas more than mine.*

When we are starting out in whatever we are believing God for, regardless of what it is, venture further than we can image because we are not just considering our plan, but the plans of God for us.

- *Don't stop praying - don't stop giving - don't stop walking in faith*
- *don't stop witnessing. So after we think we have arrived;*
- *keep praying - keep giving - keep walking in faith*
- *keep witnessing*

Meditate today on ...

For by grace you have been saved through
faith, and that not of yourselves; *it
is the gift of God, not of works, lest
anyone should boast.* For we are His
workmanship, created in Christ Jesus
for good works, which God prepared
beforehand that we should walk in them.

Eph. 2:8-10

We are treasures created by God
He enjoys His creation and said that
It is good

September 28

Toni Joy

Matthew 14:29 *Then Peter got down out of the boat, walked on the water and came toward Jesus.*

Step Out Into Traffic

I was stopped at a light driving home the other day and wondered what made me different from the world? I looked just like them (broke, busted, and discussed, and etc.). I looked at traffic and wondered what would make me different, right now, from the rest of the traffic that I see?

What if I jumped out, right in front of traffic with my car or without - I would be different!
Not the different I want. But there is a different that I do want and I would have to step out into traffic for it.

We, people in the body of Christ, have to step out into traffic. Stepping out in traffic is when you don't care about what other's think and just be fanatical about faith. John the Baptist stepped out into traffic as well as John, Peter, Paul, and many more. What do you have to lose? The scripture says giving up brothers and sisters will get you a hundredfold. Mark 10:30 And those that hold on to themselves - lose themselves, and those that lose themselves - gain everything (Mark 8:35). So how do you step out into traffic?

"Do" what you imagine in the Kingdom of God

Stop trying to **do** what you imagine in the world and **do** what you imagine in the Kingdom of God. Step out in prayer, faith, word and deed. Meditate on the Word of God. We are all "Giants in Faith" in our own imagination. We imagine in botwh worlds, but we walk out in traffic more in the world than in the Kingdom. Need proof? Examine your own life. We will go that extra mile to make a buck, get a mate, a degree, a job, etc.

Go that extra mile to be Christ-like.
Show that you are different from the world.

The Best Of Both Worlds

I was sitting outside. It was breezy but it felt really good. I mean extra good this morning with the wind blowing. I was watching my dog run around the yard chasing a leaf. I'm thinking "Lord this is good". Forgetting bills and desires that have not been manifested, life is good this morning. The Holy Spirit immediately reminded me that *This is good, all the time* and *Life is always good.*

However, at the same time, I'm thinking of a co-worker who recently made his transition from this life. I'm thinking, *did he get it right before he closed his eyes for the last time.* I began to dwell on the thoughts for today:

THAT WE CAN HAVE THE BEST OF BOTH WORLDS

It does not matter that we may have bills, sickness, needs, wants, etc. we can still have peace in the midst of all that this world throws at us. This is what I was experiencing. I is the Peace of God.

The Peace of God, lets you see and feel;

"The Lord is my light and my salvation, whom shall I fear? The Lord is the strength of my life of whom shall I be afraid."

This verse alone gives you the best of both worlds. The Lord is the light that will guide you through this life to the other side. He is ever saving you from life's destructions and self-destruction. The Lord is the strength of all you need. If you put Jesus first, middle and last in your life you can have the best of this world, which is the prerequisite for heaven.

So start today that every day when you open your eyes you will make a choice to seek him first. Then throughout the day let his light guide you. Then seal the day off with him. Now you CAN feel the Peace of God.

My Agape Walk Today

How Bold Are You

Make time
today to think about
exercising or changing your eating
habits, or tightening up the plan
you have.

✓ *I walked in love today*

CONFESSION FOR THE MONTH OF OCTOBER

Print or write out your confession; put it where you can see and confess it all month

Make your own confession for this month; write it down and speak it out for the rest of this month

_____

_____

_____

_____

_____

_____

Toni Joy

James 2:24 or he beholdeth himself, and goeth his way, and straightway forgetteth what manner of man he was.

What Matter of Man – Part I

The NKJV says, "He forgets what kind of a man he was", and the NIV says, "He forgets what he looks like". As I was reading this I couldn't help think about how easy it is for us to get up in the morning with one thought and end up going through the day with another thought. We start off with spiritual thoughts and end with carnal thoughts as the influence of the world takes precedence.

But guess what? God says that hearing the Word and doing it trumps the world, its influences and pressures. There are three things we need to see here in James:

1. *We were created in the image of God.*
2. *All three versions of this verse states that we forget who we are (meaning, we haven't ceased from being created in the image of God - we just forget)*
3. *There is a remedy of being carnal (like the world).*

The Word of God says to be a doer of the Word and not just a hearer only. So, if we constantly hear the Word and do the Word we will be victorious in whatever we do.

Sounds like the Word brings out the best in us.
It relates to our spirit man who we really are

On this note, I'm going to let the Word do the talking

Do not merely listen to the word, and so deceive yourselves. Do what it says. Anyone who listens to the word but does not do what it says is like someone who looks at his face in a mirror and, after looking at himself, goes away and immediately forgets what he looks like. **But whoever looks intently into the perfect law that gives freedom, and continues in it—not forgetting what they have heard, but doing it—they will be blessed in what they do**. James 1:22-25 (NIV)

Let's not have our time with God in the morning then go out and be like the world; or go to Church/bible study and walk out the door and apply worldly principles instead of the Word of God.

So let's not forget what matter of people we are

Toni Joy

Exodus 8:23 *I will make a distinction between my people and your people.*

Have you ever read a scripture and it lingered with you all day. Well this one I pondered on for a few days. I think it was meant for us to linger on because He mentioned it three times within the next few chapters (8:23, 9:4, and 11:7).

What Matter of Man - Part 2
As if to say "My children, please take notice that you are different because of me, special because of me, blessed because of me.

We should get up every morning knowing that we are different. The difference I'm looking at is that we are powerful people through Christ Jesus. *We dance to a different tone, walk by a different grove, sing on a different note; sickness don't belong to us; poverty don't belong to us; we are the head and not the tail; we are somebody going somewhere to happen.* We are not supposed to be like the world or act like the world. Just as Jesus said "We are in this world, but not of this world." - John 16:17.

God said, Be ye holy as I am holy
I know you are probably saying, "We can't be like God". Well, who do you think God want us to be like?
Therefore be imitators of God as dear children. And walk in love, as Christ also has loved us and given Himself for us... Eph. 5:1-2
If we have traits after our earthly parents - why not like our heavenly Father?
So as we search for ourselves in the Word of God,
Let's go through the day knowing what matter of people we are.

Do not merely listen to the word, and so deceive yourselves. Do what it says. Anyone who listens to the word but does not do what it says is like someone who looks at his face in a mirror and, after looking at himself, goes away and immediately forgets what he looks like. But whoever looks intently into the perfect law that gives freedom, and continues in it—not forgetting what they have heard, but doing it—they will be blessed in what they do. James 1:22-25

Meditate today on ...

Hatred stirs up strife,

But love covers all sins·

Prov· 10:12

And above all things have fervent

love for one another, for "love

will cover a multitude of sins·

1 Pet· 4:8

When you find yourself in the middle of
mess – find a way to walk in love· If you
can't find it – ask God, he will show you·

*Matthew 21:21 Jesus answered and said unto them, Verily I say unto you, If ye have faith, and doubt not, ye shall not only do this which is done to the fig tree, but also if ye shall say unto this **mountain**, Be **thou removed**, and be **thou** cast into the sea; it shall be done.*

"Let's Be Realistic"

We as Christians go to church like crazy, but most of us see little changes at a time if any at all during the course of our lives. When we try to walk by faith we hear "be realistic" and we mix the worlds "realistic" with the Word of God instead of "faith" and we get nothing.

There is nothing realistic about God, so why should we be realistic.

Realistic: sensible, practical, down-to-earth, reasonable, rational
Unrealistic: impractical, idealistic, impracticable, unlikely, out of reach, unworkable

**What was realistic about a steel ax floating on water?
What was realistic about Moses parting the Red Sea?
What was realistic about Jesus turning water into wine?
What is realistic about healing?
What is realistic about faith?
What is realistic about believing a God that you can't see?**

There is a certain amount of realistic that we have to deal with, let's be realistic and listen to God, be obedient, work out our salvation, our calling, being kind, having self-control and walking in all the Fruit of the Spirit. When we do this,

We control what's realistic.

My Agape Walk Today

Do something
"kind" today for
someone that
<u>You don't know</u>
and don't tell
them You did it

✓ <u>I walked in love today</u>

Columbus Day

Many countries in the New World and elsewhere celebrate the anniversary of the arrival of Christopher Columbus in the Americas which happened on October 12, 1492 as an official holiday.

Columbus Day first became an official state holiday in Colorado in 1906, and became a <u>federal holiday</u> in the United States in 1937, though people have celebrated Columbus' voyage since the colonial period. In 1792, New York City and other U.S. cities celebrated the 300th anniversary of his landing in the New World. President <u>Benjamin Harrison</u> called upon the people of the United States to celebrate Columbus Day on the 400th anniversary of the event. During the four hundredth anniversary in 1892, teachers, preachers, poets and politicians used Columbus Day rituals to teach ideals of patriotism. These patriotic rituals were framed around themes such as support for war, citizenship boundaries, the importance of loyalty to the nation, and celebrating social progress.

Christopher Columbus is often portrayed as the first European to sail to the Americas. He is sometimes portrayed as the discoverer of the New World. However, this is controversial on many counts. It is said that the land was already populated by indigenous peoples, who had 'discovered' the Americas thousands of years before.

Quotes by Christopher Columbus
- ✓ *I am a most noteworthy sinner, but I have cried out to the Lord for grace and mercy, and they have covered me completely. I have found the sweetest consolation since I made it my whole purpose to enjoy His marvelous Presence*
- ✓ *By prevailing over all obstacles and distractions, one may unfailingly arrive at his chosen goal or destination*
- ✓ *No one should fear to undertake any task in the name of our Savior, if it is just and if the intention is purely for His holy service*
- ✓ *Following the light of the sun, we left the Old World*
- ✓ *For the execution of the voyage to the Indies, I did not make use of intelligence, mathematics or maps*
- ✓ *After having dispatched a meal, I went ashore, and found no habitation save a single house, and that without an occupant; we had no doubt that the people had fled in terror at our approach, as the house was completely furnished*

Meditate today on...

Trust in the LORD with all your heart
and lean not on your own understanding;
in all your ways submit to him,
and he will make your paths straight.

Do not be wise in your own eyes;
fear the LORD and shun evil.
This will bring health to your body
and nourishment to your bones.

Proverbs 3:5-8 NIV

We have to be able to trust God
with every area of our life. Even the
things we hold most precious to us by
allowing the Word of God, the ways of
God, the Love of God to govern our
thoughts, our will, and our emotions.

John 13:35 *By this shall all men know that ye are my disciples, if ye have **love one** to **another**.*

Important - How Do I look

I wonder how many of us pass by this verse in 1 Peter without hearing it, I mean really hearing what is said:

For we have spent enough of our past lifetime in doing the will of the Gentiles... *But the end of all things is at hand; therefore be serious and watchful in your prayers....* <u>*And above all things*</u> **have fervent love for one another, for "love will cover a multitude of sins."** 1Peter 4:3-8

I was also wondering how to ask this question with a grasp on reality and not just some "in one ear and out the other" type of attitude - so I want to use this example for this question.
How important is it to walk in love?

Do we really believe we are sending our kids out into a world that will love them and treat them with tender loving care? Do we teach our kids how to act like the world because we're sending them into what some call the real world? Do we teach them about the world and send them out to become world overcomers? How do we prepare them for it? (As a saint or A sinner) As Children of God we have a choice; continue in the way of the Gentiles (trusting their way) or walk in fervent love for one another (trusting God's way). This command is not an exception because of how the world is. Let's remind ourselves that God knows what He is doing.....

<u>**God is love**</u> ...*and he who abides in love abides in God and God in him. Love has been perfected among us in this: that we may have boldness in the Day of Judgment;* **because as He is, so are we in this world**. *There is no fear in love; but perfect love casts out fear, because fear involves torment. But he who fears has not been made perfect in love. We love Him because He first loved us.* 1 John 4:16-18
If walking in love towards one another is proof that we are the children of God,
how are we looking so far?
The Spirit Himself bears witness with our spirit that we are children of God. Rom. 8:16

Look carefully then how you walk! Live purposefully and worthily and accurately, not as the unwise and witless, but as wise (sensible, intelligent people), Making the very most of the time (buying up each opportunity), because the days are evil. Ephesians 5:15-16 Amplified Bible

"Live purposefully and worthily and accurately... making the very most of the time." We're each given 24 hours every day. We have the privilege to choose how we allocate those hours. One thing I've notice about allocating our 24 hours is how much of these are broken up into **eight** hour periods. We usually work an **eight** hour shift (usually), sleep experts say we should sleep **eight** hours a night. That's **sixteen** of those 24 hours gone. That's leaves us with **eight** hours left in that day. Pause and meditate on that. Most days after we've had a normal night's sleep (eight hours) and gone to work our eight hours shifts, what do we do with the rest of those hours?

Some of us work less or more than eight hour shifts, a lot of us sleep less than eight hours each night. So, we end up with varying hours left over each day. An elderly lady I used to know use to go to sleep at 7:00pm every night. She would arise each morning between 3:00-3:30am, shower, get dressed and start her day. By going to bed at 7:00pm every night she would have had a productive day of approximately 16 hours. This elderly lady was a very close family friend. She would tell her daughters and me; *"get up early and start your day while it's still fresh. Before it gets contaminated"*. She would say, if you have shopping to do, do it when the stores first open, you'll get the best pick of the day. She went to bed early and rose early because she believed in making the most of her day while there was daylight.

How about you and me? Are we living **purposefully, worthily,** and **accurately making the most of the time?** Maybe, we could take a few hints from this elderly lady. I honestly used to think she was missing out on a lot. As I've matured, I'm thinking she had it right and I was wrong. She certainly wasn't walking around physically tired from too little sleep, which I'm sure increased her productivity. She probably also didn't have a to-do list that always ran over into the next day or next week. **In the 1ˢᵗ chapter of the book of Genesis, it says....let there be lights in the firmament of the heaven to divide the day from the night... hmm,** *Only Believe!*

Meditate today on ...

Get wisdom! Get understanding!
Do not forget, nor turn away from the words of my
mouth· Do not forsake her, and she will preserve you;
Love her, and she will keep you· Wisdom *is* the principal
thing; *Therefore* get wisdom·
And in all your getting, get understanding·
Exalt her, and she will promote you;
She will bring you honor, when you embrace her·
She will place on your head an ornament of grace;
A crown of glory she will deliver to you·"
Prov· 4:5-9

You can get all the knowledge of the world, but
truth and wisdom are only from God· So all the
understanding of the world is weak and at best "luck"

My Agape Walk Today

Don't
say any negative
words or words
That lack
Faith today
If you do, repent out loud

✓ <u>I walked in love today</u>

Toni Joy

Proverbs 20:19 *A gossip betrays a confidence; so avoid anyone who talks too much.*

The Buck Stops Here!

If all gossip ceased immediately, we would have nothing on which to build false opinions and judgments. If we never repeated something we didn't hear, see, or feel for ourselves we would not tolerate hearsay.

Psalm 39:1*"I will watch my ways and keep my tongue from sin; I will put a muzzle on my mouth while in the presence of the wicked."*

When someone tells us something and that something has value, always ask, "What is the source of this information?" With the hearsay ask, "did that person tell you that themselves?" If yes, then let's say that it's true.

What should we do with that valuable information? ***You have the privilege to intercede for that person. Pray for them.*** I remember in the very early years of my walk with God, and I was getting to know the pastor more closely, I would find myself more and more in the Pastor's presence. I found myself telling him more about me than I wanted. I would walk away thinking *no I didn't say that."* Then I would be at peace and say, *"I know he's praying me", I trust him with knowing me."*

I said that to say this: *people should feel that about you.* People should feel comfortable around you knowing that you are on their side – with their faults, weights, and blind sights. Whatever someone comes to you with, your mindset should be: **The buck stops here**. Respond with the word of God and not the word of gossip.

*He said to them, "Go into all the world and preach **the gospel** (not gossip) to all creation" (Mark 16:15)*
P.S. When someone tells us something and we, in turn, repeat this to someone else; we are guilty of he say/she say. Don't repeat but pray.

My 2Cents

On Tuesday morning of last week, a friend of mine came to speak with me about a personal matter that she wanted kept confidential. She and I have been friends over twenty years. As we finished discussing the burden she was carrying, she began to thank God for friendship. She rejoiced that God has given her friends that are prayerful and know how to conceal a matter.

A talebearer reveals secrets, But he who is of a faithful spirit conceals a matter. Proverbs 11:13 NKJV

A real friend is faithful. A real friend keeps your secrets. This particular friend and I share friends. We have a circle of friends whose company we enjoy together. The matter she shared with me was private and not meant to be shared with them. Because I value friendship and I respect her wishes to keep it private; they won't know about her situation unless she tells them.

If you find yourself revealing other's secrets that they thought was safe with you - REPENT! You know what they say, "loose lips, sinks ships".

Proverbs 16:28b says it this way, *"...a whisperer separates the best of friends."* (NKJV)

It's difficult to make friends. Why ruin the relationship because you were found unfaithful in keeping secrets. We might have heard it, we might have been told it, but we don't have to pass it on. Be a friend that sticks closer than a brother. *Have the sister's back!* Only Believe!

Toni Joy

Jer. 29:11-13 *"For I know the plans I have for you," declares the L*ORD*, "plans to prosper you and not to harm you, plans to give you hope and a future. Then you will call on me and come and pray to me, and I will listen to you. You will seek me and find me when you seek me with all your heart."*

My Heart I want to see you walk in prosperity: spirit, soul, and body

I have made a few extreme decisions about my life towards God and I truly expect to see the manifestation of my decisions to step up to a higher level concerning my finances, praying, ministering, and my parenting. Making these decisions requires a change in my thinking, how I do things, and most importantly trusting God and the leading of Holy Spirit. I realized that **I have to trust God with all my heart**. And on a personal note...**I have to do this alone** - even though I'm not alone. I have God and I know many saints are walking in faith the way I desire.

I started "My Heart" just to tell you that I want you blessed, I want the devil defeated and God's people ruling. I have to believe it can happen in my life to believe for it to happen in yours. I have to walk it out.

I know we all face a lot of challenges in life - but if we really think about it, trusting God (faith) is our biggest challenge. It's easier to do what comes physically natural to handle that which you are physically facing, than to walk by faith, believing what you don't see. What's here is here - but faith means to trust God for the manifestation of what He said. Let's accept the biggest challenge in life - one moment at a time, one day at a time by Taking **God at His Word!**

Now what I am commanding you today is not too difficult for you or beyond your reach. It is not up in heaven, so that you have to ask, "Who will ascend into heaven to get it and proclaim it to us so we may obey it?" Nor is it beyond the sea, so that you have to ask, "Who will cross the sea to get it and proclaim it to us so we may obey it?" No, the word is very near you; it is in your mouth and in your heart so you may obey it. Deut. 30:11-14

This same verse is found in Romans 10:6-13
And this is my heart that we all take God at His Word literally, with corresponding action.... Read Hebrews 11 (perfect example of faith)

Meditate today on ...

Now it shall come to pass, if you diligently obey the voice of the LORD your God, to observe carefully all His commandments which I command you today, that the LORD your God will set you high above all nations of the earth. And all these blessings shall come upon you and overtake you, because you obey the voice of the LORD your God:

Deut. 28:1-2

The command of the Lord is "Love"
Walk in "Love" and the blessings is ours
Exercise your Agape Walk "Daily"

Mark 11:23-24 *So Jesus answered and said to them, "Have faith in God. For assuredly, I say to you, whoever __says__ to this mountain, 'Be removed and be cast into the sea,' and does not doubt in his heart, but believes that those things he __says__ will come to pass, he will have whatever he __says__."*

Say the "Right Thing"

Our confession should line up with our prayers and hopes. Sometimes we negate what we believe by talking against it. We speak what the devil tells us and not what the Word of God tells us. With whose voice, word, or influence do we cooperate? We allow ourselves to be bullied by the past and the circumstances around us. We allow fear to take authority instead of letting faith and patience run its course.

__Let's sidetrack for a minute;__ **I saw a commercial one day that said "before every moment – there is a moment"** ↓ __look at this moment:__

Before every moment, there is a moment where a decision is made: to do or not to do, to say or not to say, to go or not to go, etc. We can speak up and say what our spirit wants, or the moment will pass and we will follow the flesh. Those moments are always there; we just ignore them or we are not in touch with them.

Jesus took on our sins voluntarily; He endured the cross. Some of our afflictions/temptations/trials were brought about voluntarily, some were walked into ignorantly, and some because the enemy hates us. **But regardless of the reason "Jesus handled it"**

...in the world you will have tribulation; but be of good cheer, I have overcome the world." John 16:33

We may even believe this, but without faith and actions __in what we say__, we will never overcome our tribulations. We may have the knowledge of truth but because of various reasons we don't talk it.

The Cross is our moment before "The moment", which makes us more than conquerors (Romans 8:37).

A conqueror is someone that wins a fight. A more than a conquer is one who wins before the fight starts.
And how do we win or lose before we go into a fight?
__Obey our "moment before the moment" with our confession__
For with the heart one believes unto righteousness, and with the mouth confession is made unto salvation. Romans 10:10-11

1 Peter 1:16 *because it is written, Be ye holy; for I am holy*

Beneath or Above

Holiness is the Key

We can live under or above our circumstances. Holiness and Faith in God determine the path or direction of our lives. It is not just based on faith. It doesn't matter how much faith we have without holiness. Holiness enables us to tap into the full manifestation. It is through holiness that we live above our circumstances. *Your holiness is the work of your faith.* **Faith is the substance of things hoped for, and holiness is the substance of your faith.** These works are spiritual, not works of the flesh. Holiness make us *live our lives pleasing God in our behavior and conduct.*

Faith without holiness is like:
A supervisor with an insubordinate employee or
A parent with a rebellious kid.
It's uncontrollable.

We throw faith around like it is magical – Faith prepares my mind for the changes that Holiness is about to make in my behavior, my thoughts, my attitude, my love levels, my Fruit, my willingness, AND my participation in my exit from a desire to sin.

If you want to live above your circumstances; go by way of holiness - *Faith without Works Is Dead*

What does it profit, my brethren, if someone says he has faith but does not have works? Can faith save him... ***Show me your faith without your works, and I will show you my faith by my works. For as the body without the spirit is dead, so faith without works is dead also.*** James 2:14-26

Galatians 5:22 *But the fruit of the Spirit is love, joy, peace, forbearance, kindness, goodness, faithfulness, gentleness, self-control. Against such there is no law.*
So many Christians are walking around not tapping into the real power of God. *Come out from under your circumstances, Trust God*

My Agape Walk Today

Fix it in your mind
to help everyone
that asks anything
of you today

✓ <u>I walked in love today</u>

Toni Joy

Prov. 22:6 *Start children off on the way they should go, and even when they are old they will not turn from it.*

You Do It

There are times when I'm praying for my children and right away I hear the Lord say, *"You do it"*. Like the other day, I was praying for my daughter to learn the value of having a good relationship with the people in her life – my spirit was right away challenged with a *"that's what you're there for"*. It is my responsibility to show her a right relationship (I'm her example). What I need her to know I need to be and to teach. That revelation helped me to not give up on her, but to press in loving her when she needs it the most! Especially when she is clueless.

Then my heart went out to others that for whom we need to be examples. All those that challenge us. The ones we pray for constantly. The ones that we so easily know *their* problem. Stop talking about them; start praying for them; and watch what God tells you. God is saying, ***"YOU DO IT"***.

Don't pass the buck

For I have chosen him, so that he will direct his children and his household after him to keep the way of the Lord by doing what is right and just, so that the Lord will bring about for Abraham what he has promised him." Gen. 18:19

Meditate today on ...

Beloved, I pray that you may prosper in all things and be in health, just as your soul prospers.

3 John 2

God wants us in divine health, all our financial needs met, that we are spiritually, socially, and mentally strong – that we are loved and are walking in love towards others.

I pray that for you today

Genesis 1:26 *Then God said, "Let us make mankind in our image, in our likeness."*

Identify Yourself He had me at "Our Image"

I have read and quoted this verse so many times. But this Sunday was the first time, I believe, that I looked at it this way.

> ***He made us in His Image, and According to His likeness.***
> We have the ability to walk in his likeness - ***to reflect God.***

This message was preached by my churches very own Deacon Keith Robinson, who was filling in for the Pastors while on vacation. He ministered this message that I'm sharing. *I feel sorry for those that don't go to church if their Pastor is not ministering; you miss out on a real treat. It should be very disturbing for you if you think that God can only use your Pastor. (Oops where does that leave you?).*

His message also talked about:
A good man brings good things out of the good stored up in his heart, and an evil man brings evil things out of the evil stored up in his heart. For the mouth speaks what the heart is full of. Luke 6:45

He stressed the importance of living the God kind of life; waking every morning with the purpose of being perfect in Christ. God gave us promises. Do we believe them? We can identify ourselves by what we say and do. Here are some scriptures he gave:

> **John 15:7** (NIV) *If you remain in me and my words remain in you, ask whatever you wish, and it will be done for you.*
> **Proverbs 18:21** (NIV) *The tongue has the power of life and death, and those who love it will eat its fruit.*

He also brought out not just attending to ourselves but our children too. The Word says to train up a child in the way they should go and they will not depart from it (Prov. 22:6). The NIV states it this way: *Start children off on the way they should go, and even when they are old they will not turn from it.*

"A Period of Time"

A conversation I had this morning with a young lady who was relating to me some of the difficulties she was encountering reminded me of Romans 8:28. *And we know that all things work together for good to them that love God, to them who are the called according to his purpose.*

Verse 8, really stuck out. *"And we know"*. Meaning we have this knowledge. What knowledge? That God is going to work things out on our behalf over a period of time. Over a period of time it will work out.

The New Living Translation says, **God** causes everything to work together. Who causes it? Our Heavenly Father does. We just have to get out of the way and let Him be God. He has a way of working things out.

Why does He cause everything to work out? *For the good.* For the good of whom? *Those that love Him.* Are you lovers of Jesus today? If you are, God is causing things to work out for you. He works behind the scenes. Over a period of time you'll notice it all worked out.

As I continued to converse with this young lady we discussed how we lose our joy and peace over things that just don't warrant it. Sometimes we really have to turn away from doing what seems right in our own eyes in order to come to a place of complete victory. It may take longer than we anticipated, but over a period of time, it all comes together.

From verse 29 of Romans 8, we understand, **God has a** foreordained **plan**, (a plan that develops over a period of time). In the book of Jeremiah, God said to Jeremiah, *I knew you and sanctified (set you apart) you, appointed (called) you to be a prophet before you left your mother's womb.* As we read the book of the weeping prophet (Jeremiah) we find God's plan for him played out over a period of time.

We both agreed that she would "put a little time on it" and watch all these things work together for her good. She decided she would follow the way of the Lord in her difficulties. I was born and raised in Tennessee, and there the elderly people had a saying, "time heals all wounds", I guess that's a little like saying, ***"put a little time on it".*** *Only Believe!*

Meditate today on ...

"Therefore do not worry, saying, 'What shall we eat?' or 'What shall we drink?' or 'What shall we wear?' For after all these things the Gentiles seek· For your heavenly Father knows that you need all these things· But seek first the kingdom of God and His righteousness, and all these things shall be added to you· Therefore do not worry about tomorrow, for tomorrow will worry about its own things· Sufficient for the day is its own trouble·

Matt· 6:31-34

This is my favorite scripture
My Father knows ME, loves
ME, and takes care of ME

My Agape Walk Today

How Bold Are You

Look for the opportunity

To take someone's

hand and pray

for them today

✓ _I walked in love today_

Col 1:13 *He has delivered us from the power of darkness and conveyed us into the kingdom of the Son of His love...*

Home Sweet Home - A Small Testimony

I was a cigarette smoker a long time ago. I remember trying to quit at least 500 times. *I had no power to quit.*

The day I was saved: The awesome power of God took me out of darkness into the glorious light. I knew love and joy as never before. I was a new creature in a new world. *That day, Jesus became my hero.*

When I got home I lit a cigarette and knew at that moment that it had no power over me. **I knew this in my spirit – a place that I never known before. *I wasn't in Kansas anymore! It was that moment of I'm finally home; and I knew it was real.*** I acknowledged that the spirit realm was more real than the physical realm. I decided that I would quit tomorrow (I still don't know why I said tomorrow). I lit a cigarette the next morning and remembered that I said I was quitting. I flushed my cigarettes and never had another one since. I remember a couple of times thinking about smoking, but said "NO". The thought was there, but it was powerless.

Some things in my life were supernatural deliverances and some I had to surrender and submit to God, walk by faith.

The greatest power I've seen in my life was the day I got saved, and that testimony is still inspiring me today – twenty plus years later.

Let your salvation be a witness of the power of God. Let it take you from faith to faith, miracle to miracle. If your faith is not where it should be, go back and remember what was done for you.

Get in the Word of God – Daily.
"So then faith comes by hearing, and hearing by the word of God."

Meditate today on ...

"I am the vine, you are the branches. He who abides in Me, and I in him, bears much fruit; for without Me you can do nothing. If anyone does not abide in Me, he is cast out as a branch and is withered; and they gather them and throw *them* into the fire, and they are burned. If you abide in Me, and My words abide in you, you will ask what you desire, and it shall be done for you. By this My Father is glorified, that you bear much fruit; so you will be My disciples.
John 15:5-8

We are connected to the vine – the
blood vine of Jesus Christ.
Ask the Father what you want.
Let God be gloried by our life today,
"by receiving"
How else will He be gloried?

My Agape Walk Today

How Bold Are You
Make time today to think
About your daily routine,
Is there something missing?
Is there something we need to add?
Change your daily routine today

✓ _I walked in love today_

Acts 14:8-10 And there sat a certain man at Lystra, impotent in his feet, being a cripple from his mother's womb, who never had walked: The same heard Paul speak: who steadfastly beholding him, and perceiving that he had faith to be healed, Said with a loud voice, Stand upright on thy feet. And he leaped and walked.

Relax - Faith got this

After a few moments of meditating, I thought about how blessed we are to have faith. Yet, most of the time we don't use it; at least, not to the extent where we rely on our faith to get us through life. Rom. 1:17 - *The just shall live by faith.*

God gave each of us a measure of faith and He speaks of it as it's ours to do with it as we please *(Matt. 9:29, Rom. 12:3).*

According to your faith be it unto you.

It can be perceived; it's fully loaded (powerful), and it grows by the Word of God. *Unfortunately it can be drained and weakened by lack of the Word of God.*

God's power is ignited by faith... it's like a match to fire

I believe everyone wants to be happy. Everything which with we deal steals precious moments from our life. **If only this was a perfect world... If he was... If she did... If I could... If they didn't....**

Why make faith contingent on our circumstances?
So how do we own this gift, make it ours – this commodity that gets the attention of God? Heb. 11:6

Then I went and got a cup of coffee, and said

Relax, Faith got this

If you really think about it Faith, or lack of it, has always been between you and your victory. Faith is your challenge; what are you going to do? If you really want it –

Let faith get it for you.

My 2 Cents

There have been times in my life when I was clear after the fact. WHY I didn't receive from God? It wasn't because He was saying **no** to my prayer request, but because I failed to stand in my faith to the end. One such instance occurred in 1998 when I was taught a life changing lesson about wavering in my faith. Back then there was a prayer group my husband and I prayed with weekly. During that time my husband and I were planning a vacation; it took us a year to save the money. I had made all the travel arrangements. We had a financial crisis to occur during this period and it totally wiped out our vacation savings (here was my faith test). I became despondent. We were sitting in the prayer meeting with this group and as we were praying I heard Holy Spirit minister this verse to me: ***"Let us hold fast the profession of our faith without wavering; (for he is faithful that promised)" Hebrews 10:23.***

That particular day this scripture became alive to me. I caught the revelation of what He was saying. I knew he was talking about my despondency over our vacation plans and the fact that I wasn't standing in faith anymore for it. When I heard this scripture in my spirit, HOPE rose up in me. I knew then I needed to repent over my lack of faith; and believe God to work this out. I knew this scripture meant I shouldn't give up this vacation; that I should continue to believe for this to happen. He was telling me to hold on to my FAITH stand, don't waiver in this, even though it looks bad, for He is faithful, and more than able to bring us to victory.

Our confession has a lot to do with faith. The confession of our lips is vital to our faith. This is usually a BIG reason why we don't see the victories we should see. When things appear to not be working out for us we start confessing negatively about what we are believing God to do for us. In my despondency I had begun to tell people we were **not** going on this vacation. Holy Spirit let me know that day....STOP CONFESSING THAT!!!! **Mark 11:23 "...*He shall have whatsoever he saith.*"** God had a plan to still give us the trip and needed me to SHUT UP so He could bless us. I did and so He did. Glory to God we took that nine day vacation. Yes, it was exceedingly abundantly more than we asked. **Have faith in God! Have you ever had your faith tested? Has there been a time when in the process of believing God for something, everything about it went wrong? Did you pass that faith test?** *Only Believe!*

Halloween

Ancient Origins of Halloween

Halloween's origins date back to the ancient Celtic festival of Samhain (pronounced sow-in). The Celts, who lived 2,000 years ago

On May 13, 609 A.D., Pope Boniface IV dedicated the Pantheon in Rome in honor of all Christian martyrs, and the Catholic feast of All Martyrs Day was established in the Western church. Pope Gregory

The All Saints Day celebration was also called All-hallows or All-hallowmas (from Middle English Alholowmesse meaning All Saints' Day) and the night before it, the traditional night of Samhain in the Celtic religion, began to be called All-hallows Eve and, eventually, Halloween.

Over the years, Halloween (as well as many other holidays) lost its real meaning and the origin faded..... *So we have to ask ourselves, why do we want to celebrate a particular holiday and how do we want to celebrate it?*

Do we see Halloween as demonic or not? Does it attack your beliefs? Is it dangerous?

Should we let our kids celebrate this holiday? How far do we let them go?

Do we just embrace it as a fun day? Should we celebrate it in a good way and not the tradition witches and goblins way? Or just let it pass without notice?

What I have noticed is that this is one day out of the year were people don't mind being scared. As a matter of fact, they seek it out (the more scary the better). And it's all done in the name of *fun*... **Is this a good thing?**

One suggestion I would like to offer in answering these questions is found in the bible....

Therefore, whether you eat or drink, or whatever you do, do all to the glory of God. 1 Cor. 10:31

CONFESSION FOR THE MONTH OF NOVEMBER

Print or write out your confession; put it where you can see and confess it all month

Thank you Lord for
Angels encamped all around me and my
family. I thank you that no weapon
formed against us will prosper.

Many shall fall around us, but
you shall hold us up
You are our shield and our place of refuge

We are protected by God Almighty

"Because he has set his love upon Me, therefore I will deliver him; I will set him on high, because he has known My name. He shall call upon Me, and I will answer him; I will be with him in trouble; I will deliver him and honor him. With long life I will satisfy him, And show him My salvation."
Ps. 91:14-16

Rom. 14:16 *Therefore do not let your good be spoken of as evil;*

Be Very Careful

I was on my way to work this morning and my son put it on a station that he likes to listen. This song came on that has this smooth beat to it and before I knew it my shoulders were moving to the beat.

As I was listening to the words – I put the brakes on….. What, no she didn't say that.

There are a few songs out that I have heard that has this great beat and melody to it that pulls us right in and before we know it, we are agreeing to things that we know we shouldn't. Plus, 5 hours later, that song will still be in your head.

It sounds so good. Is that enough? Is that all we need? Is that worth exposing your mind to the Devil? I just love this saying... "Wake up and smell the coffee", but for this particular instance, I would add "stop dancing to the devil's tunes".

Let's get more creative in entertaining and activities that can bring excitement to our lives. It's a lot of good music out that ministers to our soul as well as our spirit. Do we really need the help of evil and lustful music to get in the mood? Real genuine "aura" lasts a lot longer and feels a lot better - true fun! A positive and lovely atmosphere *is the real cool*.

Who we are has a lot to do with what we hear. We have to be careful in picking the music to which we listen. Be picky, very picky - we only have one "us" and God says that we are special.

If we are not careful, we won't be that special people that God created us to be; so choose well.

*Beloved, do not believe every spirit, but test the spirits, whether they are of God; because many false prophets have gone out into the world. **1 John 4:1***

Toni Joy

Isaiah 55:11 *So shall my **word** be that goeth forth out of my mouth: it shall not return unto me void, but it shall accomplish that which I please, and it shall **prosper** in the thing whereto I sent it.*

The WORD – it is what it is

As I was reading in Gen. 48:21 I was thinking about the faith that Jacob (Israel) had *"...God will be with you and bring you back to the land of your fathers"*. Looking from the time of Abraham to today, we can follow this word to be true.

Gen. 13:14-15 *And the LORD said unto Abram, after that Lot was separated from him, Lift up now thine eyes, and look from the place where thou art northward, and southward, and eastward, and westward: For all the land which thou seest, to thee will I give it, and to thy seed forever.*

Gen. 26, 2-3 *And the LORD appeared unto him (Isaac), and said, Go not down into Egypt; dwell in the land which I shall tell thee of: Sojourn in this land, and I will be with thee, and will bless thee; for unto thee, and unto thy seed, I will give all these countries, and I will perform the oath which I swore unto Abraham thy father;*

Gen. 48:3-4 *And Jacob said unto Joseph, God Almighty appeared unto me at Luz in the land of Canaan, and blessed me, And said unto me, Behold, I will make thee fruitful, and multiply thee, and I will make of thee a multitude of people; and will give this land to thy seed after thee for an everlasting possession.*

Gen 50:24-26 *And Joseph said unto his brethren, I die: and God will surely visit you, and bring you out of this land unto the land which he swore to Abraham, to Isaac, and to Jacob. And Joseph took an oath of the children of Israel, saying, God will surely visit you, and ye shall carry up my bones from hence. So Joseph died, being an hundred and ten years old: and they embalmed him, and he was put in a coffin in Egypt.*

Exo. 13:19 *And Moses took the bones of Joseph with him: for he had straightly sworn the children of Israel, saying, God will surely visit you; and ye shall carry up my bones away hence with you.*

Heb. 11:22 *By faith Joseph, when he died, made mention of the departing of the children of Israel; and gave commandment concerning his bones.*

All of this makes me wonder at times; are we believing what God told us or what we're telling God?

Are we holding fast to what we are asking God or what God is telling us? Whose words do we confess / speak every day? Are we looking out for the generations to come? Are we speaking and believing anything?

My Agape Walk Today

Tell someone
you haven't
told in a long time
that you love them.

✓ <u>I walked in love today</u>

Luke 6:41-42 *And why do you look at the speck in your brother's eye, but do not perceive the plank in your own eye? Or how can you say to your brother, 'Brother, let me remove the speck that is in your eye,' when you yourself do not see the plank that is in your own eye?*

A Stab In The Dark

It is God's desire that we help one another; bear each other's burdens. But sometimes it's hard to see the forest for the trees - and in this state of blindness we will proceed to tell others what they should do. Sometimes we give advice based on what we think, which is not the best answer for ourselves let alone for someone else. It's the blind leading the blind.

How do we know when we are blind? A lot of times we don't. Therefore, we should live our lives listening and responding to the leading of the Holy Spirit in order to comfortably and freely speak into someone else's life, as well as our own. It can be a dangerous thing to tell someone what to do about their situation. Even when we give someone a scripture to meditate on, it may lead to a wrong conclusion. We might tell someone to stay and speak to the mountain, but God wants them to leave (or vice versa). Some things we need to leave to God and/or refer them to a Christian Counselor/Minister.

Does this mean that we should not give our advice or opinion to others? No, but If we are praying and staying in the word on a daily basis, we will see the spirit flow easily and more simply through us. *Then we will find that our advice and opinions are led by God, not what we see and feel.*

I will speak to others as the Holy Spirit speaks to me. He is my guide.

But when he, the Spirit of truth, comes, he will guide you into all truth. He will not speak on his own; he will speak only what he hears, and he will tell you what is yet to come. John 16:13-14

Just say whatever is given you at the time, for it is not you speaking, but the Holy Spirit. Mark 13:11

Toni Joy

Judges 19:22 *Now as they were making their hearts merry, behold, the men of the city, certain sons of Belial, beset the house round about, and beat at the door, and spake to the master of the house, the old man, saying, "Bring forth the man that came into thine house, that we many know him".*

Déjà vu – Nothing New Under The Sun

How many of you got Déjà vu reading this chapter? You have the Angels in Genesis 19 that went to Sodom and after they went into Lot's home - the men in the city came and demanded that the men come out to know them. God knew the sin of the city and destroyed it. This story in Judges has all the characteristic of the one in Genesis except that these men were Israelites demanding their own brethren.

A Levite, his concubine, and his servant were traveling back home and was looking for some place to lodge for the night. They took the longer journey to their brethren city to keep from going to a stranger's city. **_Summary:_**
-   One of the men offered them lodging .... Just like Lot.
-   The men of the city were sinful and demanded for the Levite to come out so they could *know* him.... Just like the men in Sodom.
-   The man of the house asked them not to do this sinful thing and offered the woman instead....just like Lot.
-   The Angel's in Genesis struck the men blind, sent Lot and his family away and destroyed the city.
-   In Judges, they did send his Concubine out and they abused her until she died.

God-in-it made the difference... Read the stories, there are amazing similarities. Are we seeing Déjà vu in our lives; you know the devil is bringing it. He tries the same old things all the time. And, we fall for it.

Déjà vu, the trials and tribulations are here. Be ready, get God involved, When we're prepared, we win.

These things I have spoken unto you, that in me ye might have peace. In the world ye shall have tribulation; but be of good cheer; I have overcome the world. John 16:33

Meditate today on ...

Oh, give thanks to the LORD, for *He is* good!
  For His mercy endures forever·
Oh, give thanks to the God of gods!
  For His mercy endures forever·
Oh, give thanks to the Lord of lords!
  For His mercy endures forever:

To Him who alone does great wonders,
  For His mercy endures forever;
To Him who by wisdom made the heavens,
  For His mercy endures forever;
To Him who laid out the earth above the waters,
  For His mercy endures forever;
To Him who made great lights,
  For His mercy endures forever—
The sun to rule by day,
  For His mercy endures forever;
The moon and stars to rule by night,
  For His mercy endures forever·

Ps· 136:1-9

**Where would you be today
without the mercy of God?**

Toni Joy

Phil. 4:6,7 *Be anxious for nothing, but in everything by prayer and supplication, with thanksgiving, let your requests be made known to God; and the peace of God, which surpasses all understanding, will guard your hearts and minds through Christ Jesus.*

Don't Push

Are we bullying God, do we need to repent? I had this brilliant idea once of what I was going to do to make some drastic changes in my finances to lower some bills because the budget I had wasn't working *for what I wanted to do.*

I always discuss my ideas with someone concerning major changes. Well this time it was my Mom. (God will know just who to send you too, and it won't be the one that will always agree with you – but who agrees with God.) My mom agreed that changes needed to be made and with the end result, but, not how to get there.

I thought it was a good idea, well not really - but I really wanted it to be a good idea. For just a moment it would have changed one situation like right **NOW -** but in-turn opening up another can of worms. I sensed in my spirit that it was not God's best for me. I did everything I could to push God behind the idea and wanted Him to bless it. I prayed, I confessed. I wanted to change God's mind. We may successfully change others to see the idea, but not God. He will let us do it and help us through it, but we could have avoided it.

But in all the pushing, I was still praying and reading, and meditating on God's ways; I remembered I trusted God. I stopped pushing and started listening. The peace of God came *immediately....* **"You will get peace before you even have the answer... just knowing you are following God is answer enough".**

And we know that all things work together for good to them that love God, to them who are the called according to his purpose. Rom. 8:28

We know God's ways are better and will reap a great reward. But we want what we want, when we want it. We fool ourselves into thinking **NOW** is better and push it off on God and everyone else.

Don't Push... *But let patience have its perfect work, that you may be perfect and complete, lacking nothing - James 1:4*

Phil. 4:6,7 *Be anxious for nothing, but in everything by prayer and supplication, with thanksgiving, let your requests be made known to God; and the peace of God, which surpasses all understanding, will guard your hearts and minds through Christ Jesus.*

Don't Push - but check

I shared with you yesterday that I had this brilliant idea to make changes in my budget because the one I had wasn't working. I decided to stop pushing my ideas on God and wait on God. But there is something else we need to do.

Beloved, do not believe every spirit, but test the spirits, whether they are of God; because many false prophets have gone out into the world. **1 John 4:1**

Have you ever heard the phrase **A wolf in sheep's Clothing?** Even in our waiting, and in our faith, and our surrendering to God's plan, the devil will bring his best. God warns us of the tactics that the enemy will bring to get us to sin or to back away from God. He tells us to test the spirits.

How can we tell if it is God or a trick of the enemy? A few tips to help you see through to your answer:

Stop: don't jump at the first thing you think is the answer. He will try to get you to do something to make your answer come. He will send a wolf in sheep's clothing, but you don't have to take it or receive it.

Look: for God's love and compassion in everything. What is the motive behind it? Will it free you or bind you? Example: I was looking in my refrigerator once and as I was looking, I said Lord, how do you run out of everything at the same time? I didn't have the money to get everything I needed. My mother called a few hours later said that she got a rebate gift card. We are on the same cell phone plan. I asked, "What do you need?" So you know what I told her. I praised God. Out of love and compassion God met my need through my mother.

Listen: for the Voice and Word of God. God is not going to lead you to anything that will go against His Will, His Ways, and His Plan for you. Example: if you are anxious or impatient, you may fall for anything just to get what you want. But listen to God, hear His plan. The Holy Spirit will give you the truth. Last, but not least, make sure you are walking in the Fruit of the Spirit. *But the fruit of the Spirit is love, joy, peace, longsuffering, kindness, goodness, faithfulness, gentleness, self-control. **Against such there is no law**.* Gal. 5:22-23

Sometimes it looks like God; but we (those that seek God) will know the difference. We just have to stop, look, and listen. The enemy will emerge and be revealed. Once we really submit to God and His plan for us and walk in the supernatural forces of the Fruit of the Spirit, we will see that the devil is not that good with his weak plans. The best plan for you unveils *when you're walking In Christ.* **See God in everything you do – Don't Push**

Meditate today on ...

"Most assuredly, I say to you, he who believes
in Me, the works that I do he will do also;
and greater works than these he will do,
because I go to My Father. And whatever
you ask in My name, that I will do, that
the Father may be glorified in the Son. If
you ask anything in My name, I will do it."

John 14:12-14

We are in the family of God, We inherited
the family business. Let's Work!

Veteran's Day

Veterans Day, honors *ALL* American veterans, both living and dead. In fact, Veterans Day is largely intended to thank *LIVING* veterans for dedicated and loyal service to their country. November 11th of each year is the day that we ensure veterans know that we deeply appreciate the sacrifices they have made to keep our country free.

In America, November 11th officially became known as Armistice Day through an act of Congress in 1926. It wasn't until 12 years later, through a similar act that Armistice Day became a national holiday.

The entire World thought that World War I was the "War to end all wars." Had this been true, the holiday might still be called Armistice Day today. That dream was shattered in 1939 when World War II broke out in Europe. More than 400,000 American service members died during that horrific war.

In 1947, Raymond Weeks, of Birmingham Ala., organized a "Veterans' Day" parade on November 11th to honor all of America's veterans for their loyal and dedicated service. Shortly thereafter, Congressman Edward H. Rees (Kansas) introduced legislation to change the name of Armistice Day to Veterans Day in order to honor all veterans who have served the United States in all wars.

Veterans Day National Ceremony
At exactly 11am on November 11th a color guard, made up of members from each of the military branches, renders honors to America's fallen soldiers during a heart-moving ceremony at the Tomb of the Unknowns in Arlington National Cemetery.

I salute those men and woman that gave their lives to serve our nation. A salute also the men and women that *now* put their lives in front of ours to preserve this nation's way of living. May the peace of God preserve them and His grace and mercy be extended to them and keep them.

And may they come home to live the life that they sustain for us.

My Agape Walk Today

Smile all
day today
even if you
don't feel like it

✓ *I walked in love today*

Toni Joy

John 15:5 *I am the vine, you are the branches. He who abides in Me, and I in Him, bears much fruit; for without Me you can do nothing.*

Touched...
It doesn't matter where, who, when, or what we are...·
...··Without Christ, we are nothing·

I was thinking about the mind (my own particularly). I thought about my attention span, memory, intellect; the whole working of the brain even my personality. Then I thought about how others view their contentment, likes and dislikes, satisfaction, confidence or lack thereof and judgment.

I came to the conclusion that we are all touched! Some more or less touched than others. From the highest intellectual to the most simple-minded **No One is better than the other.**

If you are the one less touched.... What are you doing with your sanity? Those of us that are more touched.... What are we doing with our insanity? Jesus didn't separate the touched and untouched, the rich and the poor, from one sinner to another sinner or even one saved person to another. The only separation is in or out of the body of Christ. You can be smart and rich and go to hell; or dumb and poor and go to heaven. Jesus said we can do nothing without Him – so I have a question...

Are you walking according to your God given calling and purpose in life? Be Content in who you are and serve God - this is what matters.

Are we walking in love? Are we trusting God? Are we living by faith? Whatever your personality or state of mind Jesus knows each of us, every hair on our head. He died for each and every one of us. He gave a calling and purpose to each and every one of us. He knows you - He loves you! We have no excuse for not walking in **_our_** best life...the one dealt to us.

I might be touched, but I'm blessed, I'm highly favored, empowered to prosper and more than a conqueror...

Toni Joy

Rom. 8:1 *Therefore, there is now no condemnation for those who are in Christ Jesus.*

Preach out of Romans 8

Those who live according to the flesh have their minds set on what the flesh desires; but those who live in accordance with the Spirit have their minds set on what the Spirit desires... The mind governed by the flesh is death, but the mind governed by the Spirit is life and peace... Romans 8:6

Have you ever understood that some behaviors go with the territory, or the saying "that goes without saying"? If we live by the Spirit, the rest goes without saying... it's a done deal - ***it will put to death the deeds of the flesh - that's the result - LIFE***.

Ask yourself this, which is greater - the Spirit of Christ or the spirit of this world *if both show up in the ring? Ho*w many times do we get in the ring and leave God out? We think *"We got this"*. We leave the ring sick, broke, busted, and disgusted. We leave our weapons outside the ring.

Have you picked up what I want to preach yet?
Let's stop showing up without God. Jesus already did the work, won the battle. If it hasn't got serious for you yet, it will one day. What if we took a chance and walked away from some things and started doing some things, will it hurt too much? Will it cost us too much? It may feel like it is. Hey, it may hurt a lot; it may cost us a lot; but is it a pain we must go through. It's a lost we need to take to get things right, to live, and to have peace.

We will be a slave to Christ or a Slave to the world
The Word says that all things work out for the good to those that love God, to those called according to His purpose.... ***Question....*** *What, then, shall we say in response to these things? If God is for us, who can be against us? ...Who will bring any charge against those whom God has chosen? ....* ***No one....*** *Who shall separate us from the love of Christ? Shall trouble or hardship or persecution or famine or nakedness or danger or sword?* ···· ***No****, in all these things* ***we are more than conquerors through him who loved us****. For I am convinced that neither death nor life, neither angels nor demons, neither the present nor the future, nor any powers, neither height nor depth, nor anything else in all creation, will be able to separate us from the love of God that is in Christ Jesus our Lord.*

Show up with the WORD

Meditate today on ...

For you are all sons of God through faith in
Christ Jesus· For as many of you as were
baptized into Christ have put on Christ· There
is neither Jew nor Greek, there is neither slave
nor free, there is neither male nor female;
for you are all one in Christ Jesus· And if
you are Christ's, then you are Abraham's
seed, and heirs according to the promise·

Gal· 3:26-29

We are heirs of Abraham, all the promise
to Him is ours· If you don't know what you
inherited, read the will; Deut· 28:1-14

Toni Joy

1 Tim. 6:10 *For the love of money is a root of all kinds of evil, for which some have strayed from the faith in their greediness, and pierced themselves through with many sorrows.*

Money, Money,.... The all-powerful buck

It can give you a headache, cause stress, and yes, even kill you. Whether you pay tithes or not, have a lot or not, love it or not. Because we connect it to everything, we put it above everything. And sadly, it can be more important than family. If you don't believe me run out of it, lose a job, get an inheritance, or hit the lottery.

In the right perspective, we rule money and it doesn't rule us. So what's the right perspective? Jesus makes it very Clear.

"No one can serve two masters. Either you will hate the one and love the other, or you will be devoted to the one and despise the other. You cannot serve both God and money. Luke 16:13

The bible talks a lot, and I mean a lot, about money - but who's listening? Trust this, Jesus' perspective on money is quite different from the world's. We can read every one of the precepts and still join the class of people that make money the god of this life.

So how do we change that? Make God the master of our lives:

Keep reading (meditating on) the word of God over and over.
Faith cometh by hearing and hearing and hearing.
Start changing the source of our needs - all of them.
God needs to be our source.
Change your earthly desire to heavenly desires.
Make God's way of living your way of living.

We can do this once we know that God doesn't want us poor, sick, and sorrowful. As a matter of fact; God wants us to be the lender and not the borrower. We have to have something to lend. The love of money is the root of all evil only when money is your god. When money makes your decisions for you, defines you, and tells you how to treat others.

Jesus told Peter exactly where to go to get the money for taxes - He will tell us exactly where to go for our needs. Matt. 17:27

Let's get perspective on Money
And He said to them, "Render therefore to Caesar the things that are Caesar's, and to God the things that are God's." Matt. 22:21

Season Greetings

I love the month of November; not just because it's my birthday month, but because everyone is celebrating the holiday. Whether it's shopping, cooking, planning ways to be a giver, and seeing family they haven't seen in a while. Whether you have plans or not, let's get started.

Get a pencil and a piece of paper – write down your plan of what you are going to do to this holiday season to make it special – why not make it;

1. Something that you haven't done before
2. Something You have to create
3. Something that's not expensive
4. Something special you do or give to others

What are you Wishing for?

Heb. 11:1 *Now faith is the substance of things hoped for, the evidence of things not seen.*

In reading this scripture, I thought about Diana Ross's song *"Do You Know"* - remember these lyrics:

Do you know where you're going too – Do you like the things that life is showing you; Do you get what you hoping for when you look behind you there's no open door – what are you hoping for, do you know.....
Faith is the chariot that brings your hope to manifestation....

Now think about this: Faith is the substance of what we hope for, and sometimes what we hope for doesn't come to pass or we can't see it coming to pass. *I believe our hope is without substance, no chariot to bring it to pass – or there's no expectation or hope and the chariot is empty.* **Wishing is not enough**....

Listen to another verse in her song:
Once we were standing still in time - chasing the fantasies that once filled our minds....

Maybe this song came to mind because we need to stop wishing and put some real hope to our faith - get serious. The way the world is today, it seems that it is designed to kill our hopes and dreams. *But the hope that God has set before us is an anchor of the soul, both sure and steadfast.* (Heb. 6:19)

This hope won't disappoint - Rom. 5:5. Find the time to read all of Chapter 11 in Hebrews and see what faith gave to the saints of old.

Don't be afraid to hope and dream. Rejoice in hope - there are open doors. Put your hope in God - Give Faith Something to Work With. So then faith comes by hearing, and hearing by the word of God. Rom. 10:17

Our hope is in God – in the Word of God

Therefore, having been justified by faith, we have peace with God through our Lord Jesus Christ, through whom also we have access by faith into this grace in which we stand, and rejoice in hope of the glory of God. And not only that, but we also glory in tribulations, knowing that tribulation produces perseverance; and perseverance, character; and character, hope. Now hope does not disappoint, because the love of God has been poured out in our hearts by the Holy Spirit who was given to us. **Romans 5:1-5**

Meditate today on ...

Let all bitterness, wrath, anger, clamor,
and evil speaking be put away from you,
with all malice· And be kind to one another,
tenderhearted, forgiving one another,
even as God in Christ forgave you·
John 8:31-32

Live your life as if Jesus is right next
to you 24-7, that's right, He is!
As a matter of fact, He's in you

My Agape Walk Today

Do whatever you
can do today...
don't put it off
for tomorrow

✓ <u>I walked in love today</u>

Happy Thanksgiving

"The last Thursday of November is a day set aside to give thanksgiving to God for His many blessings. Congress recommends a day of... thanksgiving and praise so that the people may express the grateful feelings of their hearts...and join...their prayers that it may please God, through the merits of Jesus Christ, to forgive our sins and...to enlarge His kingdom which consists in righteousness, peace and joy in the Holy Ghost." - Continental Congress, 1777 (Samuel Adams and Richard Henry Lee)

Yes, you read that correctly. To set aside time for the people of the United States to give thanksgiving to God was a congressional request. At that time George Washington was our President. In 1863 Abraham Lincoln set aside the last Thursday of November as a day of thanksgiving and praise to God.

Fast forward to today. Some of our major retail stores will open on Thanksgiving Day so you and I can take advantage of their wonderful Christmas sales. They are going to give you just enough time to say "Thank You Lord," eat your turkey, and run out the door to buy something from them. **Really?**

Hmm, let's see, enjoy the day with family, take my time giving God thanks and meditating on His goodness - not taking for granted the original intent of the day; or rush through so I can shop and miss precious time spent with family and friends.

We have a lot to be thankful for. In my opinion the purpose of Thanksgiving is to show gratefulness to God, family togetherness, love, and stuffing my face with delicious food until I don't want to see any more food. Besides, retail strategist have said, the best shopping is done online on "Cyber Monday." The Monday after Thanksgiving. That's where the best deals really are.

Just My 2Cents

Don't forget Black Friday is the day following Thanksgiving Day,

November 22

My 2 Cents

One of the things I enjoy doing is what many refer to as "thrifting". I enjoy a good late Saturday morning of driving over to one or two of my favorite thrift stores, stopping by McDonald's first of course and picking up a high calorie ridden Caramel Mocha frozen latte. Hey don't point fingers at me, I almost always get a small one. I do it as early on a Saturday as I possibly can so that I can take my time. I only get the time to do this about once a month. You can find real treasures if you have the time to really look. I especially love buying the beautiful tea cup collections. I came home one Saturday afternoon with a "barely worn" **Ralph Lauren** blazer that I paid just mere dollars for. I dropped it off to the cleaners and I've gotten several years of wear out it.

Not only is *Black Friday* and *Cyber Monday* shopping widely advertised, but now they are also encouraging **Small Business Saturday.** That's really what got me to thinking thrifting and small retail stores.

You never know what treasures you might find when you go *thrifting*. Let's do some Small Business shopping!! Let's help keep small business owners in business. Walmart, Target, Macy's, Sears, J.C. Penny have seen enough of our dollars.

Only Believe!

Toni Joy

Luke 17:15-16 *One of them, when he saw he was healed, came back, praising God in a loud voice. He threw himself at Jesus' feet and thanked him - and he was a Samaritan.*

Explain Yourself

I was reading over last week's devotion and my prayer is that those of us that go to Jesus petitioning something, that we don't let whether or not we deserve to ask anything of God get in the way. Sometimes we need to forgive ourselves and move on. But as I was reading, something stood out in Luke 17:12-14.

As he was going into a village, ten men who had leprosy met him. They stood at a distance and called out in a loud voice, "Jesus, Master, have pity on us!" When he saw them, he said, "Go, show yourselves to the priests." And as they went, they were cleansed.

I noticed that when they asked for mercy that Jesus didn't say "Explain Yourself". He didn't stand in the judgment seat – He said, "Go." As they went they were healed.

I read further and also noticed that only one came back and gave Glory to God. Now we know all ten were not perfect and they all had different stories (Jesus didn't ask for their story). But think about the one that came back; he **may** have been the most sinful one of them all. It **may** be that the one most thankful is the one for whom the most mercy was needed; and Jesus gave it. He didn't treat any of them differently. He healed from the most innocent to the guiltiest.

Now I pose a question to you:

How can we walk in the new man when we can't let the old man go?
Just start walking in the new - Jesus didn't ask us to explain ourselves, just to receive.
Jesus asked, "Were not all ten cleansed? Where are the other nine? Has no one returned to give praise to God except this foreigner?"
Luke 17:17-19

Grace gives us what we don't deserve
Mercy keeps us from getting what we deserve

Toni Joy

Season Greetings, again

We made a plan the other day to do something we haven't done before. Now it's time to put it into action if you haven't started yet. Start working on your plan to make sure it's done in time.

Remember it's:

1. Something that you haven't done before
2. You have to create it
3. It's not expensive
4. Something you do for the holiday or give as a gift

My Agape Walk Today

End every sentence
with the words
"Be Blessed"
except when
It really doesn't
apply

✓ <u>I walked in love today</u>

Meditate today on ...

"For yet a little while,
And He who is coming will come and will not
tarry.
Now the just shall live by faith;
But if anyone draws back,
My soul has no pleasure in him."
Heb. 10:37, 38

People say that Christianity is a way of Life.
(My opinion) Christianity is life;
Faith is a way of life.
We have a lot of Christians and
faith is not their way.
A Christian is someone that
accepted Jesus as Lord;
But we still have to choose how to live!
Read Heb. 10:26-39

Toni Joy

1 Sam. 28:6 *...When Saul saw the Philistine army, he was afraid; terror filled his heart. He inquired of the LORD, but the LORD did not answer him by dreams or Urim or prophets.*

When God Doesn't Answer

What happens when we see trouble and call on the Lord and He doesn't answer? Do we do like Saul? *Saul then said to his attendants, "Find me a woman who is a medium, so I may go and inquire of her." 1 Sam. 28:7*

Oh no, not us; we wouldn't look to witch-craft, we wouldn't take matters into our own hands, go back to our old ways, panic, look to man for help, look to the lotto, make plans for our burial, cuss someone out, steal, cheat, beg, borrow or engage in behaviors that do not line up with holiness, faith, and trust?

Not a Christian with God living on the inside of us.
When we don't hear from God we should find out what's blocking the answer, why the door is closed, because

He always answers! He is always there!
When we find ourselves in a position where we can't hear from God **(and we all have moments when we will not hear – hopefully not for long) this would be a good time to fast.** It just may be "too much noise" around us.

Stop And Do Whatever It Takes To Focus On God And Not The Issue.
Blessed Is The One Who Perseveres Under Trial Because, Having Stood The Test, That Person Will Receive The Crown Of Life That The Lord Has Promised To Those Who Love Him.... Everyone Should Be Quick To Listen, Slow To Speak And Slow To Become Angry, Because Human Anger Does Not Produce The Righteousness That God Desires.
James 1:12,19-20

**When God Doesn't Answer, Take The Seal Off The Door...
And Shut Out The Noise**
*I Write These Things To You Who Believe In The Name Of The Son Of God So That You May Know That You Have Eternal Life. This Is The Confidence We Have In Approaching God: That If We Ask Anything According To His Will, He Hears Us. And If We Know That He Hears Us— Whatever We Ask—**We Know** That We Have What We Asked Of Him.*
1 John 5:13-15

John 11:3 *Therefore his sisters sent unto him, saying, Lord, behold, he whom thou lovest is sick.* John 11:39 *...by this time he stinketh: for he hath been dead four days.*

It Stinks

I don't know why it takes so long sometimes for our answer and deliverance to come, but it comes. There can be a million reasons to answer why, but this is one of those questions that you put in a box on the shelf - and ask Jesus when you see Him. In the meantime, let it go, don't get hung up on when - but know that it's coming.

Sometimes we get sick, in trouble, fall short; and we seem to think that Jesus doesn't love us anymore. This is so far from the truth. But just as Jesus came to the rescue of Lazarus - He will come to our rescue regardless of what it seems like.

God can't be God if He ain't healing, delivering, answering, blessing, raising from the dead, etc. The more impossible it is - the more it can only be a job for God, and God <u>will</u> be God if we let Him...
Has your situations got so bad that it stinks, so long that you can't take it anymore?
Martha said "Lord, he stinks."
Then Jesus said, "<u>Did I not tell you that if you believe, you will see the glory of God?</u>" vs. 40

I don't care how bad it gets, it looks, it smells, He hears you and He will come through. Trust God, trust the Word, trust Jesus... ***if you believe, you will see the glory of God?***

HE Loves Us - even in the stinky stuff
Now when He had said these things, He cried with a loud voice, "Lazarus, come forth!" John 11:43

Meditate today on ...

Therefore by Him let us continually offer
the sacrifice of praise to God, that is, the
fruit of our lips, giving thanks to His name.
Heb. 13:15

Everyone that has breath
Praise the Lord
Set aside some time to give Thanks to the Lord

November 30

Toni Joy

1 Thes 3:8 *For now we live, if ye stand fast in the Lord.*
<u>We qualify for Urgent Care</u>
Who do you call in times of "I need it Now"? How do you spell <u>urgency</u>!

Sometimes things arise and before we know it we have borrowed the money, pulled out the charge card, received sickness and deceases, slapped someone, given someone a piece of our mind, thrown a fit, worried, or *insert your own personal urgency here*.

Most of the time the decisions we make in urgency take us further away from God's help. God knows what's going on before we do; He knows what we need when we don't (Matt. 6:33). Often, we will seek 10 other ways to deal with the problem; and when nothing else works, then we go to God - *maybe*. By that time it's not in faith, it's in desperation or as our last choice.

We have to make a decision to look to the Lord and not to the world when things are pressing such as when the letter comes in the mail, a phone call comes, or the doctor enters the office. If we are going from one bad experience to another, should we rethink to whom we run in adversity? We have to make God's desire for us our way of living – and when something urgent pops up – God is our first choice. *We must spell <u>urgency</u> as prayer, seeking God, rhema (a spoken Word from God), waiting on the Lord, repentance and obedience, God's way of doing things, praise, worship, and rejoicing. **(But even if we are late in putting God first, just start where you are to listen and trust God. E<u>ve</u>n the world has an emergency room that treat hurt; <u>even for self-inflicted wounds. How much more Can God?</u>)***

Get <u>trusting-God-experience</u> *on the everyday so-called normal routine of life* so when the pressure is on, you will not be moved by what you see, feel, or think. But be steadfast and unmovable in the Word of God. Make yourself stop and...

Listen to His voice, and hold fast to Him for the LORD is your life. Deut 30:20

For Urgent Care: Room 1 Peter 5:7

CONFESSION FOR THE MONTH OF DECEMBER

Print or write out your confession; put it where you can see and confess it all month

Lord, you know me better than I know myself. Bring out in me who you created me to be. I will look to You and Your strength to do the things You commissioned me to do.

I am the righteousness of God
I am blessed
I am rich
I am prosperous
My inheritance is that of the Lord
My journey is secure

Whereby are given unto us exceeding great and precious promises: that by these ye might be partakers of the divine nature, having escaped the corruption that is in the world through lust. 2 Peter 1:4

My Agape Walk Today

Do

someone

a favor –

that

You "DO" know

✓ <u>I walked in love today</u>

John 17:22-23 *And the glory which You gave Me I have given them, that they may be one just as We are one: I in them, and You in Me*

Resurrected & Transformed

Looking from the inside out!
God gave man dominion over everything and put man in the Garden of Eden (Gen. 2:15). We gave it away. But because of the shed blood of Jesus Christ we are back in heavenly places (Eph. 2:26).

Let's look at this in a different view.
If you can believe that Adam and Eve had dominion before the fall, then believe that you can have dominion by the blood of Jesus. You have to apply it. The Blood of Jesus took us from death to life; from darkness to light, from a sin nature to God's nature (now, in this life time). John 17 describes it this way "we are not of this world but in this world".

God took Adam and Eve and put them in the Garden of Eden; He took us and sat us in heavenly places with Christ Jesus. We have access to the Garden of Eden through Christ.

Apply this in your mind. It will change something for you in you.
From being hell bound to heaven bound
Poor to rich / Sick to healed / Hated to Loved
We are: Healed and the devil is trying to make us sick
Rich and the devil is trying to make us poor
We are saved and the devil is trying to give us hell
Love lives in us and the devil is trying to make us hate
Let us now stand our ground for the battle is already won
It's a faith fight; it's just that most of us don't know it.
If you still have breathe in your lungs, Live now!

Most assuredly, I say to you, he who believes in Me, the works that I do he will do also; and greater works than these he will do, because I go to My Father. And whatever you ask in My name, that I will do, that the Father may be glorified in the Son. If you ask anything in My name I will do it. John 14:12-14

Romans 12:2 *Do not conform to the pattern of this world, but be transformed by the renewing of your mind.*

Old Dogs - New Tricks

I was pondering on how hard it was for the saints of God (Believers, Christians that lived in the world for so long) then got saved to adjust to the ways of the Kingdom of God. Sometimes it's a quick process and sometimes it's not. But the key is to keep seeking the ways of God and not get locked into this is how I am and I will die like this and resort to living less than who we can be (better yet) - **created to be.**

For the hard hats, it's difficult to conceive of doing things differently. No sex before marriage, not worrying, tithing, love our enemy, turn the other cheek....

*<u>**I have a challenge for all of us "hard core dogs"**</u>*
I double dare you to try something different –
*<u>**"Give God the benefit of the doubt"**</u>*
(we would something less)

I heard a saying the other day (I believe I heard it from Sonya Longstreet of My 2Cents)
*that if you "**want**" something different - you have to "**do**" something different*
Look at it this way...before we got saved, we couldn't conceive of being saved. But it was a good move **<u>to believe God</u>**. Why stop there? **<u>Continue to believe.....</u>**
Can you teach an old dog new tricks?
Our hearts were changed when we got saved, it's our minds that need to be renewed.
... Put off, concerning your former conduct, the old man which grows corrupt according to the deceitful lusts, and be renewed in the spirit of your mind, and that you put on the new man which was created according to God, in true righteousness and holiness. Eph. 4:22-24

Meditate today on ...

LORD, I cry out to You;
Make haste to me!
Give ear to my voice when I cry out to You.
Let my prayer be set before You as incense,
The lifting up of my hands as
the evening sacrifice.

Set a guard, O LORD, over my mouth;
Keep watch over the door of my lips.
Do not incline my heart to any evil thing,
To practice wicked works
With men who work iniquity;
And do not let me eat of their delicacies.

Ps. 141:-4

We all have to Cry sometimes, Lord help me

Psalm 1:2 *But his delight is in the law of the LORD,* ***And in His law*** ***he meditates day and night***.

Romancing God

I was listening to a song by Steven Curtis Chapman that goes something like "doing every little thing to the Glory to God". And I thought about when we live our lives giving glory to God in literally everything we do, we build a relationship with God that is secure, trusting, and intimate.

We care so much about what God can do for us. I believe we really take for granted what we can do for God. Don't you know we are romancing God when we give Him the Glory in everything we do? We romance relationships all the time, why not God? Think about the little things we do every day to please our mates, or want-to-be mates with all the charm and preparation to "wow" them. How do we "wow" God?

Let's set out to please God – *act like He's looking at you 24/7, when you walk into a room, when you're looking in the mirror getting dressed (and you know you are going to see Him), when you're talking on the phone (act like you know He's listening in or like that special person is standing behind you), when you past by someone hungry or thirsty (act like He's walking with you). When you have those opportunities to be bad, be good then give God a wink.*

Let's spend the day romancing God. See if we can get Him to say, "WOW".

"Because he has set his love upon Me, therefore I will deliver him; I will set him on high, because he has known My name. He shall call upon Me, and I will answer him; I will be with him in trouble; I will deliver him and honor him. With long life I will satisfy him, And show him My salvation." Ps. 91:14-16

Heb 11:3 *By faith we understand that the worlds were framed by the word of God, so that the things which are seen were not made of things which are visible.*

"The B-I-B-L-E"

"The B-I-B-L-E, yes that's the book for me - I stand alone on the Word of God, the B-I-B-L-E" **Do you remember this kid's song?**

The book of life – how do we read it? Theologians say that what we get out of the bible depends on how we approach it. ***If we read the bible as a sense of duty we won't get much from it***, which I also believe is true. Those are the words of Dr. R.T. Kendall, Pastor Rick Renner, and Joyce Meyer as I watched Joyce's program sometime in May 2009.

We have to be careful not to read the bible as just a quick fix. Yes, the Word of God is the answer to everything, but we have to approach it with reverence and awe of who He is to get the right answer to the right question or problem at the right time. We have to go to the Great Physician and let Him lead us and help us – and we have to take the prescribed medicine. We can't tell Him what the problem is, pick the answer we like, forge His name, and ***then think that it is God's fault that it failed***.

Read the bible with comfort and ease like you do a good novel. Let it take you to another place. The difference between this book and a novel is that it is yours for the taking to live it out in your life. It has more riches and promises than any book you can read. It's alive, full of liberty.

Here are some tips:
- Don't go to the bible to prove what you think you know or pick and choose what you like. Let God tell you something and don't over analyze it – God knows you, so He knows what to tell ***YOU***.
- Don't reduce it to your level of thinking or understanding. Just let the Holy Spirit lead you, make you wise.

There is nothing else we can stand on <u>alone</u> and it be everything.
It is the Spirit who gives life; the flesh profits nothing. The words that I speak to you are spirit, and they are life. John 6:63

Meditate today on ...

Let this mind be in you which was also in Christ Jesus, who, being in the form of God, did not consider it robbery to be equal with God, but made Himself of no reputation, taking the form of a bondservant, *and* coming in the likeness of men. And being found in appearance as a man, He humbled Himself and became obedient to *the* point of death, even the death of the cross.

Therefore God also has highly exalted Him and given Him the name which is above every name, that at the name of Jesus every knee should bow, of those in heaven, and of those on earth, and of those under the earth, and *that* every tongue should confess that Jesus Christ *is* Lord, to the glory of God the Father.
Philippians. 2:5-11

Your Name is Worthy to be Praised

My Agape Walk Today

Find time to
read a scripture
In the middle
of the day

✓ <u>I walked in love today</u>

Psalm 28:7 *The **LORD** is my **strength** and my shield; my heart trusts in him, and he helps me. My heart leaps for **joy**, and with my song I praise him.*

A WORD OF ENCOURAGEMENT

My daughter was on my heart this morning; she have some decisions that she has to make concerning her senior year. I started texting her, telling her that because she has decisions to make that the pressure was going to be "on". That it was not about her strength, but about her decision; the strength will be there once the decision is made. After I thought about that myself, it also strengthened me. I just said "Thank you Lord".

Sometimes we struggle with many things. Didn't the Lord say that "He is our Strength" that "the joy of the Lord is our strength"? It is true?

Further encouragement.... We can change
I was reading "The Two Listeners" a while back and they said something that just awakened me; "Sin only has strength because we desire it". WOW!

If we want sin out of our life.... Change our desire (regardless of what the sin is, little or big). We don't like to think we desire the sin that has hold on us, but think about it...
without the desire, the struggle is not there.

Decide to walk in the righteousness of God today, to please God...
*What does Scripture say? "Abraham believed **God**, and it was credited to him as **righteousness**." **Rom. 4:3***

John 2:1-9 *On the third day a wedding took place at Cana in Galilee. Jesus' mother was there, and Jesus and his disciples had also been invited to the wedding. When the wine was gone, Jesus' mother said to him, "They have no more wine." "Woman why do you involve me?" Jesus replied. "My hour has not yet come." His mother said to the servants, "Do whatever he tells you."*

"The Glory made Him Do It"

(Mary knew) I always wondered as I read this passage when Mary said "Do whatever He tells you to do" was Mary being difficult or was she being a mom and exerting authority? Mary was with Jesus from birth, she watched no lack in his life and I believe wherever Jesus was – lack couldn't abide. **She had to witness this** - That the answer to every question manifested through Him, that He couldn't be in a situation where the problem was not solvable. He couldn't help Himself from being wonderful... **the Glory made Him do it** - **It's in His Nature**. Mary knew her son and that if they listened or got close enough power would flow. We need to go to God like Mary, knowing the Glory will flow.

~~~~~~~~~~~~

His Glory is still flowing - We have all the answers
We have the very nature of God living on the inside of us; *wherever we go – whatever we find ourselves in...*
Do Whatever He say do.
Jesus said to the servants "Fill the jars with water"; so they filled them to the brim. They did so, and the master of the banquet tasted the water that had been turned into wine.

"You are the light of the world. A city that is set on a hill cannot be hidden..... Let your light so shine before men, that they may see your good works and glorify your Father in heaven. **Matthew 5:13-16**

Meditate today on ...

For God so loved the world that He gave His only begotten Son, that whoever believes in Him should not perish but have everlasting life.

John 3:16

Our salvation is through Jesus Christ, not by our works (being good people is not enough), He would not have had to give His Son if our righteousness could save us.

Toni Joy

Phil 4:6-7 Be anxious for nothing, but in everything by prayer and supplication, with thanksgiving, let your requests be made known to God; and the peace of God, which surpasses all understanding, will guard your hearts and minds through Christ Jesus.

Are you crazy yet?

What or who is driving you crazy? **Now this is a "What If";** *what if we see people as Jesus sees us? What if we see our children as God sees His children? What if we see our co-workers, friends, and associates as God sees us? (one more) What if we see the world as God sees the world?* (John 17:20-23)

For God so loved the world that He gave His only begotten Son (John 3:16); this was when we were at our worst.

We are supposed to see the best in people even when they are at their worst. **God didn't see anything good in us...He gave us something good so that He could see something good.** God is not in heaven pulling His hair out because we drive Him crazy. Jesus is continually interceding for us, making all things available for us. I have never messed up so bad that when I came to my senses **(or the senses that God gave me)**, that all the power was used up and there was nothing left for me. I know for a fact that He will always be there for me (Deut. 3:18 & Heb. 13:5). He will always be there for **YOU**.

Let's not let those in our lives exhaust us of all power to love and to give. Just as God sees Jesus in us, let's see Jesus in others. How do we do that?

Love like God....

Be imitators of God, therefore, as dearly loved children and live a life of love, just as Christ loved us and gave himself up for us as a fragrant offering and sacrifice to God. **Eph 5:1-2 NIV**

Luke 23:39-43 *Then one of the criminals who were hanged blasphemed Him, saying, "If You are the Christ, save Yourself and us." But the other, answering, rebuked him, saying, "Do you not even fear God, seeing you are under the same condemnation? And we indeed justly, for we receive the due reward of our deeds; but this Man has done nothing wrong." Then he said to Jesus, "Lord, remember me when You come into Your kingdom." And Jesus said to him, "Assuredly, I say to you, today you will be with Me in Paradise."*

Wow

When I was listening to this scripture being ministered about Jesus at the cross; I couldn't help thinking about the love of God.

So many people are so quick to send sinners to hell (the ones we consider sinners). Yes, it's true; we look at people all the time and say **"They're going to hell"** and to think that Jesus took one of them to heaven with him that day.

Jesus died so that we would not have to go to hell, even the ones we think belong there.

This is one of the greatest acts of the power and the love of God towards us.

Just to point out one more thing: This is the greatest example of a death bed salvation (you can't say it doesn't happen).
Let's have the compassion of Christ today
Let's not put anyone in hell
For God so loved the world that He gave His only begotten Son, that whoever believes in Him should not perish but have everlasting life. John 3:16

My 2 Cents

Toni Joy and I were having a conversation the other day about aging. She said, you should share what you told me with the Agape readers.

She mentioned to me, that she recently joined a gym. I said to her, as we mature in age, exercising is not an option. At least that's my opinion. I believe as we age, we should do what's necessary to continue to look good and feel good. Just because we pass the 40 mark doesn't mean things should go down-hill; on the contrary.

I work out 3-4 days a week. I don't do it just to maintain or lose weight. I do it to maintain my health as well. I don't want brittle bones as I age, I don't want any, nary a one of those diseases that go along with a sedentary lifestyle. The women in my family in the past have gained weight after the age of 40. I'm talking considerable weight. My sister Sherrie who lives in Florida (by the way, she's a faithful reader of Agape) agrees with me that we wouldn't do what we've seen the other women in our family do.

She and I agreed we would set a better example for the younger women in our family. So we both are very conscience of our weight and we've made great progress in the types of food we eat now. As I'm maturing, I have no plans to look my age, walk my age, or act like I'm over the hill. You know what they say, **"you're as young as you feel."**

I'm over 40 (that's all I'm going to say) and I feel good. Bless His Holy Name! Whoever told that lie that after 40 you're old; they lied. I see some signs of aging in my body. But, I continue to work at doing what's good for my body so that I can continue to feel good. When I was in my 20's and 30's I wore very little makeup. Now, I spruce what a little more with make up because I feel I need a little more help in that department than I used to. But, that comes with aging. My point is, do what is necessary to continue to look good and feel good as you increase in birthdays.

If it means you have to start an exercise plan, do it. If it means you have to change your diet, do it. If it means wearing a little more makeup, do it. What woman doesn't want to look good and feel good in her body? I'm aging gracefully, how about you? **Only Believe!**

My Agape Walk Today

Say a specific
Prayer for someone
Today

✓ I walked in love today

Toni Joy

Deuteronomy 28:13 *And the LORD will make you the head and not the tail; you shall be above only, and not be beneath.*

On Top Of The World

Deuteronomy 28 spells out where and what we are to be as Children of God.

Blessed *going in and blessed going out*
Blessed *in the city and blessed in the country*
Blessed *in the fruit of our womb*
Blessed *in our storehouses*

It also spells out where and what we are to be if we are not obedient children of God. All these blessings turn into curses. Just replace the word **blessed** with the word **cursed**.

Just do what Father tells us to do!!!

Isn't that what we tell our kids? And we wonder what is wrong with them when they don't listen. We say "If they would just listen, just trust, just do what I say".

Do we, *Just do what Father tells us to do!?!*

What did God tell Cain when Cain was angry because of Abel's offering being pleasing to God and not his offering?
"If you do well, will you not be accepted? And if you do not well, sin lies at the door. And its desire is for you, but you should rule over it." Gen. 4:7

Let's teach our kids by example. Listen to God like we want our kids to listen to us:
"Test me in this," says the LORD Almighty, "and see if I will not throw open the floodgates of heaven and pour out so much blessing that you will not have room enough for it". Mal 3:10

Obedient means...... *Living on top of the world*

Eph 5:1 *Therefore be imitators of God as dear children.*

"Told you so"

"Oh yes it is, no it ain't, yes it is, no it ain't
Ephesians 5 & 6

There are so many of us that have this same discussion with people about sin. Some really don't know what sin is. Some ask where does drinking fall on the sin scale, or gambling, and flirting. True enough that some things are not a sin, but they fall on the scale of being a heavy weight in our life; *and what's done in moderation doesn't necessarily mean it's ok.*

Weights and Sins **can keep us from God's best!**
What is a weight, as used in this reference? It could be something that doesn't bring out the best in you, takes more of your time/attention/possessions than it ought; something that takes away your goodness (whether it's mental, physical, or spiritual); it brings darkness rather than light - *like smoking, drinking, flirting, gambling, etc*

Therefore do not let your good be spoken of as evil; Rom 14:16
Sin is not a gray area. It's wide open and up front. SIN: unrighteousness for example: *adultery, murder, fornication, stealing, etc.*

Sin is a force. It may be likened to a mathematician. It **adds** *to a man's troubles,* **subtracts** *from his energies,* **multiplies** *his aches and pains,* **divides** *his mind,* **takes interest** *from his work,* **discounts** *his chances of success, and* **squares** *his conscience.* **By: A. J. Russell**

If you really what to know, **Read Eph. Chapters 5 and 6**
We could throw all those (*what some think as gray areas*) <u>not so sure</u> sins in these two chapters and cross reference them with so many scriptures that will clearly tell us what sin is.
(It really doesn't depend on the situation as we would like to think).
Therefore do not be unwise, but understand what the will of the Lord is.
Eph. 5:17-18

Again Season Greetings

We should be ready to give someone or many, a special made gift that you made yourself; you may have already given that gift to someone. Maybe you gave a party or about to give a party.

Whatever it is, we need to remember some special things about our gift:

1. Thank God for the idea
2. Be thankful that you are able to give
3. Pray over your gift, that they see the Lord in your giving
4. Share the greatest gift of all "Jesus"

1 John 5:14-15 *"Now this is the confidence that we have in Him, that if we ask anything according to His will, He hears us. And if we know that He hears us, whatever we ask, we know that we have the petitions that we have asked of Him".*

"Can We Talk"

Does God always answers our questions? I believe He will. We **_have_** to go into our conversations with God knowing and believing that He is listening and answering us or we are not in faith.

We have to ask ourselves *are we really listening,* do we really want to hear what God has to say, or do we only want to hear what we want Him to say? I believe sometimes we hear and it's not what we wanted to hear so we dismiss it just as quickly as we asked. He might even want to give us what we want, but there are some things that we may need to change, let go of, or learn in order to receive. There may be some traditions that worked years ago that don't apply today. We need to slow down and ask in faith, ready to adjust to His direction to receive. I remember telling someone that the real "you" is who you are spiritually. *Are we confusing our real desires (God given desires) with the way we may be thinking? Could our thinking be off? Good question.*

John 10:27 *My sheep hear My voice, and I know them, **_and they follow Me_**.*

God's thoughts and ways are higher than ours, so let's go into this day knowing we have to adjust to a higher way of doing and having things.

"But without faith it is impossible to please and be satisfactory to Him. For whoever would come near to God must [necessarily] believe that God exists and that He is the rewarder of those who earnestly and diligently seek Him [out]". Hebrews 11:6 AMP.

December 21

Toni Joy

Acts 12:6-7...*that night Peter was sleeping, bound with two chains between two soldiers; and the guards before the door were keeping the prison Now behold, an angel of the Lord stood by him, and a light shone in the prison; and he struck Peter on the side and raised him up, saying, **"Arise quickly!" And his chains fell off his hands"***

The Great Escape

<u>*Carnal Chains*</u> - **These chains** are just as real (and stronger) than the chains that Peter was bound with in prison. I believe some chains, if not all, come with demonic guards. Due to the lack of knowledge of Christ Jesus we don't acknowledge them as real chains; we don't even look at them as binding us. They are cords generated by the senses of the flesh and motivated by spiritual darkness of this world.

These chains are **Strongholds**. They are thoughts and feelings. They exhibit the habits of life that we have learned or inherited that goes against the knowledge of God, **His** thoughts and ways of doing things. They are strongholds we feel we can't live without. We depend on them. They even define us. You know what there are: fear, worry, anxiety, sadness, loneliness, hatred, un-forgiveness, self-righteousness, stubbornness, and there are many more we can mention. Most of us will go through situations in life where these strongholds are expected: divorce, death of someone close, sin, failure, rejection, regrets, and life styles.

These strongholds don't have to belong to us or stay. They put us in a prison without doors. Like the example I once heard about; I think it was a grasshopper. That if you put it in a jar and put the top on it that it would jump for a while, but after they try for so long and can't get out, they stop jumping. When you take the top off; they won't jump or try to get out even though they are free to go.

I like the idea that it was a grasshopper because it is the nature of a grasshopper to hop. Just like it's in our nature to live prosperous. We were created to be in the image of God. ***When you stick with God and stay in the Word, you can't help but jump, prosper, and break free from what's holding you back. The spirit inside of you will quicken you (make alive) your mind and senses to make the great escape.***

Rejoice because God has a great escape for you!

My Agape Walk Today

How Bold Are You

Everything you

Do today

Give God the Glory;

Out Loud

✓ *I walked in love today*

December 23

Toni Joy

For unto us a Child is born, Unto us a Son is given; And the government will be upon His shoulder. And His name will be called Wonderful, Counselor, Mighty God, Everlasting Father, Prince of Peace. **Isaiah 9:6**

This Christmas

Close your eyes for a moment and picture three babies of the world – beautiful babies (come on now, close your eyes for a minute - put your baby in the picture).

Now put the baby Jesus in the picture. What is the difference in all the babies? What they have? Who they belong too? You can switch the babies around, change the environment, change the status.. On the inside they all process the same thing except one baby has something the others don't. This baby has another kingdom in Him, the life/light of God, born of the Holy Spirit. He grew up in our environment, shared our life, but still possessed something we didn't have. This baby grew and chose to share His life and environment with us. A kingdom that is perfect and an environment in which we were born to live.

The rat race we see today is not the environment that God wants us to be subject. My prayer is that we all wake up Christmas morning and embrace the kingdom of God that was given to us through Jesus Christ.

..."Joseph, son of David, do not be afraid to take to you Mary your wife, for that which is conceived in her is of the Holy Spirit. And she will bring forth a Son, and you shall call His name JESUS, for He will save His people from their sins." Matthew 1:20-21

This Christmas, let's open our eyes to the kingdom of God, and the environment Jesus died to give us.
Do not be afraid to take the Kingdom of God as our Home.
He has delivered us from the power of darkness and conveyed us into the kingdom of the Son of His love. **Colossians 1:13**

Merry Christmas

Verily, verily, I say unto you, He that entereth not by the door into the sheepfold, but climbeth up some other way, the same is a thief and a robber. But he that entereth in by the door is the shepherd of the sheep. To him the porter openeth; and the sheep hear his voice: and he calleth his own sheep by name, and leadeth them out. And when he had putteth forth his own sheep, he goeth before them, and the sheep follow him: for they know his voice. John 10:1-5

<u>I want us to note two points</u>
1. Verse 3 "the sheep hear His voice" - 2. Verse 4 "for they know His voice"

The sheep hear His voice for they know His voice. Would you agree with me, to know, to recognize, someone's voice you have to be acquainted with that person? Jesus said in John 10:14 ***I am the good shepherd, and know my sheep, and am known of mine.*** That scripture makes for a promising Christmas if we mediate on the scripture fact that He is first a good shepherd, emphasis on the ***good***, and He knows us. That gives me great joy and pleasure knowing Jesus knows me. And He has given me opportunity through His shed blood to know Him. As you go about this Christmas season doing all the things you do to make Christmas happen for you and yours keep that in mind -- Jesus knows you. Powerful! Not only do you know Him and hear His voice, but **HE KNOWS YOU!**

Jesus is the Shepherd, the Good Shepherd. The bible says The Shepherd keeps the sheep. God promises to keep us, the Hebrew word for keep is ***shamar***. It means to hedge about or to guard. It's also the same word used in the confession called ***"The Blessing of the Priest"*** from Numbers 6:24-26. So this Christmas season Sister Toni Joy and I declare the ***blessing of the priest*** upon you and your family.

The Lord bless thee, and keep thee:
The Lord make his face shine upon thee, and be gracious unto thee:
The Lord lift up his countenance upon thee, and give thee peace.

Merry Christmas

December 25

Merry Christmas

Have a joyful day

Celebrating the

Birth of Jesus Christ

From : Toni Joy &

Pastor Sonya Longstreet

My Agape Walk Today

How Bold Are You
Start reading the book

Of

Revelations

If you read it before, read it again

✓ _I walked in love today_

John 14:2 *In my Father's house are many mansions: if it were not so, I would have told you. I go to prepare a place for you.*

Soon and Very Soon

Did we forget that there is a huge homecoming waiting for us?

Jesus was telling the disciples during supper that He was going away. So that they wouldn't worry, He let them in on a wonderful revelation that He was preparing a place for them.

I thought about that this morning as I was praising God. Because He longs to spend time with us, He's looking forward to us being with Him in heaven. Wow! How many people have you prepared a place for? What wonderful love this is to be waited on. He said that they could not come with Him then, but soon.

And if I go and prepare a place for you, I will come again, and receive you unto myself; that where I am, there ye may be also. John 14:3

We don't need to fear death because *being absent in the body is being present with the Lord* (2 Cor. 5:8).

So when someone say to you that he or she is in a better place, they are just reminding us of what is true (they really are in a better place). They are trying to comfort our sorrow of a loved one moving on; and I really don't think they miss us. Well, not enough to want to come back for us. This makes me think about the movie *Ghost* during the scene when the light is shining on him. Think about this, it's a love story, yet when he gets in the light he stopped looking at her. He was in awe of the glory of God. You need to see the picture again if you don't believe me. He was like, baby, it's beautiful - gotta go.

Makes me feel like singing......

Soon and very soon, We are going to see the King
Soon and very soon, We are going to see the King
Hallelujah, hallelujah, we're going to see the King

For to me to live is Christ, and to die is gain. But if I live in the flesh, this is the fruit of my labour: yet what I shall choose I wot not. For I am in a strait betwixt two, having a desire to depart, and to be with Christ; which is far better: Nevertheless to abide in the flesh is more needful for you. **Phil. 1:21-24**

Mark 2:27 *And He said unto them, The Sabbath was made for man, and not man for the Sabbath.*

The Un-religious Christian Part 1

I love how Jesus separated religion from Himself. You will find that the Pharisees challenged Jesus on being religious; Jesus simply told them in Mark 2:28, "***I run this***"

'Therefore the Son of man is Lord also of the Sabbath.

The Pharisees were the ones that opposed Jesus. (I wonder are there Pharisees in the Church today?)

What do we call righteous or religious in our behavior and acts? If someone asked you what do you **do** as a Christian, what is your answer? I hope your answer follows Galatians 5:22-23 b*ut the fruit of the Spirit is love, joy, peace, longsuffering, gentleness, goodness, faith, meekness, temperance; against such there is no law.*

Or do you say I'm a trustee, a deacon, an usher, I'm on this board, that board?
Let's separate our-selves from religion and be the un-religious Christian, take out the heart of stone and walk in the spirit

Now early in the morning He came again into the temple, and all the people came to Him; and He sat down and taught them. Then the scribes and Pharisees brought to Him a woman caught in adultery. And when they had set her in the midst, they said to Him, "Teacher, this woman was caught in adultery, in the very act. Now Moses, in the law, commanded us that such should be stoned. But what do You say?" This they said, testing Him, that they might have something of which to accuse Him. But Jesus stooped down and wrote on the ground with His finger, as though He did not hear. So when they continued asking Him, He raised Himself up and said to them, "He who is without sin among you, let him throw a stone at her first." John 8:2-7

My Agape Walk Today

How Bold Are You

Let go of all Expectations
today; Except to walk
In love towards
Yourself and others

Just do it, you will find that Love carries its own reward
just as sin carries its own punishment

✓ <u>I walked in love today</u>

Mark 3:4 *Jesus said to them, "Is it lawful on the Sabbath to do good or to do evil, to save life or to kill? But they kept silent...with anger being grieved by the "hardness" of their hearts, He said to the man, "Stretch out your hand" And he stretched it out, and his hand was restored as whole as the other... then they plotted how to destroy Him.*

The Un-religious Christian Part 2

We can get so ingrained in laws that it hardens our hearts and the good it is supposed to produce is blocked. Jesus went <u>against</u> the grain and people were healed, delivered, forgiven. Jesus <u>was not</u> what they expected. They expected a King that would sit on the throne and rule. Someone like the previous kings/prophets that would deliver them from their situations. He came to deliver and save, but not in the way they were looking for it. They wanted the kingdom they had; expecting Jesus to take the earthly throne. Jesus came with a different kind of kingdom, a heavenly kingdom: *Thy kingdom come, Thy will be done in earth, as it is in heaven...* Matt. 6:10

We are not religious

If we want to prosper (spirit, soul, and body), we must be like Jesus, **who is the head of the church**. We have to find the courage to be an un-religious Christian. They hated Jesus, they will hate us too, because....

We are not what they expect

Therefore be imitators of God as dear children. And walk in love, as Christ also has loved us and given Himself for us, an offering and a sacrifice to God for a sweet-smelling aroma. Eph. 5:1

Mark 1:12-13 *Then a voice came from heaven, "You are My beloved Son, in whom I am well pleased." Immediately the Spirit drove Him into the wilderness. And He was there in the wilderness forty days. Tempted by Satan, and was with the wild beasts; and the angels ministered to Him.*

Happy New Year's Eve
This Year – Don't be taken by surprise

Have you noticed that when we sometimes go on a fast, that as soon as we start we are defeated. I have gone on a fast and by the next day I have made some excuse as to why I can't finish.

Look at the scripture above - God was pleased...immediately The Spirit drove Him into the wilderness. He fasted, Satan tempted Him, *the world* (oops, I meant wild beasts) was with Him, then the angels ministered to Him.

Let's allow this passage to minister to us. When we start our fast this year, let's be prepared for the disturbances coming and that are around us. Let's not walk into a fight with a water gun like we are children when we should walk into battle with a two edged sword (the Word of God). We should be like a child trusting and following Jesus – but not as a child with no direction (no Father). Jesus gave the answer to it all in Matthew 4:4 *But He answered and said, "It is written, 'Man shall not live by bread alone, but by every word that proceeds from the mouth of God.'"*

Go into this year's first fast prepared for the devil to try to defeat you at the starting gate. Make "hearing from God" your biggest priority in fasting.

These things I have spoken to you, that in Me you may have peace. In the world you will have tribulation; but be of good cheer, I have overcome the world."
John 16:33

Have a wonderful New Year

Printed in the United States
By Bookmasters